GRAHAM'S STORY

DAVID W. ROBERTS

Published in Australia by Sid Harta Publishers Pty Ltd,
ABN: 34 632 585 203
17 Coleman Parade, GLEN WAVERLEY VIC 3150 Australia
Telephone: +61 3 9560 9920, Facsimile: +61 3 9545 1742
E-mail: author@sidharta.com.au

First published in Australia 2020
This edition published 2020

Cover design, typesetting: WorkingType (www.workingtype.com.au)

Roberts, David W.
Graham's Story
ISBN: 978-1-925707-34-2
pp364

ABOUT THE AUTHOR

David Roberts migrated as a qualified teacher from the United Kingdom. After seventeen years working as a teacher, deputy principal and principal in country New South Wales, he became a university academic. University appointments and consultancies enabled David to travel widely and broaden his horizons. Now retired, he lives with his wife in Adelaide. *Graham's Story* is David's third novel; the earlier ones being *One Thing Leads to Another* and *Easytimes*.

*For Wendy and Simon with thanks
for their support and technical expertise.*

CHAPTER ONE

There was an empty aching feeling inside as I trudged the dusty dirt road to school. I knew why the pain was there but I didn't know how to get rid of it. It was always like this after Mum and Dad had been arguing. From the moment I had entered the kitchen for breakfast this morning, I had sensed things weren't right. Mum had buttoned-up and wasn't talking because Dad was grumbling about anything and everything. I guess she reckoned it was better not to speak when Dad was this angry.

'Bloody dog's lame, it's got a thorn caught up in its foot and I couldn't get the bugger out. Vets are too bloody expensive so I don't know what we're going to do. I've got to move the sheep from the top paddock today too.'

Mum was at the sink, clattering about washing dishes and didn't bother to turn around to answer Dad, a sure sign things were crook on the domestic front. It must have started long before I had made it to breakfast.

'And where the hell have you been all morning, Graham? Mooning about with yer bloody books eh?'

'Just doing my homework, Dad.'

It was true. I was a few minutes late. I was supposed to be sitting down for my breakfast by eight o'clock on school days. My late arrival was because I was finishing off my cover decoration for Miss Tully. I really liked Miss Tully, my teacher, and I was doing well at school. She was pretty and kind and I knew doing my homework carefully would please her.

Yesterday, at craft, we had made notebooks to give to our dads. This had involved meticulously measuring up and cutting out pieces of stiff cardboard and producing marbling papers for the insides of the notebook covers. Homework was to get these covers decorated and I had used the new Lakeland coloured pencils Auntie Mollie and Uncle Christopher had given me for Christmas. This morning I had been up early decorating the notebook cover with things I thought Dad would like. There was a handsome red Massey Ferguson tractor at the bottom left of the front cover with lush green hills in the background covered with little white sheep. I had included a barbed-wire fence too with a couple of dead bushy-tailed foxes hanging there limply. Dad was always trying to shoot foxes because they raided our chook-house occasionally at night-time. Whenever Dad was successful, he would hang the foxes on the nearest fence as a dire warning to others that might still be prowling about. I thought Dad would be tickled pink to see a couple of dead foxes on the front of his notebook.

Mum plonked a bowl of steaming hot porridge in front of me and two pieces of cold buttered toast.

'May I have the sugar please Dad?'

A gnarled, dirt ingrained hand, propelled the sugar-bowl roughly in my direction.

'Don't forget to collect the bloody eggs before you go,' Dad fixed me with angry, mean-looking eyes; they were always mean when he was in a bad mood.

'No, I won't forget Dad.'

My little sister, Mary, even quieter than a church mouse, had finished her breakfast and was sitting at the table thoughtlessly picking her nose. Fortunately, it was Mum who noticed first, or Dad would have hit the roof.

'Run along Mary, dear, clean your teeth and get ready for school.'

Relieved to escape the tense atmosphere in the kitchen, Mary grabbed her doll, Susan, and scarpered off to the bathroom.

Dad still had one more hand grenade to throw. 'Where the hell's the newspaper today? I want to see the bloody market reports. How can a man run a bleeding farm if he doesn't know what the bloody market's doing?'

'Bill is obviously running late with his paper deliveries

today. The paper wasn't there when I looked about twenty minutes ago,' Mum reported.

'Graham, stop slobbering over your porridge and see if the bloody paper has arrived.'

'Yes Dad.'

When I ran out to the front yard, I found the newspaper lodged in one of the few bushes that still survived following years of neglect. It was out of my reach, but it eventually fell to the ground when I gave the branch a vigorous shake. Dad without his morning paper was like a dog denied his bone. I handed it to him receiving a dismissive grunt for my efforts.

Twenty minutes later, with the eggs collected and safely placed on the kitchen bench, teeth shiny clean and little Mary in tow, we were on our way. It's almost a mile to school and takes us nearly half an hour, or even longer, if Mary dawdles.

'Why's Daddy cranky?' asked Mary, holding my hand and looking up at me with her sky-blue eyes.

'I dunno,' I replied, shrugging my shoulders.

'I don't like Daddy when he gets all cranky.'

'Nor do I.'

As we approached the sharp left turn in the road at the corner of our property, old Jake from up the road came careering around the bend in his dirt-encased clapped-out ute spraying clouds of suffocating dust over us. For a moment or two we could barely see. Our attempts at being sparkling clean and neat for school were ruined. We brushed ourselves down as best we could and spat out dust.

'Bloody old fool!'

'Graham, that's naughty, that's swearing. Mummy says it's rude to swear.'

'Dad does it all the time,' I snapped back.

We walked on. That empty aching feeling simply wouldn't go away. Fortunately, I could forget the unhappiness at home, once I met up with my good mates at school, but the horrid gnawing hollowness would return as soon as Mary and I walked home after school. I knew my miserably sad feelings wouldn't completely go away until we were all feeling happy again at home. If Dad was still snarly and grumpy this evening, then there was no hope of contentment. I didn't know what, if anything, I could do to try to put things right at home. Perhaps I could ask Mum?

As we neared school, other kids were arriving from every direction. Colin, my best mate, jumped off his bike at the rusting school gate and gave me a cheery wave. He was so proud of his new gleaming BSA bike that he had been given for Christmas. My mum and dad had said I might get a bike next year, if the wool cheque was a really good one. But they had said that last year and the year before. Mike, another mate, was at the gate too, playing, as always, with his bright red yoyo. Mike was crazy about his yoyo and I had to admit that he could perform some mighty clever tricks. At the far end of the school veranda I spotted another close mate, Fred, tying up his pony, Rocky, and ensuring it had enough water and a nosebag for the day. Few of the local kids still rode their ponies to school nowadays. And there was Lynda. She was the prettiest girl in the school and made me feel fluttery every time I saw her. She was brilliant at everything; athletics, swimming, maths, composition, spelling. You name it, and she was good at it. Sometimes I managed to sit next to Lynda in class and would drool over her good looks and try to make her giggle and laugh. I'm going to marry her one day!

Mary, as usual, had brought her doll, Susan, to school. She took it everywhere. Today the doll had a new dress on and Mary was soon showing the dress off to her little classmates. She ran off happily enough with her little friends down behind the water-tank where the infants played.

Colin, Mike and I headed straight for the grassy playground down the back of the school to join the soccer game that was underway every morning before class. Rugby league, sadly, was banned, because the teachers said it was too dangerous and kids might get hurt. Soccer was acceptable as an alternative. There were heaps of protruding rocks in our playground so kids still injured themselves. Fred joined us once he had settled his pony down for the day.

The soccer game was short-lived, the bell rang and we lined up in our class rows. Mr Marsden, the School Principal, reminded us about bringing our swimming gear for tomorrow's swimming lessons and we marched into class to the sound of a pre-recorded army band. My mates and I are fourth graders. Third and fourth grade are combined as a composite class with Miss Tully, my favourite teacher. I suppose that's not saying much, since there are only three teachers at my school. There's Mr Marsden, Miss Tully and Mary's dumpy infants' teacher, Mrs Kircudbright.

Whenever there was a dull moment during the day's lessons, my empty feelings came back to haunt me and I would feel sad and gloomy. There were two kids in my class who came from what the teachers called, "broken homes". I felt sorry for these kids because they didn't have both their parents to bring them up. Their dads had scarpered off and left them alone with their mums and siblings. That's not fair!

Is our dad going to leave us? I wondered.

CHAPTER TWO

Thursdays are my favourite days at school yet I couldn't help wondering how Mum and Dad were faring. Were they talking to each other again? Did Dad come back to the house for his lunch or stay out in the paddocks sulking? Perhaps Mum had prepared an extra special tasty lunch for him in an effort to pacify him? Dad absolutely adored lamb chops and Mum told me once that the way to a man's heart was through his stomach. By my reasoning, if Dad had a few of Mum's juicy lamb chops in his tummy for lunch then he might be happier. Maybe, I speculated, everything will have blown over by the time Mary and I make it home? A plateful of lamb chops might just prevent Dad leaving the farm and turning us into another "broken home".

As always, at the end of the school day, I waited at the rusty gate for Mary. At lunchtime, Miss Tully had had a good look at my drawing on the front cover of the notebook I was going to give Dad. She said it was excellent but she felt there was too much blue sky. She had suggested I take the notebook home and put some birds in the sky, or even an aeroplane. As Dad was a farmer, and always had been, I reasoned a crop-dusting plane would be ideal, one of those two-seater Cessnas that swooped about the skies like a giant dragonfly. I reckoned I could draw one because I had watched them busy at work on surrounding properties. Dad said our farm was too small so it didn't need spraying.

Soon Mary came skipping along the path clutching her doll. She seemed to have forgotten that Mum and Dad had been fighting at breakfast time.

'Hold my hand, there are cars about.'

Mary slipped her small hand into mine but said nothing.

'Hey Graham, want to come round to my place this 'arvo?' It was my best mate, Colin, sitting on his super-duper BSA Speedster.

'Sorry Colin, I've got to take Mary home.'

'How long will that take?'

'Half an hour to get home and then at least another ten to fifteen minutes to walk back into town to where you live.'

'Oh Jeez, that's a long time. Tell you what, we can double up. Mary can sit here on my crossbar and you can run. Then we can be back at your farm quick time, eh?'

Colin was a great friend. Nothing was ever too much trouble and he was always helping people out. His old man was the postmaster at the Sandalwood Post Office. I don't know what his mum did, but I do know she made the most amazing biscuits and cakes. Whenever I went to Colin's place, I always enjoyed the yummiest of snacks.

Colin and I also shared a love of nature. We would happily spend a whole afternoon just in his backyard, where his parents grew heaps of flowers and vegetables and where innumerable insects, small creatures and bugs thrived. We would race about chasing anything that was airborne with lengthy butterfly nets. We had learnt exactly where in the garden to locate all sorts of creepy crawlies. As long as we didn't harm the garden plants, we were allowed to catch any unsuspecting little creatures and house them in containers. In Colin's garage there was an extensive array of jars with beetles in them, jars with ants, jars with millipedes and, sadly, other jars with insects that had long since passed away. We had so many animal homes on the go that Colin's mother sometimes ran out of jam-jars. Caterpillars and grasshoppers were happier in cardboard boxes, we discovered. We even boasted a large glass bowl containing several tadpoles that we had caught when we snuck out the back of Colin's yard and down to the creek one afternoon. Colin was in charge of feeding the small zoo.

Colin had been up to my place a couple of times too. The creepy crawlies were quite different on the farm and this fascinated Colin. Around the sheds we found heaps of spiders, and all sorts of moths and flying ants caught in their webs. At the right time of year, there were grasshoppers and even the occasional locust. Once we found a monster centipede travelling at a great rate of knots along the ground. We were desperate to catch it but it was too quick and scurried down a crack between two rocks. Dad said we were lucky we didn't try and pick it up as giant brown centipedes have a nasty bite.

'What do you think Mary? Do you want to have a ride home on Colin's new bike?'

Mary looked inquiringly at me with those sky-blue eyes, then at the bike and then back to me again. She nodded.

'Okay, I'll lift her up, Colin.'

Mary was six and tubby. I'm nine. I had forgotten how heavy she was. I really had to struggle to get her up onto that crossbar. Mary sat there, wobbling and uncomfortable, and I thought she was going to say she wanted to get off. But she was made of sterner stuff and was hanging on grimly and she turned to look at Colin.

'You okay to go?' Colin asked, 'We'll go slowly until you get the hang of it.' Mary nodded and handed me Susan, her doll, to carry.

Colin was true to his word, and pushed off gently.

I started to trot along beside them. Mary was doing fine. This was going to be a breeze so we'd be home in no time.

As we approached the sharp bend on the corner of our farm, I saw a plume of dust rising furiously in great belching clouds in front of us. It was that madman Jake again. I recognised the front of his ute. Colin saw Jake coming too and panicked. In his clumsy attempt to slow down and get off the road, he lost control. The bike teetered erratically, righted itself for a second, before crashing to the ground at the same time as the ute swerved, corrected, swerved again and roared past in a massive showering of dust, dirt and stones.

For a moment or two we were completely blinded by the dust cloud. I had jumped to the side of the road and was unhurt, but Colin and Mary were both lying on the road. Colin was yelling in pain and my little sister was motionless.

'Oh no, oh no, oh help!' I knew the ute had missed them, but two people who meant so much to me were now in big trouble. How could I have been so stupid to agree to let Mary ride side-saddle? A thousand thoughts ran through my mind all at once. What if Mary is dead? What should I do? How can I get help? How will I ever tell Mum and Dad? Dad will murder me! What if another car comes roaring around the corner any moment?

As I raced across the road, I remembered something

my cub-master had told us only last week. He had said that in an emergency you need to keep a cool head. Panicking was the worst thing you could do. Stay calm, and assess the situation before you act. I remembered the word "assess" because one of the cubs had asked what it meant. So, as calmly as I could, I tried to assess the situation.

Two special people were lying on the road and could have been killed if another car suddenly came zooming around the corner. I must first move them off the road, I thought to myself I grabbed Mary by her feet and dragged her over to the side of the road and parked her unceremoniously in the shade of a large eucalyptus tree. She was moaning. Then I dashed back to Colin who had stopped yelling and was now sitting up groaning and clutching his left arm. I knew he was trying to be brave. Boys don't cry.

'Hurry Colin, get off the road. Come on, quickly, before another car comes.'

'My arm's really hurting. I think it's broken.'

I grabbed him under the armpits from behind and tried to pull him up on his feet. At first, we didn't move, but then Colin started to shove his heels into the bull-dust, and between us we edged slowly towards the side of the road, like an ant dragging its prey. Next, I returned for the BSA Speedster which was filthy dirty but miraculously appeared to be virtually undamaged.

I lifted it up and wheeled it over to the same gum tree where Mary was lying and propped it up against the trunk.

The dust had settled and another car was approaching from the opposite direction, coming back from town. It was being driven more sensibly, and cornered carefully, sending up far less dust. It looked like Mrs James, who lived on a farm further along our road. I waved frantically, but she just waved back, thinking I was being extra friendly, and kept going. Mrs James must have been concentrating so much on cornering that she completely missed the sight of two injured children under the eucalypt tree.

Mary was ashen. A nasty bruise appeared on the side of her head and her eyelids were flickering as though she didn't have the strength to get them fully open. I was feeling awful, as though I was about to vomit. This was all my fault. For over two years I had been safely walking my little sister to school and back and everybody trusted me to look after her. All through kindergarten, all through first grade, Mary and I had walked the mile into school early in the morning, and the mile back again after school. Together, we had coped with rainy times, blowy times, hot days and frosts. Three times it had even snowed and once there was a flash flood at Timboola Creek and we had had to wait there in the rain for someone to help us across.

As the big brother I was trusted to protect Mary whenever unexpected things happened. In spring we were often swooped by cantankerous magpies. When this happened, we would walk along waving a stick above our heads. Mum made us special caps to wear too. Mum said that magpies don't like to see your eyes which is why they always attack from behind. Mum's special caps were white cricket caps with big colourful black eyes painted on the back. I think it worked. Instead of swooping us, the magpies would sit up in the tree branches sharpening their beaks and looking grumpy.

Summertime brought out flies, lizards and snakes. The flies buzzed about us on the hot days when we were walking home, sweaty and smelly. Once I counted eighty-three flies riding on Mary's back. She said she counted three million on mine! Blue-tongues and geckoes were frequently sunning themselves on the road. Some were squashed, leaving a messy flattened skin. Sometimes we encountered snakes such as yellow-bellied black snakes. Dad told us not to fear the snakes. He said they were more frightened of us than we were of them and wouldn't attack us unless we trod on them, or teased them in some way. So, whenever we saw a snake, we just let it cross over to the other side and admired it as it silently slithered leaving its unique wriggle marks in the dirt.

We liked it best in winter. On frosty mornings, after

rain, the puddles freeze over and we can skate about on them. Sometimes we see large cobwebs on the side of the road shimmering with hoar frost. Mary says it's like a fairy wonderland. Best of all are the rare snowy days. If we have time, we make a snowman on the side of the road where the snow has drifted. We never have any clothes to put on the snowman but we make do with sticks, stones and leaves for his face and fingers. Mary says next time it snows she wants us to make a snow-lady. Fair enough.

Once, when we were walking home, we found a dead kangaroo on the side of the road. There was a joey in its pouch so we rescued it and carried it home wrapped up in my school jumper to keep it warm. Mary fell in love with that little joey and with Mum's guidance we nursed it along until it was ready to be released back into the bush. Mary didn't want it to leave and was miserable for days afterwards.

Dad insists it isn't nature we have to worry about when we are out on the road, it's the humans. I guess he's right, because it was stupid old Jake that messed us up by speeding around that bend in the road too fast.

Our road extends on past our place for about another six or seven miles and then fizzles out where it enters a large forest plantation of radiata pines. I reckon there are wolves slinking around in there, although Dad says there are no wolves in Australia. I'm sure if they would let me go in there exploring I could find some. There are six other farms between our property and the wolf-forest at the very end. We know all the farmers and their wives and their kids, we can recognise their vehicles, tractors and horses. Mum's kitchen window looks out over the road, so frequently she knows who's going to go by and even when. Often, when Mum is doing some cooking, she will say things like, 'There go the Dennisons … off to church,' or 'Mrs Thiering's got a new hat,' or 'Tom's taking another load of sheep to market today.' Our farm is the closest one to town so Mum can keep accurate tabs on everyone.

Apart from mad old Jake, most of the folk up our road are okay. There's only one fellow that Mary and I are scared of, although I would never admit that to Mary. His name is Davey Wild and he lives with his parents next door on a farm called "Festina Lente". Nobody knew what that name meant until I asked Miss Tully, my teacher. She says it is Bahasa, a language that people in Indonesia speak. Miss Tully knows everything! She told me Festina Lente means you should improve things slowly. I suppose that's what all the cockies around here are trying to do, slowly make their farms more productive.

Davey Wild was born funny. Dad went to school with Davey and says Davey couldn't do anything at school. He never learnt to read or write and he was always being naughty and playing up. His behaviour became so bad that he was sent to a special boarding school in Sydney. Dad reckoned this was a good thing because most of the kids at Sandalwood School would tease him until he lost his temper and became violent.

Davey is a big, heavy man nowadays with a red unshaven face. He wears an old straw hat with a hole on the top. His parents have bought him new hats but he refuses to wear them. He loves his hat with a hole in it. Davey often trudges past our place to get out of the house and have some exercise. Usually he wears old jodhpurs, RM Williams boots and a check shirt. Mary and I hide if we see Davey coming.

All these things that Mary and I had encountered over the last two years now paled into insignificance. Here were the three of us stranded on the side of the road; my beautiful little sister, unresponsive, and my best mate in so much pain that he was no good to anyone. As the only able-bodied one left, I needed to take the initiative.

'Colin I'm going to get help. Stay here and look after Mary for me. I'll be as quick as I can.

Colin was clutching his wrist, which I now noticed, was twisted at a peculiar angle. Still whimpering, Colin nodded. I picked his bike up. It wasn't fit to ride; the back tyre was punctured and the handlebars were twisted.

'Bike's no-good Colin. I'll be back soon with Mum or Dad.'

I set off at an even trot. It is only about half a mile from the bend in the road to the gate at the entrance to our farm. In a few minutes I'd be there. It hadn't rained for a time, and the council hadn't been along with their grader for months, so deep corrugations had formed on both sides of the road. The corrugations are not a problem if you're walking or driving, but running across them is a different matter. It's easy to turn an ankle. I was on a mercy mission and the last thing I wanted now was a sprained ankle. I was soon puffing as a raucous kookaburra opened up with his distinctive laughing call somewhere above me. He was answered by another, sitting on the telegraph line. I developed a stitch in my left side, but the image of sweet Mary lying helpless at the foot of that large gumtree, drove me on.

I reached the farm gate and fumbled the latch to allow the gate to swing open. I hesitated about closing it behind me, but it had always been mercilessly drilled into me, like every other farm kid, that you always leave a gate as you find it. I lost valuable seconds swinging it shut and locking the latch back into position. I raced up the driveway and followed the short way to our house. I could see Mum watching me out of the kitchen window. She must have sensed something was wrong. Mary wasn't with me, and I guess I looked panicky.

'Mum, Mum,' I started yelling, before I even reached the front door, 'Come quickly, Mary's hurt, really badly.'

Mum met me at the door, worry creasing her face. 'What's happened, Graham?'

'We've had an accident on the corner. Mary and Colin are both badly hurt. We need to get Mary to the hospital.'

Mum didn't waste a moment. She flung off her apron, grabbed the keys to the ute, and tore off round to the carport at the side of the house with me in hot pursuit.

'Open the bloody gate. Hurry!'

I ran back down the drive and managed to have the gate open before Mum and the ute arrived.

'Jump in, forget about closing the gate. The sheep are safely up at the back paddock today.'

Mum was normally a sedate driver, but not today. She rammed her foot to the floorboards and we tore off creating a sandstorm behind us, fit to rival old Jake's. We pulled up a couple of minutes later in a swirl of dust, large enough to be visible a mile away. Mum jumped out and ran to Mary who was stirring and groaning, but the bruise on the side of her head had darkened and swollen more.

'Right you two, jump in the ute,' she shouted, as she gently lifted Mary. It was only then that she realised that poor Colin was incapable of jumping anywhere and certainly not into the back of a ute.

'Graham, you climb in the back and I'll pass Mary to you. Keep her as still as possible and whatever you do, don't let her bump her head. Colin, can you manage to get in the front?'

'Yes, Mrs Granger.'

Mum placed Mary into my arms and I lay back against a tarpaulin holding Mary gently but firmly. I prayed Mum wasn't going to drive like a maniac again. Next, Mum held the passenger's door open for Colin who managed to climb in without too much difficulty.

'What about my bike?' whimpered Colin.

'What about your bloody bike?'

'It's over there against the tree.'

Muttering to herself, Mum trotted back over to the tree then heaved the bike into the back of the ute, narrowly missing Mary and me. As she did so, she noticed a sad looking object lying on the road covered in dirt. Picking it up, she brushed it down vigorously to reveal Mary's favourite doll, Susan. She handed it to me for safe-keeping.

'Make sure this doll stays with Mary at all times.'

Mum took another quick look at my sister before jumping in and heading off towards Sandalwood, our little township. Aware she now had two injured children on board, Mum drove sensibly this time, and headed straight for the surgery belonging to the one and only doctor that the community had struggled so hard to retain in Sandalwood.

The road sign on the edge of town proudly announced, "Sandalwood - Population 712" The town has seen better days and no longer supported a hospital. We had a doctor for three days a week, Mondays, Wednesdays and Fridays. On Tuesdays and Thursdays, the doctor practices in Minimbah, a nearby village that's even smaller than ours. With luck, the doctor would still be in his surgery today as it was only a quarter past four and it was a Wednesday.

We were indeed fortunate. There were two cars parked outside the doctor's premises, a sure sign that the doctor was still there.

'Graham, you help Colin, and I'll carry Mary. Don't forget Susan.'

A sad little procession made its way to the outside door of the surgery, Mum nursing Mary in her arms, Colin next to her, still blubbering and holding his now swollen wrist with me bringing up the tail and feeling acutely embarrassed to be holding Mary's grubby dolly. I had to open the door for them, and we trooped in, a miserable looking bunch of souls.

'Hello Betty, what's happened here then?' I was surprised to discover that Lynda's mother was the doctor's receptionist. She looked smart and attractive; I could see where Lynda had inherited her good looks.

'We need to see the doc quick smart please Dora. Mary here has had a bad hit on the head and is semi-conscious and Colin's broken his arm.'

'You're just in time. We were about to start closing up. I'll tell the doctor.'

A moment later we traipsed into the doctor's surgery. There were only two chairs provided for patients so I had to stand.

Mum had explained to me the last time I went to see the doctor that small towns like ours, struggled to attract and retain doctors. She said most of the doctors wanted to practise in the "big smoke" and didn't relish living out in the bush. The only doctors that would come to the bush were new migrant doctors, and they only came because the law said that they had to practise in the bush for at least three years before they were allowed to return to the "big smoke." Most of the migrant doctors only stayed for a few months and then moved on somewhere else. Mum said they didn't like the accommodation in Sandalwood and the lack of facilities.

I had never seen this particular doctor before. Lynda's mother introduced us to Dr Zegalski, and then left the surgery, closing the door quietly behind her.

Dr Zegalski stood up and walked around his large wooden desk to greet us. He stopped in front of my now seated Mum, stood up straight like a soldier on parade, clicked his heels, bowed, and then extended his right hand as if about to shake hands with the Queen. Mum, who was still nursing a groggy Mary, didn't know quite what to do. After a moment's hesitation, she wiped her right hand on the side of her dress and shook Dr Zegalski's proffered hand.

I had never met anyone quite like this doctor before. He was skinny and tall, and wore an old black suit with a waistcoat and a bright red bow-tie. There was a similarly coloured red handkerchief sticking out of his breast pocket. Mum told me later that the pocket was actually called a fob pocket. The shoes he had clicked together so majestically were shiny black, like Dad's old dancing shoes. There was a small neat black moustache perched on his lip that looked as if he had stuck it on from one of those dressing-up kits. The doctor's jet-black hair was slicked back, flat, like a wet cow-pat. I was not sure I liked the look of this doctor, so I instinctively sidled up closer to Mum's chair. Looking at Dr Zegalski was one thing, but hearing him speak was a whole new ball game.

'Velcome. Vot ees the matter?' The doctor's eyes seemed to bore into Mum's.

Mum appeared surprised by this question. After all, doctors were supposed to tell their patients what the matter was.

'Pleez ...' Dr Zegalski indicated, with an elaborate hand

gesture, that Mum should put Mary on the examination table. Gently, Mum laid little Mary out, making sure her very dirty school dress, was positioned politely.

'Nah.' Dr Zegalski was shaking his head.

Mum looked up at the doctor, then realised she had placed Mary on the examination table with the wounded side of Mary's head against the wall. She blushed then picked my sister up and turned her around so that the doctor could properly conduct his examination.

'Vot happen?'

'They all fell off a bike,' I piped up. Until now, Mum had no idea how the accident had happened. 'I think Mary's head hit the road,' I added.

Mum turned and glared at me; she couldn't contain herself. 'What the hell was Mary doing on a bicycle?'

Before I could muster up a response, Dr Zegalski spoke again.

'I tink vis is concussion. Is best go 'ospital for check. Ve vill call da ambulance. Now, vot is the matter 'ere?'

The doctor moved over to examine Colin's swollen wrist. My best mate warily surrendered his painful arm for the doctor's inspection. Dr Zegalski pressed it in several places and asked repeatedly, 'It hurt, no? It hurt, no?' to which Colin obliged either with a loud 'ow!' or a shake of his head.

'Is broken,' the doctor announced finally, after a few

more painful prods. 'Also, ambulance. No fix 'ere.' Dr Zegalski shook his head sadly and managed a trace of a smile.

And so it was that an ambulance was dispatched from Goulburn, our nearest large town, and wound its way along the thirty-five miles of twisting dirt road to the doctor's surgery at Sandalwood. By the time the ambulance arrived, nearly an hour later, Mary was sitting up and talking in a funny rambling way and had vomited on the doctor's floor twice. Lynda's kindly mother stayed to help, whilst my mum and Colin's mum, who had hastily been contacted, were fussing about waiting to go in the ambulance. As soon as the ambulance left Sandalwood, Lynda's mum drove me home. I only wish Lynda had been there too.

I was dreading telling Dad what had happened. I thought he would explode and rant and rave at me. If I was in trouble for being a few minutes late for breakfast, what would Dad think if I had almost killed his daughter and my best mate at the same time? But he just shrugged his shoulders and said, 'These things happen, mate.'

Sometimes, I don't understand grown-ups!

CHAPTER THREE

Dad said we would have to "batch" for the night, which simply meant looking after ourselves. He pulled half a dozen good-sized lamb chops from the fridge and set me to work peeling spuds and pumpkin. The meat and vegetables were, of course, home produce. Dad reckoned Mum had green thumbs and that everything she tried to grow in the garden prospered. For dessert we opened another bottle of Mum's preserved apricots and, as a treat, Dad said we could have some Peter's strawberry ice cream. Mum and Dad often worked together in the orchard where we grew apricots as well as plums, nectarines, quinces, apples and pears. Mum always seemed to be making jams or preserving fruits. We often shared our produce with our friends and they would reciprocate by giving us foodstuffs that we didn't have.

I was helping Dad with the washing up when the phone rang. It was Mum with news about Mary and

Colin. Apparently, the doctors were concerned about my sister. They said she had been concussed, but that the injury should right itself in a couple of days. They were far more worried about an injury she had suffered in the small of her back, where they thought she must have fallen onto the bike's handlebars. Mum pronounced the next few words very carefully because she had written them down on a piece of paper when the doctors had explained what the problem was. The doctors think Mary's suffering "acute renal injury".

'And what the hell does that mean?' demanded Dad.

'It means she has badly bruised one of her kidneys, dear.'

'Well she's got two of the buggers. Why's that a problem?'

'Well, I don't really know. The doctors have asked a kidney specialist to come and see Mary tomorrow. He's going to drive down from Canberra.'

'And what about Graham's mate, Colin? How's he going?'

'They x-rayed his arm, set it in plaster and he went home with his mum a few minutes ago. He's tired but seemed cheerful enough.'

'So, what happens now Betty?'

'Well, I have to stay here with Mary. She's frightened, confused and miserable. They've given her stuff for the pain and that has calmed her down a bit. They're bringing a trestle bed into the ward so I can stay the night with her. You'll just have to manage without me for a couple of days, I'm afraid. I'll ring you again tomorrow to let you know how things are going.'

This news made me feel awful. My poor little sister was having to stay in hospital because I had so stupidly said she could ride side-saddle on Colin's bike. I promised Mary, there and then, that I would never make such a stupid decision again.

Dad sent me off to bed at the usual time. Most nights, Mum came in and read a story to the two of us, but tonight there was no Mum, and no Mary, so there was no story. Dad came in to say goodnight, but he never read us stories. I think he thought reading out loud to kids was sooky. Most nights he just popped in, gave us a quick kiss and left. That was how Dad was, the strong, silent type.

But tonight, things were different. Dad came in and sat on the end of my bed, something I couldn't remember him doing before.

'You and I need to have a bit of a chat, mate. Your mother and I think you are old enough to hear the truth now.'

It was a warm night so I only had a sheet over me. I peered at Dad over my sheet and wondered what "the truth" was. I could see that whatever Dad was going to talk to me about, was proving difficult for him. He seemed embarrassed and wouldn't look me in the eye.

Suddenly, to my horror, I remembered John, who was eleven and in grade six, telling us in the playground about a talk his dad had given him one night. It was all about sex and John had done his very best to keep a straight face. Was sex the topic my dad was stealing himself up to talk about? If so, I dreaded what was coming. I reckoned I already knew what sex was all about, it was when the dogs, or cows, or sheep coupled in order to make babies. Pretty straightforward. What the heck was there to talk about? I had seen it happening on the farm often enough. Even the rooster did it.

'You have to keep what I'm going to tell you a secret, Graham. You are definitely not to talk to Mary about it, she's too young to understand. This is something between me, you, and your Mum, and nobody else. Do you get my drift?'

Yup, I thought, this is certainly a sex talk coming up.
'Sure Dad.'

'It's going to be a bit of a shock for you mate, but we want to tell you before someone else does. I'm going to tell you tonight and when Mary's about your age mum will explain it to her also. That sound okay?'

We had been doing "commonly used expressions" at school this last week and one of the expressions we had discussed popped into my mind now, "making a mountain out of a mole hill". Dad was certainly fumbling about in a silly way and making a big fuss over nothing. If animals wanted to have babies, they coupled. If married people wanted to have babies, they must do it too, although I wasn't sure just how they did it. Perhaps Dad was about to explain?

'Have you ever noticed Graham, that you and Mary look very different?'

This is getting weirder and weirder. Of course, we look different, Mary's a girl and I'm a boy. We have different parts.

'Mary has curly red hair but you have straight black hair. Mary has deep blue eyes and yours are hazel.'

I waited silently, unsure where this was all leading. Dad looked more embarrassed than ever.

'Have you ever wondered about how different you two are?'

'Not really, Dad.'

'Well…it's because you have different parents.'

This short statement floored me. I said nothing for a moment or two, trying to digest what Dad had just said.

'So … Mary's not part of our family, Dad?'

'Of course, she's part of our family. We love her very much.'

'I don't understand.'

'Mum and I are not Mary's mum and dad.'

'So, why's she living here then?'

'We adopted her.'

'What's that mean?'

'Mary lost both her real parents in a car accident, so mum and I said we would be her parents instead.'

I was so amazed to hear this that I was temporarily lost for words. Finally, I found my tongue again.

'Does ... does Mary know this Dad?'

'No. It happened when she was a baby. She was in the car too and was thrown out. At first the police couldn't even find her. She was badly hurt and taken to a special children's hospital in Sydney until she was better. The reason I'm telling you all this now is that she injured her kidneys in that awful car accident when she was a baby and now it has happened again.'

'Is that serious, Dad?'

'Quite possibly.'

Once again, I felt terribly guilty. If Mary was badly hurt this second time it would be my fault. If only I had behaved more responsibly, like a big brother should. Dad was speaking again.

'There's more, son.'

I looked at Dad who reminded me of a tortoise wanting desperately to disappear back into its shell. I waited.

'We are not your parents, either.'

This statement hit me like a sledge-hammer. I was still trying to digest the extraordinary fact that Mary was not really my sister, although in every way she felt and behaved like my sister, now I was being told something even more shattering. My head was reeling, it was all too much. Words seemed useless, I just gawped.

'We adopted you too mate. Your mum and I couldn't have children of our own, so the next best thing was to adopt other children who needed parents.'

'So, what happened to my real parents?'

Dad coloured a bit and looked away, 'I don't know.'

'But you must have known, Dad?'

'I had some idea at the time, but remember, it was many years ago. I don't know where they are now.'

'So, my proper mum and dad are still alive then?'

'Probably.'

'I want to find them. I want to know who they are, and everything about them,' I blurted out without thinking.

'Sorry mate, we can't help you with that. What's important now is that *we* are your parents and we love you very much.'

It was all too much. I couldn't face hearing anymore. I rolled over and buried my face in my pillow. Dad put his hand on my shoulder and tried to comfort me as I sobbed quietly. I don't know how long Dad stayed but I must eventually have fallen asleep.

CHAPTER FOUR

Usually the morning chorus of boastful hens proclaiming their successes woke me up, but not this Thursday morning. Late to bed and trying to comprehend all that Dad had told me had kept me awake. I was clearly short on sleep and feeling tired and irritable. I went through my morning duties in a semi-trance and landed back in the kitchen for breakfast just as the phone rang. It was Mum informing us this time that the specialist kidney doctor had ordered little Mary be transferred to a renal ward at the children's hospital in Sydney. Mum was going down with her in the ambulance.

'Is she going to get better Dad?'

'I guess that's in God's hands, mate.'

I remembered I hadn't said my prayers last night. Saying my prayers was something that happened when Mum came in to read us a story at bedtime, but last night Mum was away. How was Mary going to get better if I didn't ask God to fix her up? For a moment I contemplated returning to my bedroom to say a quick belated prayer. Perhaps it would help?

I hadn't fathomed God out yet. My Scripture teacher, at school, told us that God was omnipotent. She explained this meant he was all powerful and could do anything he wanted. Apparently, he was everywhere, saw everything and you couldn't do anything without God seeing it. So, he would have watched me encouraging Mary to ride side-saddle on Colin's bike. Did God make Mary fall off and hurt herself then? Mrs Adams, the Scripture teacher, would say that it was the devil who made bad things happen. So, was the devil there watching us as well? I decided to say a double lot of prayers when I went to bed this evening and to apologise to God for forgetting to pray last night. Mrs Adams had assured us that prayers helped, but she had also said that God didn't always do what we asked of him. It was all very confusing. God must be mighty busy listening to everyone's prayers and trying to decide which ones to answer and which ones to ignore.

Mum was not around to make my sandwiches for school, so I grabbed a couple of pieces of bread, cut a hunk of cheese, and picked out an apple that still looked reasonable and threw everything into my picnic box. I would also have my free bottle of milk at school during morning break.

'Bye, Dad.'

'Bye, mate. When you get back, I'll probably be up at the shed fixing the tractor.'

For the first time in two years there was no Mary to cajole, tease or encourage to complete the dusty walk to school. I missed her happy innocent chatter. Often, we would find something interesting to examine along the way. It might be an ant's nest, or a discarded cicada shell, or a trap-door spider. Sometimes we would imagine we could recognise shapes in the clouds, or play pooh sticks if Timboola Creek was up. Today I felt lonely and fell to wondering more and more about what Dad had spoken about last night. It was hard to believe that Mary and I did not completely belong to Mum and Dad. Perhaps we shouldn't even call them Mum and Dad? Then I remembered that Dad had told me it was a secret and I must not mention it to Mary or anyone else. That was going to be hard, I wanted to share this scary news with my best mate, Colin.

It was a relief to get to school and find everything was still normal there after such a tumultuous time at home, and with Mary. Soccer was on in the playground at the back of the school, so I dropped my school bag, raced down, and joined in. The bell rang far too soon and there was a stampede for the toilets before school assembly started. There was no sign of Colin anywhere, so I assumed he must have been kept home to have a day to rest after yesterday's events. Mike, with his bright red yoyo spinning up and down furiously, Fred and pretty Lynda came over to ask about Mary and Colin. I filled them in as best I could. I was also longing to tell them what I had discovered about my parents, but I kept silent. It was a family secret and I had promised not to speak to anyone about the matter. I could be trusted to keep a promise even if I had let my sister down.

The morning lessons went okay and I had cricket training with Mr Marsden, the principal, at lunchtime. It was a hot day, and during the afternoon lessons, Miss Tully talked about Wentworth, Blaxland and Lawson, the three intrepid white explorers who attempted a crossing of the challenging Blue Mountains. Normally I love Social Studies, but this afternoon I just couldn't concentrate. My eyelids felt heavy, as though they had weights attached, and I desperately wanted to put my head on my arms and go to sleep. Miss Tully's voice became a lulling, soothing drone ...

'Graham, are you feeling all right?'

I woke with a start, 'I'm sorry, Miss Tully.' Then I realised, with a nasty sinking feeling, that I must have completely missed hearing what it was we were supposed to be doing. The kids in the class were busy doing something, but I didn't have a clue what it was. I looked up, helplessly, at Miss Tully.

'I'm sorry,' I said again feebly, 'I didn't get much sleep last night.'

Miss Tully smiled and didn't get angry with me. 'Would you like me to explain what you have to do again?'

'Yes, please.'

I never did find out whether Wentworth, Blaxland and Lawson made it over those mountains.

I managed to stay awake for the rest of the afternoon. When the bell sounded and our class had left the classroom in an orderly manner, Miss Tully cornered me.

'Graham, it's not like you to fall asleep in class. Is everything okay?'

'Yes, thanks, Miss Tully. Mary has had to go to a special hospital in Sydney, and Mum's away, so I was up late last night and then I couldn't get to sleep.'

'Yes, I heard about little Mary. I'm so sorry. Do you think she'll be in hospital long?'

'I don't know.'

'Well, if there's anything I can do to help, just let me know Graham,' Miss Tully gave me one of her lovely reassuring smiles. 'Try not to worry too much about your sister and make sure you get to bed nice and early tonight. I want to see you sparking on all four cylinders at school tomorrow.'

'I'll do my best, Miss Tully.'

Again, I longed to open up to someone and share my concerns about my parents not really being my parents.

I would have felt so much better if I didn't have to keep it all bottled up as a secret. Miss Tully would be very understanding if I spoke to her.

—•—

It takes but a few minutes to walk from school to Colin's place, so I thought I would nip around to say "Hi". The sun was beating down relentlessly from a cloudless azure sky, the air buzzing with the sounds of summer. I teamed up with Mike and his constantly rotating red yoyo, along the way. Mike lived in the same street as Colin but further down. He was becoming really skilled with his yoyo. As we wandered along, he showed off a few of his newest tricks, "The Throw Down", "The Sleeper" and "The Three Leaf Clover". Mike had been busily researching the yoyo in his family's Encyclopedia Britannica and informed me they had been around for three thousand years. In some parts of the world, yoyos were even used as weapons.

Because Colin's dad was the Sandalwood postmaster, his family lived in the especially appointed postmaster's house. This was a solid, rather boring, red-brick, late-Victorian building with the Post Office on the ground floor and the living quarters above. There was a family entrance at the side of the building. Mike dazzled me with one more "Three Leaf Clover" display as he said his farewells and I rang the bell. Colin's mum came down the stairs to open the door and welcome me.

'How lovely to see you, Graham. Do come in. Colin is upstairs resting but already missing school.'

I followed Mrs Trent's wobbling posterior up the narrow flight of stairs. Colin's mum was a large, jovial woman who loved to wear jewellery. Today, massive purple earrings jangled from her ears like candelabras and a matching necklace surrounded her formidable neck. When we reached the top of the stairs, I expected to see purple rings on her hands too and was not disappointed. The best thing about Mrs Trent though, was her superb cooking. Whenever I visited, she would say, 'Now, I wonder if I can find a little something in the cupboard?' Out would come a pile of freshly baked biscuits or dark chocolate cake layered with cream, or even a pavlova. Today's "little something" turned out to be brandy snaps. Mrs Trent plonked down a plateful of these yummy treats next to my cool orange juice with blocks of ice floating about.

'Now young Graham, have you been beating up my son again?' challenged Mrs Trent, with her hands on her substantial hips and wearing a full-length apron covered in colourful pieces of fruit and wine glasses. I could tell she was joking from the look on her face.

'No,' I mumbled, my mouth full of brandy snap, 'He fell off his bike. Honestly.' I looked at Colin for support.

'I told you Mum; it was that old fool mad Jake that made me come off my bike. The police should stop him driving.'

'It's a pity there were no grown-up witnesses,' remarked Mrs Trent, as she grabbed another brandy snap. 'That man's a perfect menace.'

Colin was keen to show off his clean white plaster of Paris that stretched from his knuckles almost up to his elbow. There were three signatures on it already; his parents, and older sister, Michelle. 'Here you are,' he said, and passed me a biro. As I scribbled my name, as best I could on the rough surface, Colin told me his arm ached a bit still, but he would definitely be back at school tomorrow.

'Only if he eats his tea tonight and doesn't vomit it all up like he did last night,' added Mrs Trent.

Colin ignored his mother's remark and asked if there was any more news of Mary. I explained that she had been in a car accident when she was a baby, and had damaged her kidneys back then. Now, she had done it again. Doing it once was bad enough, but doing it twice was so serious that she had to be sent to Sydney so the specialist kidney doctors there could look after her.

'Were you in that car accident also?' asked Mrs Trent innocently. Suddenly, I realised I shouldn't have said anything about the car accident that had killed Mary's parents. Mary was now six year's old so the accident would have been only five years back. Another of the commonly used expressions we had been studying at school came to mind, perhaps I had "let the cat out of the bag?" Then I remembered, with relief, that my best mate, Colin, and his family, had only come to Sandalwood at the beginning of last year, so could not possibly know anything about Mary and her car accident. I determined, there and then, to keep my mouth shut about Mary's car accident five years ago.

I scoffed one more brandy snap, licked my creamy fingers clean and thanked Mrs Trent politely for afternoon tea. I picked up my school bag as Mrs Trent handed me one more brandy snap, 'Here you are Graham, one more to keep the wolf from the door,' she laughed.

'Wow, that's another commonly used expression,' I sang out, as I clattered down the stairs, and wended my way home, full of cold orange cordial and delicious brandy snaps.

CHAPTER FIVE

True to his word, Dad was in the open shed working on the tractor when I arrived home, hot and sweaty. Our two farm dogs, Dum and Dee, lay sprawled on the straw enjoying the shade and showed little interest in my arrival, except for a casual twitch of their tails. A couple of sparrows flew out as I entered the darkened shed, adding their high-pitched twittering to the racket of the deafening cicadas all about us. The warm, familiar, musty smell of the shed enveloped me. I could see Dad now spreadeagled under the engine of his beloved red Massey Ferguson.

'Hi Dad.'

'You took your time? It's nearly five.'

'I went to see how Colin was, he didn't come to school today.'

'Is he okay? A bit better than Mary, I hope?'

'Yup, he's okay. I wrote my name on his plaster. I

was only the fourth person to do it. Any news of Mum and Mary, Dad?'

Dad eased himself out slowly from under the tractor and stood up, wiping his dirty hands on an oily rag. The dogs sat up, alert, sensing something might be about to happen.

'Mum rang again. They think Mary's going to be okay but she's never going to be really healthy again. She's got permanent damage to her kidneys and they can't fix 'em. Chronic renal failure they reckon.'

'What do the kidneys do, Dad?'

'Your Mum was telling me about them on the phone this 'arvo. They're a bit like the bloody filter in my tractor. Blood runs into the kidneys and they filter out the good stuff that your body needs and then you pee out the rubbish. Clever eh? Filter in the tractor does much the same.'

'It's a pity Mary can't get a new kidney filter like you can for the tractor, Dad.'

'Well, Mum says the scientists are working on doing exactly what you just said. One day they reckon they will be able to give new kidneys to people whose kidneys are shot.'

'Are they going to make kidneys?'

'Nope. They'll transplant them.'

'What's that mean?'

'When someone dies, they'll whip out their two good

kidneys and stick 'em in somebody who needs new kidneys.'

'Crikey, that's weird Dad. Do the kidneys still work after you die?'

'For a short time apparently, the Yanks are experimenting on kidney transplants right now.'

'Wow. So, one day Mary could get a dead person's kidney?'

'Possibly son. Now, I've got a couple more jobs to do, so you're going to be chief cook tonight. Grab some more of those lamb chops from the freezer, get some spuds organised and cook up some onions and carrots. Reckon you can do that?'

'I think so, Dad. Can we have some more ice cream tonight too?'

'You had bloody ice cream last night, so just get out some more of Mum's preserved fruit. Don't go raiding the ice cream. Do you hear me?'

'Yes, Dad.'

I gave Dee and Dum a quick pat and trailed off to the kitchen to spend the next hour preparing the vegetables and cooking. Dad came in about six o'clock, fixed himself a beer and collapsed into his favourite chair.

And so, new routines were established on school days for the next couple of weeks, until Mum and Mary returned. Dad worked until six o'clock, or later, and I did the cooking. Gradually I became more proficient and quicker, but the meals were deadly boring. I like lamb chops, but after two weeks of nothing else you get really tired of them. Dad didn't seem to mind though.

One night, I gave Dad his notebook after I had finished making the improvements to the cover along the lines Miss Tully had suggested. Altogether, I had spent considerable time and care on Dad's notebook and was proud of my efforts. He just glanced at the notebook and grunted.

Often, I spent time thinking about my adoption. It was never easy talking to Dad in the evenings, he was usually tired and grumpy, but I badly wanted to find out more. Dad always turned the radio on at seven o'clock in the evenings to listen to the ABC National News and I was never allowed to talk during the broadcast. By the time I had finished the washing up, it was time for me to retire to my bedroom. This was the time of day when I most missed Mum and Mary. There were no good night kisses and cuddles, no bedtime stories, no being tucked up snugly in bed or interesting chats. All that happened now was that Dad would come in to turn off my light and say goodnight in a gruff sort of way. Sometimes I cried myself to sleep.

One Sunday night, when Dad had had a rare day off work and was enjoying a couple of extra beers, I sensed he might be more open to some conversation. I decided to be brave.

'Dad, if you and Mum are not my parents, then who are?'

He looked at me over his half-finished bottle of beer and laughed, 'Got yer worried has it?'

I didn't want to admit that I was worried, so I put on a brave face and tried to "man-up".

'Well, it would be handy to know. I might bump into my real dad somewhere or my proper mum.'

For a moment Dad looked angry. I don't think he liked the words I had used.

'Listen mate, *we* are your parents now. Sure, we didn't produce you, but we look after you, feed you, educate you and everything else. If I hadn't told you you're adopted you would never have known about it and wouldn't be worrying.'

'That's true Dad, but now that you have told me, I would really like to know who are my other mum and dad.'

'I guess I can understand that, but we're not allowed to tell you. Sorry mate.'

And that was the end of that. Sometimes, I would lie awake at night wondering and imagining what my biological parents might look like, what they did, whether they were still alive, and where they lived. I would imagine film stars, or doctors or maybe teachers. Perhaps they were off the land and were like us, farming sheep and cattle? Or maybe they were scientists working on kidney transplants in America and would come back one day in the future to help little Mary?

But I always came back to one worrying question, why did my parents get rid of me? Surely, having a child was something special and you wouldn't have one if you didn't want it? Did my parents have no money to look after me? Were they too ill to care for me? Had they died like Mary's parents? Something terrible must surely have happened. People simply don't give children away like a brandy snap or a couple of lamb chops. Perhaps my adoptive parents had to buy me from a shop somewhere? Maybe there were places where you could go if you wanted to buy a child for adoption? Was I expensive? Not knowing the answers to all these vexing questions was so frustrating!

Dad had said that he and Mum couldn't have children, which is why they had adopted Mary and me. But why couldn't they have children of their own? Do you have to get permission to have children? Living on a farm, I had often seen the ram servicing the sheep, the bull mounting the cows and the rooster chasing the hens. I also knew that these encounters were not always successful. Dad would often mention to Mum at meal times how many of his ewes were lambing and sometimes he would be excited if twins were born. Other interesting remarks I overheard from time to time, 'the bull did a good job this year, almost all the cows are in calf.' On another occasion, 'the ram was not performing, half the sheep missed out.' So, humans must do it too. Perhaps, like the farm animals, it was not always successful? I decided to interrogate Mum when she got home.

—•—

At last Mum rang to say they were coming home on Friday, and it was arranged that Dad and I would drive into Goulburn to pick them up from the railway station. The train didn't arrive until five minutes past five so there was ample time for Dad to pick me up from school and drive the thirty-five miles. I was so excited at school I found it difficult to concentrate. I managed to get all my spelling correct but stuffed up on the day's multiplication table quiz. Usually, I'm the best in the class, but today Colin, Mike, Fred and Lynda all beat me. Lynda stuck her tongue out at me, just to rub it in, when Miss Tully wasn't looking and then I was in trouble when I did it back to her.

Friday afternoon is always devoted to sport, and today it was cricket for grades three and four. We play a kind of tip and run so everybody has a chance to field, bowl and bat. Miss Tully was taking us. I'm good at cricket and slogged a couple of Lynda's balls over the fence. It was my turn to stick my tongue out at her. If Miss Tully saw it, she didn't say anything. I ended up taking two catches, forcing a run out and then I clean-bowled Fred, who didn't take it well. Whilst I was fielding near Miss Tully, I told her that Mum and Mary were coming home today. She gave a little clap and said she was so pleased for me.

The trip into Goulburn was uneventful and we arrived early. Dad had picked a bunch of red roses for Mum from our garden which he had wrapped in brown paper. Next, he bought a cute cuddly koala from the station cafeteria for Mary. We sat on a heavy green wooden bench on platform two waiting for the 5.05 from Sydney. We had been the first people waiting on the platform but as the arrival time crept closer, more and more people arrived until the platform was packed. The station master announced, three times, in a dull, monotonous tone, 'The 5.05 from Sydney, due on platform two, is running three minutes late,' but nobody seemed to mind.

I have never ridden on a train and was amazed at how noisy and long it was. In fact, I wondered whether the platform was going to be long enough. Dad and I were on our feet, hoping to catch sight of Mum and Mary. Many of the passengers had their windows down as the train slowed and were frantically waving to friends and relatives. There was no sign of Mum or Mary though, not that I could see much. With a screeching of brakes, the train ground to a halt and doors were flung open as the platform welcoming crowd surged forward to embrace loved ones. A large man with a walking stick pushed me rudely out of the way as he barged through to embrace an equally portly woman. Excited voices and smooching couples surrounded me.

The second wave of disembarking passengers was soon on the platform taking up much of the space with multiple hugs, kisses and embraces before we finally caught sight of Mum standing at a door two carriages away looking about trying to spot us. Dad started to wave his roses above his head as we elbowed our way towards her. Progress was slow. I noticed the younger couples spent far longer with their kisses and hugs and didn't seem to want to stop, but the older couples just had a quick peck and parted. Dad and Mum were quick peckers.

Dad helped Mum down the steps, gave her the bunch of red roses and then leaned in to pick up my sister. I think she had been sleeping because she looked dopey.

'Little Mary, how are you love? Graham and I have missed you.' He planted a wet kiss on her forehead.

Mary's blue eyes were as intense as ever as she gave Dad a hug and a sloppy kiss.

'Here you are, this is for you,' and Dad placed the koala into Mary's hands.

'Got any more bags, love?'

'Yes, I had to buy an extra suitcase. If I carry Mary,

could you go and collect it please? Here's the ticket. We'll be in the waiting room.'

At last, I had a chance to give Mum a big hug and she was able to give me a kiss while still holding Mary in her arms.

'And have you been helping your Dad while I've been away, Graham dear?'

'Sure have. I've been cooking tea every night and I've been watering your flowers and the vegie patch. The tommies are huge and there are lots of pumpkins ready. And I hit Lynda for two sixes in cricket this 'arvo.'

'Oh, you're wonderful, Graham. Come on, let's find a seat in the waiting room while Dad collects our suitcases; Mary's getting too heavy to carry about.'

I prattled on cheerfully about Dum and Dee, Colin's plaster, school and Mrs Trent's brandy snaps for several minutes while we waited. What I really wanted to do though was ask Mum about my being adopted, and who my parents were, but I knew I couldn't with Mary present. Mary was lying back quietly in Mum's lap hugging her beloved Susan and her new koala but she looked as though she wanted to go back to sleep. I noticed she was sucking her thumb, something she had given up doing years ago.

'Don't suck your thumb Mary,' Mum picked up the fluffy koala and wiggled it about and Mary's eyes lit up momentarily. She cuddled it briefly before again appearing to fall asleep.

Dad reappeared lugging two large brown suitcases with name tags attached to the handles. 'Is Mary okay to walk to the car? It's about fifty yards away.'

'I think so.'

I spent most of the hour it takes to travel to Sandalwood looking out of the back seat window and half listening to what Mum and Dad were discussing. Mary slept in Mum's lap all the way. Travelling at some speed along a dirt road with corrugations, makes it difficult to hear conversations, so I only caught snatches of their exchanges. Dad chatted about the farm, the condition of the sheep while Mum spent most of her time talking about Mary and her kidney disease. She was full of praise for the children's hospital in Sydney but hated the constant noise and frantic pace of Sydney. She was longing to get back to the peace and quiet of our farm and to sleep in her own bed again. The doctors had explained that Mary was never going to be healthy again because her kidney disease was chronic. That was still a new word for me but I worked out that "chronic" meant Mary had a disease that would never go away. Mary had to learn to live with it, Mum said. I felt so sorry for my little sister and again longed to tell mad Joe what I thought of him and his stupid ute.

Mum cooked tea that night and we didn't have lamb

chops and spuds! Mum knocked up a lovely quiche and we had Brussel sprouts and spinach from her veggie patch. We capped that with blackberry tart and ice cream for afters. I think Dad was glad not to have to sit down to my lamb chops and spuds yet again. Mary wasn't hungry, so Mum gave her a small helping of quiche and then some ice cream and put her to bed.

That night, Mum came into my room and sat on my bed just like old times to say a special "goodnight". We talked for a long time. Mum explained that Mary could still go to school and do everything but that she was going to be "listless". This was another new word for me. Kidney disease meant Mary would often be tired and not feel well, so I was going to have to be an especially loving and patient brother. Mary would not be fit enough to walk to school anymore and either Mum or Dad would need to drive her there and back every day.

Then Mum gave me a terrific surprise. They had decided, now that I was nearly ten, to buy me a bicycle. It would help me be more independent and I wouldn't have to come to school in the car all the time. It would have to be a second-hand bike, she warned, because new bikes were so expensive. They would look in the local newspaper to see if any bikes were being advertised and Dad had promised to help me learn to ride. As soon as Colin's arm was better, we could go riding about town together. Yippee!

I was so excited about the possibility of getting my first bike, I almost forgot to ask Mum about my adoption.

'Mum … Dad told me you are not my real parents and that you are my adopted parents.'

A look of surprise flashed across Mum's face but she recovered her composure quickly.

'Oh, did Dad tell you that already?'

'Yup.'

It was easy to see Mum was unsure what to say next. She looked down at her hands and hesitated; then looked me in the eyes, 'Well your dad's right, but Graham, darling, we love you just as much as proper parents do, probably more. Don't ever forget that. You belong to us now. And you are both very *very* precious.'

'Why didn't my real parents want to keep me? Didn't they like me?'

'It's a long story, Graham, and I think you have had more than enough excitement for one day. It's getting late too and you have to help Dad on the farm tomorrow. Maybe we can talk about it another time?'

When Mum makes up her mind about something, a stern look comes over her face and her eyes change from being smiley and loving to cold and firm. This happened then and I realised she had shut up shop and I would have to wait until another time.

'Good night dear.' She bent over and gave me a kiss

and was out of the room in a flash turning the light out as she went.

Sleep didn't come easily. All shapes, types, makes and colours of bikes came and went in my mind's eye as I pictured Colin and I careering down the local roads at a hundred miles an hour, doing massive skids in the dirt before just pulling up in time. Then I would think of sweet little Mary having to go to school in the car and feeling "listless". I was also angry at Mum for not telling me about my real parents and why they had given me away. My emotions were all over the place; I was excited about my future bike, sad about Mary yet angry at Mum.

I must have remained awake until late because I heard Mum and Dad going to bed and then some weird noises coming from their bedroom that I had never heard before. My parents' bedroom is right next to mine. There were strange thumping sounds that went on for several minutes and then Mum squealed out loud several times. Was Dad hurting her? The squeals didn't sound normal. Then everything went quiet again.

Finally, I fell into a restless sleep.

CHAPTER SIX

'Wakey, Wakey, rise and shine.' It was Dad standing at my bedroom door dressed and ready for work. 'Get your clobber on and meet me at the shed in ten. Breakfast when we get back.'

I was tired after such a bad night and longed to stay in bed and sleep more. Dad had flung open my curtains to reveal the early morning pink glow in the sky before the sun rose above the hills at the back of our place. Looking at my alarm clock, I noted it was only ten past six. Outside, the pre-dawn bird chorus was in full swing with the cheerful chirrups of blackbirds accompanied by the gentle cooing of doves and pigeons. Somewhere in the distance a kookaburra opened up and was quickly answered by another. Magpies were in the mix too. I yawned, stretched, then ran to the bathroom.

I probably didn't make it in ten minutes, but I was close. I had my new watch, neat shiny and secure on my wrist, an extra special Christmas present from Mum and Dad. The tractor was already chugging away and I was met by our two enthusiastic sheepdogs, Dum and Dee who went through their usual routine of snuffling around my legs and wagging their tails energetically to express their pleasure at seeing me. 'Okay son, hop on.'

I clambered onto the trailer together with Dum and Dee who were clearly ecstatic about the possibilities of the day ahead. 'What are we doing Dad?' I yelled, as we backed slowly out of the shed.

'Checking the newborns, mate. Last night's rain and the cool change may have been a bit tough for some of them. If we find any that look crook, we'll bring them in, together with their mothers, and put them in the home paddock for a day or two. They're out of the wind there and can shelter under the trees. This cold wind is a potential killer for the new lambs.'

Dad's long-serving Massey Ferguson trundled steadily up the rocky hillside along the rough track that hugged the barb-wire fence. I needed to hang on tight. Most of our property was granite country with smooth eroded outcrops on the hilltops called tors. These tors can create the weirdest of shapes and at night look scary in the moonlight. The lambing paddock was over on the other side of the ridge exposed to the cold southerlies. It seemed an odd place to choose for the lambing paddock but Dad reckoned the best feed was there and cold snaps, like this one, were rare during the summer months.

It was just as well we came to check. When we paused on the crest to view the ewes and their newborn lambs, it was clear some were in trouble. A couple of hungry eagles were already circling above as a blast of cold air hit us. I wished I'd donned my jacket as well as my jumper. The flock seemed instinctively to know why we had arrived. The ewes with the fit stronger lambs moved off briskly, leaving the mothers who were concerned about their newborns behind. We counted six of these. On closer inspection, three lambs had already died, so we ended up bundling the three remaining cold, distressed lambs, together with their Mums, into the trailer. Dad kept a couple of old dry blankets handy, so my job was to wrap the lambs up as best I could to warm them, while the three perplexed mums watched on, anxiously.

It was past eight when we finally parked the tractor back in the shed, having settled the three lambs with their mums safely in the shelter of the home paddock. The lambs were looking stronger already and pumping their mums for milk. The smell of bacon frying greeted us as we left our dirty boots and coats by the door and escaped the icy cold wind. Mum had done us proud. Breakfast for me was a big fry up of egg, sausage, bacon, a chop with tomatoes and mushrooms. If there was any room left after this, there was toast with butter and some of Mum's chunky orange and lemon marmalade.

My meal was all washed down with a glass of milk whilst Dad managed a couple of mugs of tea.

I was so hungry that I gobbled up my meal without saying a word, and it was only when I was contemplating whether I could squeeze in a second piece of toast, that I noticed Mary. My cute little sister had been lying asleep all this time on a stretcher bed in the corner of the dining room. She was pale but seemed comfortable enough. My heart went out to her. Here I was, healthy and hungry, while my sister lay there with barely any energy, sleeping. It wasn't fair.

'Did Mary have any breakfast?' I inquired.

'Yes, dear, she had some porridge with lots of brown sugar and half a glass of milk.'

'Will her kidneys get better?'

Mum looked over to see if Mary was still asleep. Not wanting Mary to hear her answer, Mum looked back at me and slowly shook her head.

'She's got to get better,' I blurted out, 'I love my sister, she has to get well.'

Again, Mum shook her head and came over to where I was sitting to put her arms around me.

'I'm so sorry Graham, love, but the doctors are not hopeful. She is very unwell and there is no cure for kidney disease. All we can do is keep her as comfortable as possible and love her to bits.'

'Is it because we had that accident with the bike, Mum?'

'No dear, the doctors believe she was born with a kidney disease. Mary has had two accidents in her short life. They didn't help, but the doctors say that the kidneys were only bruised. She would be fine by now if she hadn't been born with this horrid disease. Don't ever feel bad about that accident. In no way have you made things worse for Mary. Okay?'

I nodded and asked, 'Are we going to catch her disease?'

Dad answered this time, 'No mate, it's not the kind of disease that can be spread to anyone else. We are all quite safe. It's not infectious like a cold or the measles.'

I jumped down and went over to Mary who was stirring.

'Hey Mary, would you like me to read to you?'

She fixed me with those beautiful blue eyes but didn't say anything.

'I know which is your favourite book Mary and I'm a really good reader you know.'

She smiled.

I ran from the room and found Mary's precious copy of *The House at Pooh Corner* sitting on her book shelf. This was a present from our grandparents who lived in England. A couple of years ago they had sent me a copy of *Winnie the Pooh* and for Christmas this year Mary had received *The House at Pooh Corner*. We had both fallen in love with Christopher

Robin and the adorable creatures that lived in the *Hundred Acre Wood*. I sat on the floor leaning up against Mary's stretcher bed.

'Which story do you want Mary?'

'The one about Tigger coming to the forest for breakfast.'

And so, I settled down and read the whole story to Mary, all seventeen pages, stopping only to show her the pictures. When I'd finished, she sat up and asked for the rest of her milk.

'Why do you like that one, Mary?'

'Because Kanga's in it and he's a kangaroo.'

At this moment Dad reappeared at the door waving the local paper about. 'There are two boys' bikes advertised in the local rag and they both sound promising. Mum, can you give both the numbers a ring please to see if the bikes are still available and, if so, we'll drive in and take a look. Get ready Graham, this might be your lucky day.'

Dad went off to find his wallet, Mum did the phoning and I put on my shoes and did my hair.

'Shall we all go? queried Mum, 'both bikes are still for sale. Are you feeling well enough to drive into Goulburn, Mary? We'll get back in time for a late lunch.'

Mary nodded and stood up.

'I need a pee,' was all she said, so we assumed that it was a "yes".

Five minutes later we were on our way.

It always takes at least an hour to travel the tricky dirt road into Goulburn. We stopped at the golf course on the edge of town so Dad could study the street map. We were looking for number 15 Zenathon Road. We located the house down near the railway line and I was all of a quiver with excitement as we tumbled out of the car. I grabbed Mary's hand.

'Now Graham, calm down and don't get too bloody excited. You might think the bike is great, but the price has got to be right too, and remember, there's another bike to look at. Let me do the talking and you keep your trap shut; then you might learn a thing or two.'

Mary gave my hand a sympathetic squeeze, I had been put back in my place.

As we approached the gate, a monstrous Alsatian came bouncing out from a garage barking and barring its teeth. It then stuck its front paws aggressively onto the wicker fence. The fence shook and I reared back fearing it might collapse and allow the dog to escape. The drooling dog seemed determined to attack us if we entered his domain.

'Hey come away you, you silly bugger.'

The cranky voice belonged to a man who also

appeared from inside the garage. I stared because I had never seen such a large person, he seemed to be all stomach as he waddled towards the gate. The giant wore a faded blue singlet that barely covered the top half of his stomach and his legs resembled tree trunks. A soiled fag was stuck to his bottom lip. I wondered how he managed to talk without it falling out. Apart from the singlet, he sported a grubby pair of khaki shorts that looked like they hadn't ever seen the inside of a washing machine and a pair of well-worn thongs. A battered slouch hat resided on his head and matched the colour of his substantial bushy beard.

'Don't worry,' he said, chuckling, 'his bite is far worse than his bark.'

That didn't sound promising so I stood rooted to the spot hanging on grimly to Mary's hand.

'Get away Fang, get away.' Fang reluctantly obeyed his master and slunk off back to the garage.

'John Granger,' said Dad, extending his hand across the still closed gate.

An enormous hand enclosed Dad's. 'Arthur,' the man replied. Dad introduced us and Arthur acknowledged each of us with a single grunt. Then he flicked the latch on the gate, sniffed loudly and inquired, 'You from Sandalwood then?'

Not waiting to hear Dad's answer, Arthur turned and slowly lumbered to the other side of his house, away from the garage, much to our relief, since Fang was standing guard and salivating hungrily at the garage door. Mary let go of my hand and quickly grabbed Mum's for greater security.

'Ere she is,' announced Arthur, wheeling out a surprisingly clean, bright red Triumph. 'She's a bloody beauty and goes like the clappers. Won it in the big raffle.'

'Looks like it's almost new,' remarked Dad as he glanced over it.

'I ain't got any young'uns anymore, so I don't need it.' Arthur replied. 'I lent it to the young bloke next door, thinking they might buy it, but the parents are unemployed and ain't got no money. Waste of bloody time.'

'What sort of a price are you asking?' inquired Dad.

'Twenty quid,' Arthur responded.

'Seventeen,' Dad offered.

'No, I ain't budging. You won't get a better deal than this anywhere,' asserted Arthur.

'Are you sure? We have another bike to look at right now.'

Arthur shrugged his massive shoulders.

'Good luck to yer mate,' and Arthur placed the bike back up against the wall and started to waddle off. Fang growled aggressively as we hurriedly let ourselves out.

Little Mary couldn't get back into the safety of the

car quickly enough. I pretended I wasn't scared of the evil-looking dog, but was more than pleased when all the car doors were firmly shut and Dad pulled away from the kerb. Fang obliged us with a snarly farewell, his paws up on the fence again.

'Where's the other place, Betty?'

Mum looked at the map and gave directions. Ten minutes later we pulled up at number 3 Thompson Street in one of Goulburn's newest suburbs. Here, there were no front fences and the gardens were better kept. Number 3 Thompson Street boasted a well mown lawn, a handsome stone letterbox and a concrete path that curved its way up to the front door.

'No dogs here Mary, so it's okay.' Again, I took her hand and we followed Mum and Dad along the path. A mat at the foot of the front door said, "WELCOME" in large letters. There was a window right next to the front door with a colourful picture of parrots.

'Nice stained-glass window,' Mum remarked.

Dad pressed the bell.

A moment later an attractive lady came to the door. I reckoned she was about the same age as Mum, but she didn't have Mum's well-worn, tanned face from working long hours outdoors.

'Hello,' she said, cheerfully, 'You must be the Grangers who rang me a couple of hours ago? Please come in. My name is Lucy Davies and the cat's called Bubbles.'

Dad did the introductions again, although I'm not sure Mrs Davies saw Mary because she was shy and stayed hidden behind Mum.

'Now, before you look at the bike, would you care for a cool drink? It must have been a hot and dusty drive in from Sandalwood?'

This was more like it. I immediately warmed to Mrs Davies and decided there and then that her bike was going to be far better than Arthur's.

A couple of minutes later we were sitting on comfy posh armchairs with icy cool drinks and a large plate on the coffee table containing chocolate biscuits that were getting fewer by the minute. I woofed down three before Mum said that that was enough. Even Mary managed one. I reckon Dad had three, although Mum didn't tell *him* to stop eating them. Bubbles was doing the rounds, purring and rubbing up against legs as cats do.

'Now, Rob, my husband, is out this morning with my son, who is about the same age and size as you, Graham, so, he has left me to handle things. The bike's a Malvern Star, Youngster, 20-inch Boys Super Quality and it's virtually brand new. Would you like to come and see it?'

'Yes please!' I couldn't contain myself.

Everyone found my enthusiasm infectious and we all jumped up and followed Mrs Davies through the kitchen, out the back door, and around to the garage. There, leaning up against the wall, was the shiny blue Malvern Star.

'Wow!' I exclaimed, and ran towards this exciting new prospect. The bike had a shiny bell, a pump and even a tray at the back for carrying stuff. 'This is great, Dad, can we buy this one?' Already, I had visions of turning up at school on Monday morning and all the kids coming over and drooling over my new blue Malvern Star. Miss Tully would be sure to admire it as well.

'Not so fast, son. It may be out of our price range.' Dad looked across at Mrs Davies, inquiringly.

'We are asking twenty-four pounds.'

'Ouch, that's too much. We can only spare twenty. Any chance you can bring the price down to twenty?'

'I've had an offer of twenty-two pounds already this morning, so you need to match it or better it.' Looking at Mrs Davies, I could see she meant it. A horrid sinking feeling came over me; I was going to miss out and I so desperately wanted this bike. My first ever.

'Oh please, Dad.' I looked pleadingly at Dad, and then Mum, and then at Dad again.

Dad shook his head. 'I'm sorry mate, we just can't afford that much right now. There'll be other bikes coming up for sale, or we can go and buy that bike that Arthur showed us. It was twenty.'

'No, this bike is far better. Please Dad, it's only four more pounds.'

Dad turned to leave. 'Thank you, Lucy. Sorry we can't do business.' A despondent family group started to follow Dad. Little Mary came and held my hand to try and cheer me up. Even Mrs Davies looked sad. Then I had a brilliant idea.

'Dad, how about I give you the extra two pounds from my pocket money?'

'Graham, you don't have anything like two pounds of pocket money saved up,' laughed Mum.

'I've got some of it. Last time I counted, it was fourteen shillings and sixpence. I get sixpence a week, so I'll be able to pay off the rest by early next year. I promise Dad. Instead of giving me pocket money, you just keep it to pay off the bike. That way we can do it Dad. Please?'

I could see I was making progress. Dad and Mum were looking at each other in the way that grown-ups look at each other when they are weakening. Even Mrs Davies was watching intently. Dad shoved his hand into his back pocket and pulled out twenty pounds in notes.

'This is all I've got,' he said, waving them about and looking across at Mum.

'I have two pounds here in my handbag, which is this fortnight's housekeeping,' Mum replied, diving in to check she was right.

Mrs Davies interrupted. 'Look, I don't want to sound rude, but the asking price is twenty-four pounds and I know that is what my husband is hoping to get. I don't think I can let this bike go for twenty-two pounds without first discussing it with Rob. And don't forget somebody else might come and see us later this weekend and offer us the full price. Remember also that someone offered us twenty-two pounds before you came along, so, by rights, this bike should definitely be going to them before you.'

I felt like a deflated balloon. A moment ago, I thought the deal was sealed and the bike was mine, now it was anybody's guess. Then it was Mum's turn to come up with a clever idea.

'Graham, every time you have a birthday, Uncle Christopher and Auntie Mollie send you a pound for your birthday present. Would you like to put that pound towards the bike, in advance, so that we can offer Mrs Davies twenty-three pounds? If we do this, it will better the twenty-two-pound offer Mrs Davies received earlier. What do you think?'

'Mum, you're a genius!'

Dad turned to Mrs Davies again, 'So, we are now offering you a total of twenty-three pounds. It's the very best we can do.'

Mrs Davies smiled, 'I do hope your offer is the best one, because I can see young Graham has set his heart on the bike. Please leave me your phone number and I'll ring you by tomorrow night to let you know whether or not it's yours. We paid twenty-five pounds for the brand new Malvern Star only last week and it has hardly ever been ridden.'

'Do you mind if I ask why you are selling it then?' inquired Mum.

'We bought it for my son's birthday last week, but a few days ago, we had some bad news. My son has been suffering some strange fits and a couple of days ago the doctors informed us he has epilepsy and that he'll never be allowed to ride again. Too dangerous.'

I felt really sorry for Mrs Davies but especially for her son. I didn't know what this epilepsy thing was, but I sure hoped I didn't ever get it.

We left with mixed feelings. Now I had to wait until Sunday evening to find out whether somebody had trumped our twenty-three-pound offer. Dad promised he would drive over to pay for the bike on Monday if the news was good.

The trip home was uneventful. Mary fell asleep and Mum explained to me what epilepsy was. Both my parents assured me that if I became the proud owner of the Malvern Star, they would give me riding lessons every day until I was proficient. Mary woke up at one stage and told me she would, "do driving lessons" for me too. Very cute!

Time dragged over the weekend. I helped Dad on the farm on Saturday afternoon by helping him deal with a new rabbit infestation. We took the tractor and ripped out the rabbit burrows in what we called the "Wet Paddock". Being a bit damper there, rabbits found it easier to dig their network of burrows. We didn't see any rabbits because Dad had poisoned them with 1080 a couple of months back. In the evening we played Monopoly. Mary played, but she didn't really understand what she was doing and after half an hour became terribly cranky and threw her money on the floor. Mum took her off to bed, but sadly, that was the end of Monopoly for the night.

There was a kid at school called Norman Crocker whose Dad was the manager of the Sandalwood branch of the Bank of New South Wales. Norman's family was famous about town because the Crocker's were the first people in the whole of the Sandalwood district to purchase a television. The kids at school sucked up to Norman, hoping he would invite them back to his place to watch this amazing invention. Norman's parents had bought their television for Christmas and the news was around town by the time school started late January. Suddenly, everyone at school respected Norman more. He was special, he had television! Wow! Well, Norman could have his new-fangled television, I much preferred a new bike.

Getting to sleep on Saturday night was not easy. I pictured myself turning up at school one morning with my shiny blue Malvern Star Youngster Super Bike and the schoolkids coming over to admire it. They would all want a ride but nobody was going to get one. I would allow only a few of my closest mates to have a ride after school occasionally. That meant Colin, Mike and Fred. I would love to let Lynda have a go; except she wouldn't be able to ride a boy's bike. On weekends the four of us boys would cruise about town, go down to the general store, watch the tennis or ride up Pioneer Hill to the Sandalwood Lookout.

Sunday dawned hot again, a strong northerly rustled the leaves and swayed the branches. I admired the birds adjusting skilfully to the variable wind gusts whenever they prepared to land. The occasional grasshopper or locust was flung about almost uncontrollably. High cirrus clouds had begun streaming in from the south; a sure sign a change was on its way. Somewhere a shed door relentlessly slammed open and closed, open and closed. Gloomily, I realised my morning would be spent at Sunday school.

My family was Anglican, or "C of E" as we are referred to at school when it's Scripture time. I had learnt that C of E stood for "Church of England". What I couldn't understand was why we were known as "Church of England" when we lived in Australia.

When Mum called in to wake me, she put out the clothes she wanted me to wear for Sunday school with a warning to be careful not to get dirty when I collected the eggs. Most Sundays we went to Saint Ninian's Church of England as a family. Several of the kids from school were there usually, although the kids who lived farther out of town, in the bush, went to their own little churches closer to their homes. The Reverend Tomlinson was okay and cracked a few jokes, but my Sunday school teacher, Mrs Creighton, was a dead loss. We kids ran all over her, at some stage the Sunday School Superintendent would have to come in to restore order.

Now, Mrs Creighton hated creepy crawlies. If she saw a mouse, or a centipede, she would squeal and ask one of us boys to remove it. On this particular Sunday, Dave, who lived next door to Colin, turned up with a cardboard shoebox. Before things got too much out of control, he put his hand up, a rare thing for Dave to do.

'Mrs Creighton, I've brought you a present.'

'Oh, how sweet of you, David. Is it something to eat?'

'Oh yes, Mrs Creighton, these are really tasty.'

The class had more or less quietened down by now, sensing that something interesting might be about to happen. Dave had a reputation.

'Shall I bring it up, Mrs Creighton?'

'Oh yes please, David. I'm sure we can all share whatever it is.'

Dave stood up, clambered over a couple of the other kids, and made his way to the front, where Mrs Creighton was sitting on her chair with her Bible open. He had a funny looking smirk on his face as he handed the cardboard box to Mrs Creighton. Mrs Creighton put her Bible down on the floor and held the box in her lap for a moment.

'Well, children, what do you think David has brought us?'

The girls in the class suggested lollies, chocolates and smarties.

'Well, shall we have a look?' The tension in the room had been rising steadily and Mrs Creighton was relishing this rare moment when she had managed to get the attention of the entire class.

'Yea, open it up Mrs Creighton,' several kids yelled out in unison.

Adjusting her glasses, Mrs Creighton did as she was bid and flicked open the lid of the box.

What happened next was something like an explosion. Mrs Creighton jumped straight up in the air like a rocket emitting a scream loud enough to be heard right across Sandalwood. By the time she landed back on the chair it was clear that the box had contained a nest of cockroaches that, thrilled to finally escape from their cramped prison, went charging off in all directions seeking shelter in dark places. Mrs Creighton's blood-curdling scream was followed by a series of high-pitched squeals from several of the sissy girls in the class intermingled with yells of delight and laughter from the boys. Mrs Creighton and most of the girls stayed rooted to their chairs with their legs up for fear the cockroaches would climb up their dresses, whilst the boys began charging all over the room chasing the offenders and squashing them underfoot, at the same time yelling, 'I got one, and another and another ...'

The hunting down of the 'roaches reminded me of an Easter egg hunt, except this was far more fun. Easter eggs don't move about! We boys were in hot pursuit of the speediest cockroaches that had by now managed to get to the walls, and were desperately seeking little hidey-holes, when there was an almighty bellow from the door.

'What on earth is going on in here?' It was Mr Snaid, the Sunday School Superintendent.

Mr Snaid was a large, roly-poly sort of a man. He stood at the door, red faced, with his hands on his hips glaring at the chaotic scene before him. Mrs Creighton and the girls with their legs tucked up perched on chairs, and the boys scattered across the room with gleeful looks on their faces.

'I repeat, what has been happening in here?' Mr Snaid's face was turning beetrooty.

Mrs Creighton, sensing an answer was required

bravely lowered her legs to the ground and, looking about to check no more cockroaches lurked near her chair, bravely stood up.

'Mr Snaid, David Simpson brought a box full of cockroaches to show me. It was a horrid trick! I thought the box contained lollies or something else nice to share around.'

Mr Snaid didn't have a chance to answer because at that precise moment a particularly large evil-looking cockroach belatedly appeared from inside the cardboard box that had been hurriedly discarded, and headed straight for Mrs Creighton. Seeing the shiny monster gathering speed, Mrs Creighton heaved herself back on her chair where she stood holding her dress with a look of horror on her face. There was another round of squeals from the girls which continued until my friend, Fred, approached the marauding beast from behind and thwacked it with his shoe. A scattering of cockroach body parts, sitting in a small puddle of yellow coloured blood, lay on the ground horribly close to Mrs Creighton's chair. There were more yellow blobs visible around the room where other 'roaches had been too slow to make their escape.

'Where is David Simpson?' demanded Mr Snaid.

We all looked around but Dave was nowhere to be seen. Realising the extent of the near riot he had created, Dave had bolted straight for the door and fled.

There was no sign of him except for a cardboard shoe box lying abandoned on the floor. I'm not sure what happened to Dave after this particular drama but I do know Dave never attended Sunday school again.

The rest of the day dragged on interminably while I awaited a call from Mrs Davies. Mum did her usual roast lamb for lunch, one of her top dishes of the week. I spent the afternoon with Dad stacking logs for firewood for next winter. In the Southern Highlands cold nights can start early in March so we needed to be ready. I kept dashing back to the house to see if there had been a phone call from Mrs Davies. Finally, Mum told me to stay with Dad, and if a call came, she would send Mary out to tell me what the news was. Five o'clock passed, and Dad declared that was enough work for the day, so we came in, showered and changed into clean gear. Mary was looking a bit miserable so I said I would read to her again. She was pleased about that. Still no phone call …

I finished off my homework, making sure I did my best modified cursive writing to impress Miss Tully, laid the table for tea and checked the eggs again. Still no phone call …

'Dad, can we ring Mrs Davies, please? It's coming up to seven o'clock?'

'Sorry mate. She said she would ring, and I'm sure she will.'

Tea was scrambled eggs and bacon. There was gramma pie with cream for dessert. I helped to clear the table and Mum asked me to give her a hand with the drying up. Still no phone call …

The grandfather clock in the hall chimed eight, my signal to go to bed. I couldn't stand it anymore. I felt tears starting to well up and I avoided looking at Mum and Dad. I didn't want anyone to see I was about to start crying. Surely, if the bike was going to be mine, we would have heard by now? At teatime Dad had said that "no news is good news" but I didn't believe him. Mum came over and put an arm around my shoulders. 'Time for bed, mate. Clean your teeth and I'll be there in a minute.'

I felt like shit as I moped out of the kitchen. This wasn't fair, I had set my heart on that bike and now some other kid was going to be enjoying it. I couldn't hold the tears back anymore and they flooded out. I reached the bathroom and angrily squeezed my toothpaste out. I didn't want Mum to come in tonight, no more stupid stories. I went to bed sulking. I pulled the bed-clothes back, climbed in and hid underneath them.

Then the phone rang! I jumped back out of bed, raced down the hall to the kitchen, and stood at the door in my pyjamas looking hopeful. Dad was on the phone. He looked straight at me and slowly shook his head. It was as I had feared all along, somebody else had bought it. I started crying as I ran back to my bedroom. I pulled the pillow over my head because I knew Mum would come down and try to console me, but I was inconsolable. A moment later the door opened, and sure enough Mum came in and sat on my bed.

'Graham, that was your Uncle Christopher. Given half a chance, he'll chat on for hours, so Dad will ask him to ring back tomorrow, just in case Mrs Davies rings.'

I didn't reply. What was the point? All weekend I had been fretting about the phone call from Mrs Davies and now, well after eight o'clock, it looked as though she wasn't going to even bother to ring. It must mean that I had missed out and she didn't want to tell me. My tears were coming again so I rolled over so Mum wouldn't see and tried to cry silently. I heard Dad put the receiver down and did my best to stifle my sniffles. Mum put her hand on my shoulder and said things to comfort me, but I wasn't listening. Eventually, I fell into an uneasy, restless sleep.

Monday morning, I awoke with a heavy heart. It was a school day, but I felt sad and had no enthusiasm for school. Perhaps Mum would let me stay home? Even the chooks seemed despondent when I went to collect their eggs. Between them, they had only managed two eggs, which was a paltry effort because usually I would collect five or six and we would have enough to sell a dozen to a couple of people in town. Dee and Dum were still tied up and barely flicked a tail to acknowledge me. It was shaping up to be a seriously crap day.

Mary was sitting at the kitchen table picking her nose again when I came in with my two eggs and handed them over to Mum. I looked at Mary and shook my head. It was a habit she had started recently, probably copying one of the kids in her class. She looked at me with her cute blue eyes, daring me to say something but I couldn't be bothered. If she wants to pick her nose, she can pick her bloody nose! I sat down in my usual seat and reached for the milk.

Suddenly, the phone rang. Dad was closest so he walked over to pick up the receiver. I wasn't allowed to answer the phone, unless Mum and Dad were both out.

'G'day, John Granger.'

We were all quiet, listening intently, trying to hear who it was. Mum stopped what she was doing at the sink and I held my spoon, motionless and suspended, above my cereal.

'Oh, I'm sorry to hear that Lucy.'

So that was it, Mrs Davies had rung after all but the news was, as I had expected, not good. I watched Dad and could feel my tears welling up again. Mary had fastened her blue eyes on me but I was determined not to let her see me crying.

As I watched Dad, a broad smile came across his face and he raised a hand and gave me a "thumbs-up" sign.

'Yes, I can come into Goulburn today Lucy and I'll have the twenty-three pounds with me. I'm sorry your phone was out of operation last night.'

CHAPTER SEVEN

I couldn't believe it! A minute ago, the world was grey and miserable and I didn't know how I would survive the day. Now, in a flash, everything was wonderful again. Everyone was full of smiles and Mary ran around the table and gave me a great big smoochy kiss and a hug.

'Can I ride your bike too, Graham?' she asked, with her blue eyes looking pleadingly at me. Mum was really thrilled and as soon as she had given me a big cuddle, left the room to get the two pounds from her handbag to give to Dad.

'I hope you realise we'll be living off bread and water for the next fortnight,' she laughed, when she returned.

Dad promised to take Mary to school and then drive straight on to Goulburn to pick up my blue Malvern Star Youngster Boys Super Quality bike.

'When you get home, Graham, your bike will be here and I'll give you your first lesson this 'arvo.'

I was on top of the world. It was a beautiful sunny day and I was sure all the birds were singing for me as I walked to school.

My mates, who already owned bikes, were excited for me too and I'm sure Lynda, when she hears the good news, would spend more time with me than ever before. Classes went well and Miss Tully, who also rode a bike to school, said she was looking forward to seeing me riding about town. At last the bell rang signalling the end of the day's lessons and I tore out of the classroom to collect my school bag. Dad was parked out the front to collect Mary, so I jumped aboard too.

Ten minutes later we were home. Mum insisted we have an afternoon snack and a drink before Dad and I went out for lesson number one. Dad then infuriated me by spending at least fifteen minutes, with me sitting on the lawn, while he droned on about such things as, which brake to use, tyre pressures, never taking Mary on the bike, where to keep my bike safely, and some of the basic highway rules. I don't think I took any of it in, I just wanted to get started.

Finally, I clambered on with Dad holding the bike steady, and together we began a slow wobble around the front yard. After a few circles without serious mishap, Dad suggested we go along the dirt track that led down to Timboola Creek. The track was in reasonable condition without too much loose gravel and we made steady progress. I could tell that Dad was getting really puffed though. He played tennis most weekends, but that was not the same as running and hanging onto a bike for twenty minutes without stopping once for a rest.

'Stop here I'm buggered,' Dad panted when we reached the meagre trickle of water that professed to be Timboola Creek. 'Hop off and let me have a breather.' I did as I was told; it was vital to keep in Dad's good books because I expected I would need at least a couple more lessons before I got the hang of it and felt confident enough to go out on the road on my own. Five minutes later Dad had his breath back and we headed unsteadily back home.

I needed another three sessions with Mum or Dad jogging along beside me before they felt I was ready to ride on the road at the front of our place. After school on Friday was to be the first test run. The four of us, together with the excited Dee and Dum, headed for the road with me proudly pushing my not-quite-so-clean, blue Malvern Star Youngster Boys Super Quality bike. Mary was permitted to sit on the bike-seat as I carefully steered it through the front gate and lined the bike up in readiness to ride towards town.

'How far can I go, Dad?'

'Go as far as the corner of our property. Then stop, turn around and ride back. Be sure to keep an eye out for traffic.'

'Can't I go a bit farther?'

'That will do fine for your first go. If that bloody idiot, old Jake, shows up, pull over to the side and dismount. You understand?'

Old Jake was nowhere to be seen, and after one false start, I was up on my bike and away. Boy, did it feel good! At last I could join my mates on weekends and ride about town. I resolved to ride over to Lynda's place so I could show off. I was just thinking how clever I was when I saw a car approaching, ploughing up the dust as it came. I was only about a hundred yards from our gate, but I reckoned the car would reach me before I made it there. What if it's mad old Jake? I pulled over and successfully dismounted. It wasn't old Jake, as it turned out, but the vehicle covered me in a good layer of dust all the same. When I returned to our gate I was clapped in and Dad said that because I had the good sense to get off my bike when the car approached, I would be allowed to ride my bike to school next week. Yippee!

I was not allowed to ride into town over the weekend but Dad promised I would be permitted to next weekend if I rode to and from school safely and sensibly all week. By Friday, I felt I had been riding for years and no longer had any fear of meeting traffic. I was motivated to behave myself and subsequently it was agreed that, come Saturday morning, I could ride in and join my good mates, Colin, Mike and Fred.

That first Saturday together was bliss. The other three, who had had their bikes for a year or more, wanted to show me heaps of things. There was the "slippery dip" a place near Timboola Creek that became excitingly treacherous after rain. Up the back of old Mrs Pendle's place there were the remnants of an orchard and, in season, there were plums, apples, pears and even boysenberries to be gorged. Then there was cranky Bill Brooks, who definitely had a screw loose and resided alone on the edge of town. He had a couple of nasty big dogs that, fortunately, he kept chained up. Riding near the dogs set them off barking like crazy and their noise would really infuriate Bill, who would then threaten to let the dogs off their chains to chase us. Finally, the boys took me to a swimming hole further down the creek. There was not enough water to go swimming today, but when it rained, they assured me, it filled up fast and we could use the tyre-swing to crash-bomb the water.

I arrived home exhausted. It was the first time I had spent most of my day cycling about town and every muscle in my body ached. Mum advised a long hot bath, which helped, I think.

Mary was not looking too well so I played with her for half an hour or so before tea. She enjoyed that, but after half an hour she quietly climbed back onto the sofa and fell asleep. That night, when Mum came in to read to me, I questioned her about Mary.

'Mum, is Mary going to get a little bit better?'

Mum looked as though she was going to cry. She held my hand, and hesitated, before she answered.

'The doctors don't think she will, Graham.'

'They know it's her kidneys, so why can't they give her some medicine for the kidneys? There must be some?'

'Doctors are very clever people but they don't have the answers for all the illnesses we can suffer. Sadly, nobody has discovered a way to help Mary with her particular kind of kidney disease yet.'

'But what about in other countries? Do the Americans or Poms have doctors that can fix her?'

'No dear, nobody in the whole wide world knows what to do for little Mary.'

'Then I'm going to be a doctor when I grow up and I'll discover a special medicine to help Mary.'

'That's a beautiful idea, Graham, and I hope you do. But Mary needs help now, not in fifteen or twenty-years' time when you become a clever doctor.'

'What's going to happen to Mary then?'

Mum was reluctant to answer this question. She looked down at her fidgety hands and then asked, 'Would you like me to read to you?'

'No Mum, I want you to answer my question, please.'

I could see Mum felt trapped, but I was determined to find out more about Mary and her kidneys.

Taking a deep breath, Mum began, 'It's not good news, Graham. Mary will gradually get worse. The doctors can give her medicines that will stop her having any pain, but ...' Mum started to cry quietly and fished around up her sleeve to find a handkerchief.

'Is she going to die?'

Mum was weeping now and she just nodded. I felt bad because I had been so pushy and had made Mum cry, but I still needed to know more.

'When? When will she die, Mum?

Recovering slightly Mum looked at me, put down her hanky, and replied. 'Nobody really knows dear. When we came back from Sydney, last month, the doctors thought around six months. I'm praying hard that she will still be here to have her seventh birthday on July 7th.'

I reached out my hand and placed it lovingly on Mum's. 'Come on Mum, we have to be brave, it might never happen. I'm going to ask God to fix her up. We need another miracle. There have been lots of miracles and we just need one more. Doctors might not know how to fix Mary, but God does. He made everything, so making a better kidney for Mary will be a pushover for him.'

Mum smiled, 'I hope you're right darling.'

'Does Mary know?'

'Know what?'

'That she might die?'

'No, we haven't told her. She knows she is very ill and that it's her kidneys that are making her unwell. She is so brave and never complains ...' Mum started to sniffle again and the handkerchief was back in service, 'how do you tell a six-year-old she's dying?'

I had no answer.

'One thing you must never do Graham, is tell anybody about Mary's condition. Will you promise me? Only the doctors, Dad, you, and I, know. If we mention it to anyone else, the news will spread around town before you can say, Jack Robinson.'

For a moment I thought I would ask who Jack Robinson was, but then I realised Mum wanted me to make my promise, so I did.

'I promise Mum, I'll only tell God.'

'I think He knows already, Graham.'

'Then why doesn't He do something about it?'

'Well, let's both pray that He does. Now it's getting late and it's time for you to go to sleep.' Mum gave me an extra special kiss, turned the light off and closed the door quietly.

I was so tired from all my cycling adventures that I fell asleep almost immediately.

CHAPTER EIGHT

A couple of days later Mum came out with some surprising news.

'Tomorrow, I'm going to take Mary with me to Sydney so we can spend a couple of weeks with Auntie Mollie and Uncle Christopher.'

'Can I come too?'

'No dear, this is a special treat for Mary.' Mum gave me a harrowing stare and then I realised that this might be Mary's last chance to be with her uncle and aunt. 'You and Dad will be looking after the farm on your own and I know you will do a great job together.'

'There are still heaps of lamb chops in the freezer,' remarked Dad, giving me a wink.

'Yes, we can manage fine Mum,' I agreed.

Uncle Christopher and Auntie Mollie owned an old house less than a mile from Bondi Beach. We had stayed with them a couple of times during the long summer holidays. I had many happy memories of lazy days on the beach playing cricket, swimming, making sandcastles and walking along the cliffs. If it was wet, we went to the pictures or played board games. Auntie Mollie was a terrific cook and was always making yummy cakes and biscuits. Uncle Christopher was a bank manager and was at work every day during the week and even on Saturday mornings, but was always around in the evenings. Uncle Christopher was a real wag and heaps of fun.

That evening Mary was exhausted and Mum tucked her into bed early. I asked if I could go and read to her. When I went in, she was chatting away happily to one of her dolls and then propped the doll up so she could listen to the story as well. Mary snuggled down and gazed at me expectantly with those beautiful bright blue eyes.

'What's the name of this doll, Mary?'

'Her name is Melanie and she's got kidney disease.'

'Oh dear, how do you know Melanie has kidney disease?'

'Because she gets pains in her back and feels very, very, very tired.'

I started to read the story but after only a few minutes Mary was asleep. I reached across for Melanie and gently tucked her in under the blankets. Mary looked so peaceful and I felt sorry for her.

Next morning everyone was extra busy. Mum

was fussing about giving Dad instructions about the washing, what food we could eat from the fridge, and what we would have to buy in the next couple of days. Mary wanted to pack all her dolls (about fifteen of them!) and had to be told she must pick three favourites only. This made Mary cry and uncooperative. Dad was trying to find a couple of invoices that he needed in order to pay some bills whilst in Goulburn. Finally, they drove off heading for the Goulburn Railway Station to catch the 10.23 for Sydney and all stops along the way. Suddenly, I was all alone in the house and feeling rather sad. I found my school bag, remembered to pack my lunch, and cycled away. I badly wanted to get to school and play with my friends and, of course, see Lynda.

School was great and I received a special award at assembly for "Most improved in Spelling" in Miss Tully's class and later scored a scorcher of a goal in lunchtime soccer. When the final bell went, the gang (Colin, Mike, Fred and me) rode around the block planning next weekend's adventures. On Saturday, we arranged to meet behind Mrs Pendle's place to raid her apple trees. Mike reported they were almost ripe and we needed to get them now before the birds did. Sandalwood had reached the semi-finals of the district cricket competition and was to play the Crookwell Seconds on Sunday. The match started at eleven o'clock and we decided we would be there to barrack. Mike and

Fred's Dads were both playing for Sandalwood. With Mum away, I reckoned it would be easy to convince Dad that I could skip Sunday school for once.

I rode home in a cheerful mood expecting to find Dad out and about somewhere. But there was no sign of him and the car was not in the garage. He must have been held up in town, I thought, so I raided the fridge, poured myself a drink and settled down to do my homework. When that was done, and still no sign of Dad, I went out to feed Dee and Dum. They had been tied up all day so I let them loose and they charged happily about the yard doing what dogs do. Around six o'clock, Dad finally made it home.

'Did you get delayed, Dad?'

'Sure did, son. I had a few people to see.'

I could tell he didn't want to talk about it, so I changed the subject and told him about my spelling award and the fantastic goal I'd scored from the left wing. He grunted but wasn't particularly interested.

'Looks like I'll get my sixpence pocket money for my spelling too, Dad.' Again, just a grunt.

'Have you got tea organised, son?'

'Not yet, Dad.'

'Well, look sharpish. You know what we usually have when Mum's away. I'm going to have a shower.'

When Dad was grumpy, I knew to keep my mouth shut and do what I was told. I did my best with the cooking and it was almost ready when he emerged from his shower. He went to the fridge and took out a cold bottle of beer. We ate in silence. Something must have been worrying him but he wasn't going to tell a nine-year-old about it. After tea I washed up and took myself off to bed. Already, I was missing my Mum and Mary and wished we could chat on the phone.

Next morning, Dad announced he had to go to town again. He wasn't dressed in his working gear for the farm and looked as though he was off to a meeting or to Sunday church. Again, that evening, he was late home. This business of going off to Goulburn became almost a daily occurrence on school days, although he didn't go to town at weekends, choosing instead, to catch up on work around the farm. This routine was quite different to normal. Usually, Dad worked hard all week on the farm and went into town on Saturdays and we would often go with him. Weekends were reserved for family activities. Unless it was a market day, Dad hardly ever went to Goulburn during the working week. Why this sudden change I wondered?

On Thursday evening of the second week, as I ploughed my way yet again through Dad's favourite lamb chops with potatoes, the phone rang. It was Mum, and Dad took the call. I couldn't hear what was being discussed but Dad explained afterwards that Mum had decided to stay a third week in Sydney because

Mary was just loving the beach and her time at Uncle Christopher and Auntie Mollie's weatherboard house. The doctors had put Mary onto some new medication that took away almost all her pain but made her a bit dopey, according to Mum. What surprised me though, was Dad's strange reaction to this news. He appeared to be genuinely delighted that Mum and Mary would be away for a third week. I desperately wanted them home because I missed them so badly, even though Dad appeared unfazed. Again, I wondered why?

The gang and I had arranged to meet at the Sandalwood Showgrounds around nine o'clock on the next Saturday morning. The plan was to have a picnic lunch made up by our mothers which we would then share. Now, of course, my mum would not be home to make up a picnic lunch for me, so I would have to get it myself. I was used to fending for myself for school lunches, so I did the usual. I grabbed about a dozen small cherry tomatoes from the garden patch, buttered three slices of bread and dolloped on some of Mum's strawberry jam. There were a few small apples left in the fruit bowl, so I grabbed them as well. At least I had something to share around!

While I was getting myself organised, I noticed Dad seemed particularly nervy. He watched me for a few minutes and then asked, 'What are you doing today, son?'

'I'm meeting up with Colin, Mike and Fred at nine o'clock. We're taking a picnic lunch to share.'

'Sounds good. When do you think you'll be back?'

'Is five o'clock okay, Dad?'

'Suits me fine. I hope you have a great day.'

'Are you going into town again today Dad?'

'Nope. I've got a few things that need doing about the place, so I'll be staying home.'

I was pleased to hear this, because I knew that Dad had been neglecting many of the tasks he normally carried out around the farm on a regular basis. The sheep needed shifting to a new paddock and the fences hadn't been inspected and repaired for weeks. I doubted whether Dad had even checked that the water troughs were all functioning properly and Mum's veggie patch was becoming seriously overgrown. I had been bringing in a few of the new season's apples and plums from the orchard but much of the fruit was being allowed to drop and rot. Dad usually insisted that fruit could never be permitted to lie about rotting as it attracted vermin and encouraged fruit flies. If Mum was home, she would be jumping up and down by now and picking loads of fruit to preserve, make into jam, or sell at the markets at weekends. The truth of the matter was that Dad had become slack and was spending far too much of his time in Goulburn instead of on the farm.

'Now, you are quite sure that you won't be back until five o'clock, Graham?'

'Sure Dad. We are doing a big ride today. We're going down to Paddy's Gorge and back and that's a long way for us to ride.'

This seemed a strange question to ask me a second time. It was usually the other way round with my parents making sure I would definitely be home by a particular time. Typically, they would be saying things like, 'don't you dare be late home this evening' or 'make sure you are home right on time.'

Time was getting away and I had to ride into town to meet up with my mates by nine. I grabbed my picnic lunch with a bottle of cordial and put them in my backpack, found my plastic raincoat and yelled a farewell to Dad as I flew out the door. Dad was on the phone and just gave me a wave. Today was a day full of promise. Paddy's Gorge is where Paddy, an Irishman, is supposed to have been shot by the police after he, and his ferocious gang, had held up a coach near Sandalwood. This morning we would be journeying there to see if there was anything left. We reckoned it would take the best part of an hour along the rough dirt road just to get there. The weather was warm and sunny with a slight southerly keeping the temperature under control.

When I arrived at the showground only Colin was there. We chatted about school and the test series against the Poms. Mike and Fred arrived together about twenty past nine. Fred then realised he had forgotten to bring any lunch so we had to go back to his place for his mum to get something together in a hurry. Mike, as always, had his yoyo with him, and while we waited, he kept us amused by showing off his latest tricks, "Walk the Cat", "Skin the Cat" and "Rock the Baby". There was to be a yoyo competition in Goulburn in a couple of months' time and Fred was going to enter the junior championship.

Finally, Fred emerged with his picnic box and we set off for Paddy's Gorge an hour late.

We made good progress. The road down to Paddy's Gorge was a quiet one. Only a few families lived along the road as it was not productive land for farming because it was too rocky, and the last part of the road was a Conservation Park.

About half way there, as we negotiated a sharp corner, Colin, who was in the front let out a yell and swerved violently to his right. He had narrowly missed a large red-bellied black snake slithering across the road. The near miss shook us up a bit and we stopped about a hundred yards on, at the bottom of the hill, to recover. By the time we'd fully discussed this chance encounter, we reckoned the snake had grown to at least eight-foot-long, was as thick as a man's arm and was definitely about to climb up Colin's bike!

A few minutes later I noticed my front tyre was going down.

'Shit, I've got a puncture.'

The others crowded round giving the tyre several presses with their fingers.

'Could just be needing a bit more air,' suggested Mike, 'pump her up again Graham.'

I did as I was bid but it was useless; it was definitely a puncture.

'You'll have to go back home and push your bike all the way,' lamented Fred. 'Pity I don't have my pony here, she seldom gets a puncture.'

There was a ripple of laughter but we knew we had a big decision to make. I had no option, I had to go back, but I didn't want to return on my own. Naturally enough, the others wanted to keep going. In the end it was my best mate Colin who volunteered to escort me home, leaving Mike and Fred to continue on.

Pushing our bikes was hot work since much of it was uphill. It took us almost two hours to get back into Sandalwood where we parted company. I really appreciated what Colin had done. I pushed on, up our dusty lane to our property, finally arriving there about two o'clock, three hours early. I was hot and thirsty, not to say disappointed. I had not yet opened my lunch box and was starving.

As I pushed my bike through the gate and walked up

our short driveway, I was surprised to find Dad had a visitor. Parked in the shade, under our one and only oak tree, was a white Mini, caked in dust. We don't see many Minis in Sandalwood because most people drive utes, trucks, Fords or Holdens; vehicles that are especially designed to cope with the rough roads and corrugations. Although Minis are great cars, and do well at Mount Panorama at the Bathurst 1000 races, they could rattle to pieces out here in the bush. I looked in through the car's windows as I passed by and noticed a pretty pink umbrella on the floor of the passenger's seat. On the back seat there was a lady's hat. I didn't recognise the car and wondered if this was a cousin or some distant relative calling in, unexpectedly. Dad would be annoyed, I reckoned, as he would have to be entertaining someone instead of getting his farm work done.

I stowed my bike in the shed and gave Dee and Dum a decent pat and a kind word. I thought the dogs were starting to put on weight because they were not getting the exercise to which they were accustomed. I topped up their drinking bowls and made for the back door. Everything was quiet.

Pushing open the back door there was still no sound of talking. I entered the largest room in our house, the lounge, or living room, as Mum preferred to call it. Nobody here either. In the middle of the room there is a low wooden coffee table and on the table I noticed a smart-looking lady's hand bag and next to it a small packet of something I didn't recognise. I read the label which didn't help me either, it said "condoms".

I left the lounge and entered the kitchen; nobody was there either. Where were they? Perhaps they were outside looking around the farm? But there had been no sign of anyone when I had been out the back putting my bike away and Dad's ute was still there in the garage. We never took visitors down the short hallway to the three bedrooms, although occasionally a visitor wanted to go to the bathroom. I was dying to have a pee myself so I headed down the hallway. Mum and Dad's bedroom door was open which was unusual because Dad often didn't put his clothes away and just threw them on the floor. This annoyed Mum so much that she always shut their bedroom door. As I went past my parents' bedroom, I saw something extraordinary. Dad was there on the bed with nothing on and he was lying on top of a woman!

I couldn't believe what I had just glimpsed and hastily moved on into the bathroom and closed the door. A thousand thoughts rushed through my mind as I started to relieve myself. What were they doing? Who was this woman? Why were they in Mum's bed? I knew instinctively that what I had seen was wrong, terribly wrong. I was just finishing when the bathroom door flew open and Dad stood there with a dressing gown on.

'What the fucking hell are you doing here?'

Dad was in a terrible rage and the few times I had seen him like this before I knew it meant danger. He was likely to hit me or slap me. My piss went all over the place as I looked up at him and stammered, 'I'm very sorry Dad, I had to come home early, I'm really sorry, Dad. I had a puncture.

'Get out of the bloody house and I'll talk to you later. I'll teach you to break your bloody promises! Go on, get out!'

I had made a mess of myself and there was urine all over the floor and the toilet seat. I raced out the bathroom door as Dad glowered and took a massive swipe at me as I passed him. Down the hallway I scampered, through the kitchen, through the lounge and out the back door. I kept running, whimpering now and terrified. What was Dad going to do to me? I ran about a hundred yards out to the orchard to an old mulberry tree. This was a special private place where I went if the world seemed to be caving in and I felt helpless. I threw myself down where the grass was still green and screamed and thrashed the ground violently with my fists.

After a couple of minutes, I lay still, exhausted. Everything was so totally confusing. What I had just witnessed must be what humans do to make babies. But why was Dad trying to have a baby with this stranger who obviously had arrived in the Mini? Surely it was only mothers and fathers who made the babies, that's how they became mothers and fathers? One thing I knew for sure was that Dad was furious with me because I had seen him doing it with this strange woman. I knew I was in deep trouble, so for a few minutes I contemplated running away.

But then some other thoughts began to surface. I knew what Dad had been doing was awfully wrong because he should be trying to have his babies with Mum and nobody else. But I had seen him doing it with another woman. I could tell Mum all about it and then Dad's secret wouldn't be a secret anymore. Mum would be absolutely ropable if she knew what Dad had been doing. It was then I realised what Dad had been doing almost every day for the last two weeks when he went off to Goulburn. All along he must have been trying to make babies with this stranger. So, I reasoned, I should definitely tell Mum.

Who was this mystery woman? Mum would want to know. If I moved quickly, I might be able to find out. I left the safety of my mulberry tree and scampered through the orchard dodging between the fruit trees until I reached the side of our house. Nobody had appeared at the back of the house so I kept going. The orchard gives way to a miscellaneous collection of shrubs and bushes at the front of the house and I knew

I could remain hidden there to watch who came out to drive the car away. I didn't have to wait long. Dad and the mystery woman soon came to the front door, both now fully dressed, where they had a quick kiss and a hug. The woman skipped lightly over to her white Mini. When she walked around to the driver's door, I had an excellent view of her. She was slim and pretty with long blonde hair and I knew immediately that I had seen her somewhere before.

I watched intently as the car turned around to leave and the mystery woman waved and blew a kiss to Dad, who sent a kiss back. But who was she? Just as the car reached our gate, it came to me. The mystery woman was Mrs Lucy Davies, the lady who had sold us my bike in Goulburn. Now, I could tell Mum everything. I let my mind run back to the Saturday we all went to Mrs Davies' house to inspect the bike. I clearly remembered Mrs Davies talking about her husband and her son, who were at some sporting event together. The son must be about my age, but he had to give up bike riding suddenly, because he had been diagnosed with epilepsy. Now, it all fit together. Dad had gone to Goulburn to collect my bike from Mrs Davies and to pay for it, and somehow, they had become close. It was now clear that Mrs Davies' house was where Dad had been going almost every day for the past fortnight.

My immediate problem though was facing up to Dad.

I couldn't stay out in the garden for ever. I made my way back to my special mulberry tree where I lay down in the shade to think it through. Perhaps I would be wise to wait a couple of hours to let Dad calm down more? But I badly needed Dad's help to fix my puncture. I was still tossing up what to do when the backdoor swung open and Dad yelled out at the top of his voice.

'Graham, Graham, come in, I want to talk to you. Now!'

I didn't want Dad to find out about my special mulberry tree retreat so I took a circuitous route back through the orchard and appeared innocently between a Granny Smith apple tree and an ancient Victorian plum. I tried not to look scared but my heart was thumping like mad. On a number of occasions, Dad had laid into me when I had been naughty and what had transpired this afternoon could mean really big trouble. I had assured Dad I would not be back until five o'clock but then turned up at two o'clock and caught them at it. But who was the real sinner here? Surely, trying to make babies with a strange woman was far more serious than me turning up unexpectedly because I'd had a puncture?

'I'm here Dad.' I tried to look relaxed, as if I had not done anything wrong, and gave Dee and Dum another pat and a kind word as I passed. Dad saw me coming, turned around and disappeared back into the house. I followed him in. He went to the fridge and took out a beer.

'Sit down, son.'

'Can I get a drink too please, Dad?'

'Help yourself.'

I found a glass filled it with cold water and sat down nervously across the table from Dad.

Dad took a gulp of his beer and glared at me; he didn't quite know how to begin. I was hugely relieved he didn't think beating me was going to work. I had a quick slurp of water and waited.

'So, you had a puncture?'

'Yes Dad. I was wondering if you could show me how to fix it please?' Dad liked being asked to do things that required his special skills, so I thought this was a promising way to start our conversation.

'How'd you do it?'

'I don't know. We were half way to Paddy's Gorge when I noticed it.'

'That's bad luck.'

Silence.

I sat there nervously waiting and fidgeting between slurps of water.

'You saw something you weren't meant to see today, son.'

I nodded.

'Sometimes adults have affairs: Lucy and I are having an affair.'

I had not heard this word before. What exactly was

an "affair"? Did all adults have them? How come I hadn't heard about "affairs" before now? Was Mum going to have an "affair" down in Sydney? What about Miss Tully. Did she have "affairs". What about old Jake? A whole new mysterious window on the world of adults was suddenly opening up. Was having an "affair" normal? Was it acceptable? Perhaps Mum wouldn't mind if Dad was having an affair? I felt hopelessly confused, so I simply remained silent, just looking at Dad.

'Whatever you do you must never say anything to Mum about what you saw today. Do you understand me Graham? It's a secret that only you and I share.'

'And Mrs Davies,' I said rather cheekily.

'Yes, and Lucy,' Dad reiterated.

Another few seconds of silence.

'We love each other,' Dad added.

'Who Dad? You and Mum or you and Mrs Davies?'

I could see this question had struck home and Dad didn't want to answer. He looked down at his hands, had another gulp of beer, and sighed deeply.

'It's complicated son. Of course, I love your Mum. She's my wife and we've been married for nearly fifteen years. But I love Lucy too, in a different way.'

'I don't understand, Dad.'

'Well, that's because you are only a kid. When you're grown up, you'll understand these things better. All you have to remember now is to keep your trap shut. Never say anything about Lucy to anybody. Is that quite clear? Not to Mum, or your mates, or your teacher, not even to Mary. If you and I keep this a secret, we'll get along well. But if I ever even suspect that you have told anyone about me and Lucy your life won't be worth living.'

Dad glared threateningly at me; I knew he was serious.

'Do you promise to keep this a secret, son?'

'Yes, Dad,' I said limply.

'Good, now we've got that sorted, where's your bike? Let's get that tyre fixed.'

CHAPTER NINE

That evening, Dad ordered me to bed promptly at eight o'clock. Usually on Saturday evenings I was allowed to stay up a bit later because there was no school next day. But tonight, Dad wanted me out of the way. I said goodnight, carried out my ablutions, and was in bed ten minutes later feeling neglected and lonely. I was longing for Mum and Mary to return to bring some warmth back into the house. I turned my light off and lay there brooding about the day's happenings. I decided, when I went to school on Monday, I would go to the school library where there was a big dictionary in two volumes called "The Concise Oxford Dictionary". Miss Tully had been teaching us how to use dictionaries and had explained how they were helpful if you didn't know the meaning of a word. I felt confident I could find out the meaning of the two new words I had come across today, "condom" and "affair".

Before I fell asleep, I heard snippets of a conversation

Dad was having on the phone. I could only catch bits of Dad's conversation but enough to conclude it was Mrs Davies at the other end.

'Is it safe to talk to you for a few minutes? ... No, he's asleep ... everything's okay ... he'll keep quiet ... no need to worry ... Monday, as usual ... love you, darling.'

Dad sent me off to Sunday school next morning and I rode my bike to Saint Ninian's. Dad had done a great job fixing the puncture. I was pleased I went because the rest of the gang were there and Mike and Fred were full of their time down in Paddy's Gorge. They reckoned there was a ghost down there and they claimed they had even found blood on the ground. It was totally spooky they said and were desperate to revisit the place next weekend. Sadly, I couldn't commit to going with them because we expected Mum and Mary to be coming home next weekend.

The rest of Sunday dragged. I helped Dad finally to move the sheep. The paddock they had been in for weeks was critically over-grazed and the sheep had started to lose condition. Dee and Dum thoroughly enjoyed the rounding-up activities and fortunately demonstrated they had not lost any of their herding skills. Next, we spent a couple of hours picking the Granny Smiths and sorting them according to size. Mum would really appreciate this work being done as she had charge of the orchard. The fruit was mostly large and certainly tasty with surprisingly few blemishes. Some were destined for storage others would be turned into apple pies, apple crumbles and apple-anything-else that Mum might create.

I was up early on Monday, did my chores and organised my breakfast and some lunch for school. I kept a watchful eye on Dad, after over-hearing snatches of his conversation with Mrs Davies on Saturday evening, and sure enough he was dressed up in his smart "going-to-town" gear again. I knew to keep my mouth shut and made no comment. The "affair" was still on.

As soon as I reached school, I headed for the small school library. Children were allowed to use the library before school started even though there was no librarian present. The librarian came only on Wednesdays when all the classes had their library lessons and we could borrow books. I went over to the non-fiction shelves that held some of the largest books in the library like atlases, almanacs, encyclopaedias and dictionaries. The Concise Oxford Dictionary was huge in comparison to the small ones we had used in class for learning our dictionary skills. The volume I wanted was so heavy I was worried I might drop it. Once I had it safely on the table, I began to search for the word "affair".

It was not difficult to find the word, but what I didn't expect was that there were seven different ways you could use the word "affair". I struggled through the seven definitions, and in the end, decided that the fifth was the one that best applied to Dad and Mrs Davies. The dictionary explanation was:

"5. An amorous or romantic experience, especially a temporary one; love affair; romance."

I sort of understood what all this meant and was pleased to read it was *"especially a temporary one"*. Perhaps this "affair" would be all over by the time Mum came home?

Next, I looked for the strange word I had seen written on the small packet left lying on our coffee table. The word was "condom".

This time there was only one meaning listed. The dictionary stated:

"condom: a rubber or plastic sheath used by men as a contraceptive or to prevent venereal disease (origin uncertain)."

This was starting to get horribly tricky. Here were three more new words that I didn't know; sheath, contraceptive and venereal disease.

I was about to start looking for each of these words in the dictionary when the library door flew open and two of the big secondary school girls bowled in. Because our school was considered to be "remote" we had about thirty secondary kids who came to the school every day and did correspondence lessons. They were supervised by the teachers and some of them sat up the back of my classroom.

'What yer doing Graham?'

'Just looking up some words in the dictionary.'

'I bet you're looking up rude words,' laughed Eileen, a large buxom girl nearly as wide as she was tall.

'Come on Graham, tell us what you're looking up or I'll thump you good and hard,' chimed in Felicity, the other girl, with a sneer on her face.

The dictionary was still open at the page where I had found the word "condom."

'Show us the page Graham,' and the two girls stood on either side of me like members of the gestapo and looked at the open pages. 'Tell us Graham or we'll thump you.' Felicity now grabbed my arm and started to twist it.

'I don't know, I was just looking to see what a big dictionary looked like.'

'Bullshit. You're a good reader. Eileen have a look will yer.'

Eileen ran her finger down the page and soon found the word "condom". She let out a squeal of delight, and announced with glee, 'Condom! Graham you were looking up condom!' and the two girls collapsed into peals of laughter. They found it hugely amusing that I was looking up this word.

'Why do yer wanna know about condoms?' giggled Felicity.

'I bet you can't even get it up yet?' added Eileen. Felicity burst out laughing again at her friend's remark.

I had no idea what the girls were on about and I felt very small and silly.

'Got a girlfriend have yer?' questioned Felicity.

'Going to give it to her are yer?' chortled Eileen.

I was saved by the bell.

'Better put your condoms away then ...' was Felicity's passing shot and they both squealed with laughter again as they left the library.

Hastily I closed the dictionary, returned it to its rightful place on the shelf, and ran out for morning assembly.

CHAPTER TEN

All day I felt unsettled, and school work became a drag. Normally, I looked forward to school and enjoyed all my lessons. Miss Tully was a terrific teacher because she was fun and explained things so well. But today I seemed to lack the energy and enthusiasm for any work. I didn't bother to put my hand up to answer questions and just sat there in my own little private world. Instead of concentrating on school work, I found that I kept drifting off to think about my worries. I reckoned I had far too many problems on my plate from my little sister dying of kidney failure and Mum away in Sydney leaving me at home alone with my Dad, to his affair with a strange woman called Mrs Davies. Also, still haunting me was the discovery that I was adopted and that I didn't really belong to my mum and dad. I desperately wanted to know more about this whole adoption business.

If only I had someone I could talk to about these

adult kinds of things. Dad was too difficult to approach and Mum was away. I loved knocking around with my mates but they were not adults and wouldn't know about such things as "adoption", "affairs", "condoms", "sheaths" and "contraceptives". I felt as though I was being thrown, unwillingly, into the world of adults when I was only a nine-year-old child. I didn't want any of this. I didn't know how to deal with these issues. Why couldn't I just be a happy fourth grader like everyone else? It wasn't fair, I didn't want all this shit.

At last the bell went for the end of the day's classes. I handed in my book for marking realising, as I did so, that I had only written down about half of the stuff Miss Tully had told us to copy off the blackboard. Usually, I managed to have everything written down in neat modified cursive writing, but not today. I felt no pride in handing in my poor, half-finished work. I was letting Miss Tully down too. I really liked her and she was so encouraging. What was wrong with me?

As I was leaving the classroom to collect my school bag, Miss Tully stopped me.

'Graham, can you stay back for a moment please, I want to talk to you?'

Oh no, surely, I'm not in trouble for something in school as well?

'Yes, Miss Tully.'

'Sit down for a moment, I'll be back in a tick.'

Miss Tully left the classroom to check that the rest of the class had collected their belongings and those that caught school buses were lined up in an orderly fashion. A few minutes later she returned and gave me a lovely warm smile.

'Thanks for waiting, Graham.'

'That's all right, Miss Tully. Am I in trouble?'

'No, of course not. You are one of my very best pupils.'

Miss Tully took down one of the chairs from a desk and sat down opposite me.

'Graham, you haven't been your usual sparky self today. Are you feeling okay?'

'Yes, thank you, Miss Tully, I'm fine.'

'Well, if you are feeling okay, then there must be something worrying you, because you were not your usual happy, hardworking self today?'

'I'm sorry, Miss Tully. I'll try harder tomorrow.'

'Sometimes Graham, it's good to talk to someone if there is something worrying you. Now, I know that your lovely sister, Mary, is very unwell and is down in Sydney with your Mum. Perhaps you are really missing them?'

I didn't want it to happen but I could feel my eyes watering up and my nose running. I looked down because I didn't want Miss Tully to see me crying. She said nothing and then the flood gates opened and I cried openly. I fumbled in my pocket for a handkerchief but there wasn't one there. Miss Tully passed me one of hers. She let me cry for a moment or two and then spoke again.

'Graham, it is perfectly normal for you to be feeling sad about Mum and Mary being away but I expect they will be coming home soon?'

I nodded and sniffed. After wiping my nose, I replied.

'I think they're coming home this weekend.'

'Oh, that's great Graham. You must be looking forward to that?'

I nodded again, but I didn't feel any better. Miss Tully persisted ever so gently.

'Mary is very sick, isn't she?'

'Yup. The doctors think she's going to die.'

Miss Tully reached forward and took my hands in hers. They felt warm and soft, nothing like Mum and Dad's that were dry and hardened from daily farm work.

'I'm so sorry to hear that, Graham. You have been wonderfully brave about it, but today you allowed it to get on top of you, I think? People often say that when you are facing something sad and difficult, like Mary's illness, the best way to deal with it is to work even harder. When you are really busy doing good things, you have less time to worry about the bad things.'

I sniffed; what Miss Tully was saying made sense. I wiped my nose again and looked up for a brief moment. Miss Tully had such a lovely face and her eyes were twinkling. I felt a strong urge to open up and tell her about all my other problems, however, I had promised Dad I wouldn't speak to anyone about his affair. Perhaps I could ask her about adoption, but Miss Tully was speaking again.

'So, Graham, do you think you can come to school tomorrow and again be one of my star pupils?'

'Yes Miss Tully, I'll try.'

'That's the way. And remember, if ever things get a bit too much, you can always share it with me if you want to.'

'Thanks, Miss Tully,' and I managed a sort of a smile as I stood up and left the classroom.

CHAPTER ELEVEN

Things at home were no better during the third week.
Dad made no attempt to hide the fact that he was
visiting Mrs Davies virtually every work day. He would
return from Goulburn about the same time I arrived
home from school on my bike. Then he would change
into his working gear and get me to come out with him
to do jobs around the farm.

We were well into March now and the days were
noticeably shorter so that there was only about three
hours of daylight left for us to do any outside work after
school. Consequently, Dad never had enough time to
do the big time-consuming jobs, instead we tinkered
around doing things that were quick and easy. A large
eucalypt had fallen across a fence in the Hill Paddock
but to clean it up with the chain-saw, collect the logs
and stack them, was a whole day's work, so it was
simply ignored. The sheep required drenching but that
was out of the question whilst the "affair" was still on.

Fences needed checking and repairs made in several places. Finally, Mum's veggie patch and the orchard had been allowed to get well out of hand. This part of the farm was Mum's pride and joy and I knew she would be most disappointed to see how it had been neglected in her absence.

The evenings with Dad were not much fun either. I had to do my best to please him and stay out of his way at the same time. This "affair" didn't seem to be making him any happier. He remained grumpy and seldom showed any interest in anything I was doing at school. He never even asked about school, and if I mentioned something, he would just grunt to show he had heard me. Every night he ordered me off to bed before eight o'clock. I managed to get through the week by taking Miss Tully's advice to heart and made sure I worked hard at school and completed my homework in my bedroom as well as I could. Miss Tully was so encouraging throughout the week that I felt she was more like a friend.

Mum and Mary's train was due in at Goulburn Station on Saturday morning at 10.29am and Dad told me to be ready to leave at nine. I couldn't help wondering what would happen with the "affair" when Mum came home. Surely, Dad wouldn't keep sneaking off to Goulburn almost every day? Mum would soon see how the farm, her vegetables, and the orchard had been neglected and she would definitely not be impressed.

My pocket money was helping to pay off the bike so I had no money to buy presents for Mum and Mary. I asked Miss Tully if I could have some coloured cardboard to make a "Welcome Home" card for Mum. She gave me some pink cardboard and I decorated it using my Lakeside coloured pencils. I tried to draw pictures of things I knew Mum liked on the card. I wasn't a good drawer but I managed to produce passable pictures of a selection of fruits and vegetables around the outside of the card. I wrote inside in my best modified cursive. I was one of the best writers in the class, Miss Tully said.

In school craft we had been making papier-mâché puppets. The one I had made was a clown and I planned to give it to Mary. I had used heaps of colourful paints and the clown had a stack of unruly hair stuck on top of its head like a scarecrow. I gave it bright blue eyes like Mary's and huge red lips. It looked a bit silly, but I thought Mary would like it. Our Mums were asked to provide clothing for the puppets to wear and to hide our hands when we were making the puppets do things. Miss Tully, realising my Mum was still in Sydney and couldn't help me, promised to make a colourful clown's jacket for me. The final result looked terrific and I was so proud of my efforts.

I completed my morning's chores and was ready for Dad well before nine o'clock, clutching a shoe box in which Mary's clown and the card for Mum was lying. As far as I could see, Dad didn't have any presents to give them. We left on time, stopping for a moment outside the Sandalwood Post Office, where Dad gave me what looked like a card to post. Before I dropped it into the letter box, I unobtrusively glanced at the address. It was addressed to Mrs Lucy Davies. Not a good sign!

The train from Sydney pulled into the station on time. I was so excited I couldn't stand still; it was nearly a month since I had seen Mum and Mary. Dad had told me to leave my shoe box with its contents in the car and give my presents to them later. When I saw Mum, I gave her an almighty hug and hung on for as long as I could. Then I went to Mary but gave her a far gentler hug. Dad disappeared to collect the luggage from the carriage at the back of the train. Mum and Mary looked surprisingly well and sun-tanned, although I noticed Mary seemed even thinner than when she had left us.

When we reached the car, I couldn't wait any longer, so I flipped the lid off my shoebox and gave Mum her card and Mary her clown. Mum gave me another kiss and cuddle and Mary played with the puppet clown most of the way home until she fell asleep, exhausted.

Mum chatted away all the way home. She loved Bondi and had been swimming several times in the sea. She described many of the things they had seen there including young women wearing new swimming gear called "bikinis". The place was so alive, she said, and Mary's health seemed to pick up for a week or two. Uncle Christopher and Auntie Mollie had been generous hosts and had looked after them wonderfully well. Mary loved it at Bondi so much that she didn't want to come back to school and Sandalwood. Then Mum started quizzing Dad about the farm.

'So, dear, have you had any rain?'

'Only a couple of showers, it's been pretty dry.'

'And how's the farm looking?'

'Not marvellous. I haven't been able to get out to do the work. Painful back! Could barely get out of bed some mornings.'

I couldn't believe what I was hearing. Dad was telling a massive lie. He had never once complained of a bad back in all the time Mum had been away. Not once! He was telling a huge porky to explain why so little had been done around the place. How could he do this to Mum? I desperately wanted to contradict him and tell Mum what Dad had really been doing with Lucy Davies almost every day.

'I'm so sorry to hear about your sore back, you never mentioned it when I rang you?'

'I didn't want to worry you. You deserved a good break love, and the beach was great for little Mary. If I'd told you about my crook back you would've felt obliged to come back early and I didn't want to spoil your fun.'

Dad was piling bullshit on top of bullshit. In truth, he had wanted Mum to stay away as long as possible so she didn't come home and spoil *his* fun with Mrs Davies. He disgusted me! How could he be so brazenly dishonest?

'Have you been to see Dr Zegalski?'

'Nah what's the point? Backs get better with time. If it gets real crook, I take a Bex and have a lie down, just like the advertisements say.'

'Well, if it gets really bad you can always drive into Goulburn to see one of those physiotherapists or chiropractors dear. But you would have to get a referral from Dr Zegalski first.'

There were a couple of minutes of silence. I was sure Mum had inadvertently given Dad the perfect excuse to go to Goulburn whenever he wanted to visit Mrs Davies again. All he had to do was pretend to have a crook back and then get a referral from Dr Zegalski.

'So, dear how is my orchard? The apples, pears and plums should be ripe by now. Have you been able to pick them?'

'With a bad back, picking fruit has been almost impossible. Graham has picked some grannies for you, but my back has been too painful. Isn't that so Graham?'

I didn't answer.

'Isn't that so, Graham?' Dad had raised his voice this time and was glaring at me in the rear vision mirror.

'Yes Dad,' I mumbled.

'And the veggies?' inquired Mum.

'Same story. love.'

'Oh dear! The carrots, onions and spuds will be okay staying in the ground, but you should have had heaps of rhubarb, tomatoes, lettuce, cabbage and beans by now?'

'Sorry dear, I guess there's a lot of catching up to do, then.'

'I'll help you, Mum,' I piped up from the back of the car.

'You're a sweetie Graham. We'll get stuck into the veggies after lunch.'

It was almost twelve o'clock when we parked outside Sandalwood's general store so Mum could buy some urgent groceries.

Lunch was very late but it was bliss when it was served up. Mum rustled up a fantastic salad from our veggie patch where she had hurriedly retrieved lettuce, radishes, snow-peas, tomatoes and cucumber. These she served with generous helpings of ham that she had picked up at the general store and then added our very own hard-boiled eggs. Wonderful to have Mum home and in charge of the kitchen again. Things were looking up already.

During lunch I watched Mary carefully. She didn't

seem interested in her food and picked at it like an overfed bird. She had taken a real liking to my clown though, which as a special treat, had been allowed to sit on the dining room table propped up against the toaster. Toys are not usually allowed on our table during meals, but I guess with Mary's condition, a few special concessions were permissible. Mary hummed happily enough whilst Mum did her best to coax her into eating a bit more of her meal.

After the meal, with the dishes washed up and put away, Mum announced she was changing into her gardening gear and everyone was welcome to join her in the veggie patch. Mary carried out "Clowny," as he was now christened, and several other dolls to enjoy a picnic on the lawn in the shade. Mum and I were dressed and ready for serious action. Dad surprised us by declaring a short spell in the garden probably wouldn't aggravate his back too much, and actually asked Mum what she would like him to do.

We spent a surprisingly happy time out in the veggie patch as a family, and I began to wonder if things could perhaps get back to normal again and Mrs Davies would simply disappear like a wisp of smoke. Mary fell asleep again in the shade of a Cox's Pippins apple tree and after an hour Dad said he needed to go indoors and lie down for half an hour to ease his back pain. He promised to come back.

While Dad was indoors, Mum sent me in to get the Yates Garden Guide. She wanted to check when to start pruning some of the trees in the orchard. When I wandered in, I spied Dad sitting with his back to me chatting on the phone. I tip-toed to the office to find the Garden Guide and, as I did so, overheard Dad asking Mrs Davies if she liked the sexy underwear he had given her.

So much for his sore back and the longed-for disappearance of Mrs Davies!

CHAPTER TWELVE

Towards the end of March every year, the primary schools' athletics carnival is held in one of the larger towns in the district. Unfortunately, Sandalwood is never deemed big enough to host this event, and anyway, we didn't have the facilities, such as proper jumping pits and smooth well-manicured running tracks. This year, the carnival was to be held in Goulburn and all the primary school kids at Sandalwood Public School were going to attend. There were about forty of us altogether, from third grade through to sixth grade, so a bus had to be organised to get us to Goulburn.

Over the last month or so, the teachers had been selecting the team to represent Sandalwood. I was excited because I qualified for three events and I was competing in the nine-year-old boys seventy yards, the junior high jump and the junior long jump. Apparently, Miss Tully used to be a good jumper so she had been taking the boys and girls who qualified for the jumping events in Goulburn for some extra training sessions during lunchtime. I especially enjoyed these extra practices because Lynda was there. She was in the junior girls' high jump. I was better than Lynda at long jump but she usually beat me in the high jump. Lynda was a fast runner too but I always beat her.

At teatime one evening, Mum announced that she would be one of the parents who would be travelling on the bus on Friday with all of us kids to the carnival. The teachers, she said, needed a few parents to come along to help look after us during the day. This was great news, because Dad said he needed the car on Friday to go to a Field Day over at Crookwell to learn about new experimental pastures that were being developed for sheep graziers. A clever move on Mum's part because she could now come to the carnival after all, and watch me perform.

Friday couldn't come quickly enough, and you could feel the excitement building at school throughout the week. The school's colours were red and white so the kids who were competing had to wear white shorts and socks with these crazy bright red T-shirts. There were special team events too, such as relays and ball games called "tunnel ball" and "over and under". Some of the kids made red and white streamers to wave about when cheering our team on.

On Friday morning we had to hurry as the bus was

leaving before school normally started. Dad drove us to school and then drove off to his Field Day in Crookwell. He promised he would be back at the school to pick us up at 3.30pm when the bus was expected to return from Goulburn. Mary had her usual classes because she was still in the infants' school.

When we arrived, the bus was already parked outside the school and there was a real buzz of excitement about the place. We were told to line up in our classes to be checked off before getting on the bus. Mum was there, holding a large bag that contained our picnic lunches and drinks, together with hats and jumpers, so I didn't have to worry about carrying anything. I sat next to Colin; he wasn't much of a runner but was terrific at ball games. Fred and Mike were in the seat immediately in front of us and, whoopee, Lynda was just across the aisle from me.

The big fifth and sixth grade kids got on last and walked up to the back of the bus as if they owned it. They made plenty of noise and playfully punched a couple of us younger kids as they went by. I was surprised to observe that a couple of the big sixth grade girls were starting to form breasts. I glanced across at Lynda but there was nothing to see there. I wondered, idly, how old girls have to be to have affairs and babies. Perhaps I could ask Mum?

Mr Marsden, the School Principal, boarded and laid

down the law. There was to be no standing or getting out of our seats and no littering of the bus. It was okay to have the windows open but we mustn't put our arms or heads out of the window or throw anything out. Miss Tully was also on the bus looking glamorous in a white dress with bright red roses. Mr Marsden then climbed off the bus because he would be driving his car into Goulburn. Finally, the three mums who were escorting us climbed aboard, including my mum. I was proud that my mum has volunteered to give up her day to come and support us.

Johnno was driving the bus; he flicked his indicator and pulled out. The bus soon became noisy with the kids at the back horsing around. We four boys nattered happily together, and of course, Mike had his yoyo with him, but he found it difficult to do his tricks in the bus as it rattled and bumped over the rough road. At one point Lynda leant over and offered me a polo mint. I felt really chuffed about this, but then she spoilt it by offering polo mints to my three mates as well. She was looking so pretty and had her hair cut short so it wouldn't knock the high jump bar off.

We made excellent time and in a bit over an hour were into the outskirts of Goulburn. We had to travel through town and out to the new suburbs on the other side where the newest athletics oval was. We were barely a couple of miles from our destination when the bus's engine began coughing and spluttering. Johnno looked worried. After a minute or so the engine died completely and Johnno was forced to bring the bus to a gentle stop outside somebody's house. The street looked vaguely familiar and then I remembered this was where our family came to inspect the Malvern Star bike that eventually became mine.

In fact, the very next house in the street was the one we visited. This was where Mrs Davies lived, the woman with whom Dad was having his affair. Mum realised that she had been here before and walked over to speak to Johnny. Miss Tully joined them and the three talked for a minute or two before Miss Tully called out for quiet on the bus.

'Listen-up everybody. Our bus has developed some kind of a mechanical problem. Graham's mum, Mrs Granger, knows the people in the next house so she and Johnny are going there to ask if we can phone another bus company to come and pick us up and get us to the carnival on time. The oval is only about two miles away but it's too far to walk. Hopefully another bus can get here soon. So, stay in your seats but gather up your belongings so we can transfer to another bus as quickly as possible.'

I was explaining to Colin, Mike and Fred that this house was where we had bought my almost brand new bike, when I saw something that stopped me mid-sentence.

I couldn't believe what I saw. There, parked in the driveway of the house that Mum and Johnny were now hastily walking into, was Dad's car. It was unmistakeably his. I could clearly read the number plate from where I was sitting. There was absolutely no doubt; Dad's story about going to a Field Day in Crookwell was another shocking lie. There was no way Mum wouldn't see our car parked in Mrs Davies's driveway.

I watched in horror. Mum stopped momentarily at our car and looked inside. Double-checking, I suppose, that she wasn't dreaming. Then she and Johnny walked on up to the front door and rang the bell. I sat there spell-bound. They rang a second time.

The door opened. Standing there was Mrs Davies wearing a dressing gown. I could only imagine the way the conversation went. Mrs Davies stood there shaking her head vigorously. Clearly, she was not going to allow Mum and Johnny to enter and use her phone. I suppose, on reflection, that it could have been even worse, Dad might have come to the door! Mrs Davies was now strenuously pointing to her next-door neighbour's house, presumably suggesting to Johnny and Mum that her next-door neighbour might be able to help.

In small, tight-knit communities, like Sandalwood, everybody knows everybody's business and that includes knowing what type of car your family drives. Colin, Fred, Mike and Lynda and half the kids on the bus, knew immediately that it was my family's car parked in the driveway of the house Mum had visited to ask permission to use the phone.

One of the sixth-grade kids, called Greg, yelled out from the back of the bus.

'Hey, Graham, that's your old man's car in the driveway. What the heck's he doing here?' The bus went quiet, waiting to hear my reply.

'Yeah, that's our car,' I replied, trying to sound matter of fact and unsurprised. Now everyone on the bus craned their necks to look at the car in question.

'What's he doing mate? A sheila came to the door, I saw her,' called out Chris, another sixth grader. Chris stopped short of saying anything more, but a few of the older kids on the bus knew exactly what he was implying. I was blushing like a beetroot. How could I possibly answer? I took evasive action and ducked down to be out of sight and kept silent. My mates didn't know what to do; I could tell they were mystified. Lynda did the nicest thing of all, she looked at me sympathetically and passed another polo mint across. I whispered 'thanks,' and popped it in my mouth.

A few minutes later Johnny and Mum returned to the bus. Mum was visibly shaken. For an awful moment, I thought she might get off the bus again and go straight back to Mrs Davies's house to confront Dad. Most likely she was too shocked to do anything, because she just sat down lamely, and it was Johnny who told us that they had rung another bus company and a back-up bus would arrive in about ten minutes. We would, he promised, still get to the oval on time.

After this horrendous start to the day, I decided getting completely caught up in the carnival and all the fun, was the only way to handle matters. Sandalwood Public School was the last to arrive, but that didn't matter. First up was the march past. There was a special prize for the best school in the march past. Soon the loud-speaker system was pumping out familiar marching tunes and every school smartly marched past the Australian flag. Sandalwood did a reasonable job but didn't win. One of the small schools, with only one teacher, claimed the cup for "Best School March Past – 1960".

Next up, were the heats for the age races for boys and girls. Fred and I were to represent Sandalwood in the nine-year-old boys. As we sat in our rows awaiting our heat to be called to the starting line, I surveyed the others in my heat. I reckoned I had a good chance. There were eight in my heat but only four would qualify to go through to the next round. Seventy yards is a long sprint for nine-year-olds but I had been training and came home strongly. I finished third so was into the next round. Fred just missed out in his heat.

There were sixteen of us into the semi-finals and again only four from each of the two heats would advance to the final. I scraped in fourth so made the final, much to the joy of Mum and my Sandalwood supporters. By the time the finals were on, in the afternoon, I was getting tired. I had already jumped in the long jump and the high jump without much success and taken part in the ball games. I did my best, but was coming last, until one of the other runners tripped, allowing me to finish seventh.

My last event was the junior boys' relay. Relays always end in grief for some schools. Teams are disqualified for going over the change-over line, or somebody drops the baton, or runs into the wrong lane. Our team had been well trained though and made no mistakes. We came fifth but then two schools that came in ahead of us were disqualified so we were promoted to third place and won bronze ribbons. Fantastic effort! Fred and I proudly lined up to receive our certificates and bronze ribbons at the end of the day.

Overall, Sandalwood had fared well. There were eight schools about our size and we ended up a very respectable second. Three boys and two girls from our school were selected to go to the District Championships to be held next month in Canberra. The wonderful news was that Lynda was one of the two girls. She was runner up in the junior high jump and Miss Tully was absolutely thrilled because she had trained her. Lynda's legs were not just nice to look at but were athletic too.

There was a festive mood in the bus on the long way home. We had a different bus and bus driver this time. When we drove past Mrs Davies's house, I was relieved to see there was no sign of Dad's car and this time nobody on the bus made any snide remarks. Mrs Davies had probably remembered Mum from the time we went to her house to purchase my bike, and would definitely have warned Dad.

Dad had promised to pick Mum, Mary and me up from school at 3.30pm. I was dreading it!

CHAPTER THIRTEEN

Our bus pulled up outside Sandalwood Public School ten minutes late. I could see Dad chatting to a couple of other dads several cars down the road. Mary was already safely sitting in the back of the car playing with Clowny.

Mum and I had hardly spoken all day, except when she had given me my lunch, or had congratulated me. It was actually a bit embarrassing having your mum come along on the bus as a parent supervisor. Ever since Mum and Johnny had called in at Mrs Davies's place on the way to the oval, I had been worried about her. Did she actually see Dad in the house when Mrs Davies opened the door? Was he in his pyjamas like Mrs Davies? What did Mum think was happening? Surely, she was going to ask Dad why his car was parked in Mrs Davies's front yard. Was I about to witness a massive argument? Would Mum ask me later what I knew? The more I thought about this whole ghastly situation, the more uneasy I became. I was truly dreading being in the car with Mum and Dad on the short drive home.

When the bus pulled in, Mum gathered up her gear and helped to see us kids off the bus. Then she had a few parting words with the teachers and a couple of other parents she knew. While she chatted, Colin, Fred, Mike and I made final plans for tomorrow which was a Saturday. We were determined that this time the four of us would make it down to Paddy's Gorge. As before, we would take a picnic lunch and explore along the creek. We reckoned there could be caves further down the gorge. Fred warned us that we might encounter the ghost they had sensed was watching them the first time they were down there. It all sounded really exciting. We arranged to meet at the show ground at 10:00 a.m. and not be late.

When Mum finished yakking, we made our way down together to the car. I watched closely to see the reaction when Mum greeted Dad. The meeting was best described as frosty, they just nodded at each other. There were no kisses, hugs or even pleasantries exchanged. As usual, Mum sat in the front passenger seat and I climbed in the back next to Mary, who had abandoned Clowny and was now playing with Susan, her favourite doll. I gave her a quick tickle. She laughed and said, 'Don't do that Graham,' which really meant, please do it again. I obliged, and this time she squealed out loudly.

'Hey, stop that racket,' Dad could never abide Mary's squeals.

We relapsed into silence, which was broken only once, when Dad asked, 'How did you go son?'

Mum filled him in with most of the details. The rest of the short trip home was again in silence.

As soon as Dad parked the car, he headed off up the paddock and Mum retired to the kitchen with Mary. I didn't quite know what to do. I didn't want to go with Dad because I hated what he was doing to Mum, but I found stuff in the kitchen helping Mum was usually boring. I decided instead I would play with Mary. Mary was dog-tired. School seemed to take it out of her even though her teacher, Mrs Kircudbright, let her have a sleep after lunch every day because of her special needs. I always let Mary pick what games or activities she wanted to play so there were no arguments that way, and if she was going to die soon, this seemed only right. Today, Mary wanted to play "mums and dads". I was so pleased that Mary was too young to know about "affairs" and that her dad was having a big one behind Mum's back.

All that evening I played the part of the silent observer; I reckoned I would make a good spy one day. Few words were exchanged between Mum and Dad and I don't think they even looked at each other once during teatime. It was my turn to help Mum with the washing up, whilst Dad mooched off to his study on the pretext he had some accounts to deal with. The washing up done, I read a story to Mary. Mum then bathed Mary and put her to bed. I sensed there had to be a time later this evening when Mum would get stuck into Dad, and I was determined to stay awake and listen to everything.

I was right. I had been fighting a losing battle and kept dropping off to sleep only to wake with a sudden start. Then I would do whatever I could to help me stay awake longer. I twiddled my toes and counted to a hundred or did fifty arm stretches. Pretending to be a pig on a spit was a good one, but it made a terrible mess of the bed. I didn't do anything I wasn't allowed to do, such as getting out of bed or turning the light on. Then, just as I felt I couldn't stay awake any longer, I heard raised voices coming from the study at the other end of the house.

It was an argument all right, but I couldn't hear what was being said. For a moment or two I contemplated creeping down the corridor to listen, but the thought of what Dad would do to me if he caught me, was a powerful deterrent, so I stayed put. Then, I started to think what might happen if Mum and Dad decided they would split, separate or divorce. There were two kids at school whose parents had broken up. Both the kids lived now with their Mums. What would it be like? If my parents couldn't resolve their differences, would Dad kick us all out of the house? Perhaps Mum, Mary and I would have to go down to Bondi and live with Uncle Christopher and Auntie Mollie? Being near the beach could be okay, though.

I don't know how long they argued, but it ended with doors being slammed. Eventually everything in the house went quiet and I fell into a restless sleep.

I awoke much later than usual on Saturday morning and felt tired and stressed. I needed my full night's sleep and when I missed out I became cranky quickly. I turned up for breakfast to find Dad had already left, and Mum was washing up their dishes. Mary was playing happily on the floor with her dolls.

Life on a farm often required early morning outside work, even when it was miserable and cold, so a decent cooked breakfast was fortifying and comforting. Mum and Dad never missed out on a cooked breakfast and I always enjoyed one too. Today, Mum cooked me tomatoes and sausage with scrambled eggs and served it all up with hot buttered toast. Mary didn't have much of an appetite these days, but Mum was pleased that she had enjoyed some porridge with brown sugar this morning.

Mum was not saying much. When I told her the gang

was meeting at ten o'clock and I needed some lunch, she set to and made up a picnic for me. Next, she gave me a bag and told me to go and pick some plums to share with my mates. I didn't think Mum looked happy this morning. Little wonder, I reckoned, after last night's arguments. At least they were both still living in the same house so they hadn't divorced, I reasoned.

I packed my small backpack with the plums, a water bottle and my picnic and gave Mum and Mary a hug and a kiss. I jumped on my bike and pedalled like mad to make the rendezvous by ten o'clock only to find I was the first to arrive. I'm the one living out of town, yet I was the only one to arrive on time. Typical! The other three arrived soon after and the mood was upbeat. Mike and Greg were waffling on about the ghost of Paddy's Gorge and Colin had even remembered to bring a torch so we could explore the caves that were supposed to exist along the side of the creek. The only concern was the weather. High cirrus cloud had been thickening since yesterday and now the clouds were looking threatening. Colin assured us he had heard the forecast on the ABC that morning and rain wasn't expected until the late evening.

We made excellent progress this time and had no dramas, like punctures, along the way. We didn't see a single vehicle and in a bit over an hour we pulled into a small parking area at the end of the road. A sign informed us that we were entering Paddy's Gorge Conservation Park and listed the things we could, and could not, do in the park.

'A load of bullshit,' commented Mike, who was already getting out his yoyo for a quick practice.

'No, it's not you drongo,' asserted Fred, who was into nature and wildlife and was one of the few kids to still ride his pony to school.

'Course it is. Who's ever going to know what we do here?'

'That's not the point,' Fred responded, 'We have to be trusted to look after the bush. If we look after the place then the animals will thrive and it'll keep its beauty; then everybody can keep coming here to enjoy it.'

'Gee, you talk a lot of bloody rubbish,' Mike snapped back.

'Okay, shut up you two. We don't want any arguments. We're a team of explorers, remember, and we may need to work together if something goes wrong.' These were the wise words of Colin, the peacemaker.

We stowed our bikes behind some thick purple flowering lantana bushes so they were out of sight, unless someone seriously went looking for them. I was the only one with a safety chain and padlock which I used to lock Colin's and my bike together. Better than nothing, I thought. Then we set off with Mike in the lead.

We headed down to the gorge following a narrow,

seldom used track, that wound its way snake-like down to the side of Paddy's Creek. It was pleasantly shady in amongst the thick bush and I was relieved it was a reasonable track because it would have been easy to get lost if you wandered away too far from the creek. Nobody knew the names of any of the trees around although Fred informed us that this was a strip of rain forest that ran along both sides of the sheltered creek and this explained why the trees were so different here to the ones we saw in the more open country at the top. It was surprisingly quiet with few birds about. We stopped from time to time to admire a bright red fungus or a group of attractive blue flowers. Fred said they were orchids.

It was obvious that the track was used occasionally because we came across a few places where branches that had started to grow across the track had been broken or slashed. We reckoned it would be one of the rangers who looked after the Conservation Park who had done the slashing.

Mike simply couldn't help himself and did his best to scare us several times. At one point he turned around and told us he had just seen a deadly brown snake slither under a log and that he had nearly trodden on it. Another time he rambled on about how his Dad had told him to watch out for the leaves of the giant native stinging tree, one touch of its leaves would kill you in ten minutes, Mike claimed. Next, he carried on about the vicious bite of the blue-bottomed ant that was deadly if you were bitten more than twice, he declared. The rest of us had never heard of blue-bottomed ants so dismissed this as another example of Mike's weird imagination. We were genuinely scared once though when we disturbed a couple of large grey kangaroos that suddenly crashed off through the undergrowth.

The track was slippery in places and protruding tree roots often made the going difficult. In a couple of places along the creek we passed dark coloured rock pools that looked deep, cold and uninviting. Between the rock pools there was but a trickle of water and sometimes the creek dried up completely. We had to negotiate beds of stinging nettles and massive scotch thistles that had taken root even down here along the creek.

After about half an hour, Colin came up with the question we had all been thinking, but didn't want to be the one to ask it, in case the others thought we were scared.

'How much farther are we going to go?'

We had already passed the place along the track where Mike and Fred had turned back on their first exploration of Paddy's Gorge a few weeks back.

'Yeah, I'm bloody starving,' claimed Mike.

'Me too,' Fred seconded.

'Let's go on for ten more minutes and then stop for

lunch,' I suggested. 'We may find a clearing, or a cliff overlooking the creek.'

'Okay,' agreed Colin, so we kept going.

The creek, and the track we were following swung sharply around to the left where there was a rough ford over the water and a treacherous looking four-wheel drive track coming steeply down from the hills on the other side of the gorge.

'Wow, where does that track come from?' asked Fred.

Nobody had any idea, but the ford and the surrounding rocks provided an ideal spot for our picnic lunch. We opened our backpacks and started eating hungrily. Each of us had brought something to share, be it plums, chocolates, biscuits or lollies.

Once our appetites were satiated, we lay back on the warm rocks to watch the trickling creek and the dragonflies that darted about or hovered above the water. It was a peaceful sunny spot. A family of blue wrens flitted around a little distance away and high above us an eagle circled graciously eying the ground below, intently, for unsuspecting prey.

Mike could never stay still for long, however, and clambering to his feet announced, 'I'm going for a pee' and wandered off into the bushes. The rest of us were thinking we might also need to answer the call of nature, when Mike came charging back, still fumbling with his fly-buttons, and in an agitated state.

'Hey, guess what? I've found a den; someone lives down here. Come and have a gander.'

We jumped to our feet and scrambled after Mike back through the dark bushes. He was right. There in front of us rose a craggy rock wall as high as a church and at its foot a small entrance to what looked like a cave. All about us were clear signs of camping. A rough circle of large stones created a fire place, complete with hot plate. In addition, two large logs had been felled and rolled into position to provide basic seating for several people around the fire place. The camping site looked to be still in use because someone had piled up fresh firewood nearby ready for use.

'Let's look in the cave,' I yelled, excited about this amazing find.

'Wait, till I get my torch,' Colin responded, and went scrambling back to where we had picnicked to retrieve our only torch from his backpack. 'Okay, follow me,' he ordered on his return. We fell into line behind him full of anticipation.

The entrance to the cave was not much bigger than the size of a large man, but once we were through, we discovered it opened up into a substantial, almost circular shaped cavern, with a smooth dry dirt floor. As Colin flashed his torch about, we realised we had entered a really interesting place. This cave was clearly being used as accommodation. Two sleeping bags were rolled up and sat on stretchers, there were wooden seats and a rough-hewn table. On the table sat a paraffin lamp, an ashtray and a packet of Woodbines. Against the wall leaned two fishing rods and close by stood a small cupboard which we opened to reveal cutlery, basic cooking utensils and enamel plates and cups. A shelf nearby held saucepans, a billy and two frying pans. Under the shelf was a wooden box containing bottles of unopened beer and a couple of bottles of half consumed sherry.

'Hey, whoever is living here could come back at any moment,' exclaimed Fred. 'We might get done for trespassing?'

'Nah,' replied Colin. 'You can only trespass on someone's private land. This is a cave, it's not private land. Anybody can stay here if they want to.'

'Whoever stays here comes often,' I added. 'And they might come back any moment and trap us inside. We'd better scarper.'

'That's right,' Colin agreed. Perhaps they come here at weekends, and this being a Saturday, they could be on their way here right now.'

We looked at each other and written across everyone's face was a look that said, "Get out quickly!" We headed for the cave's opening and scrambled back into the intensely bright, glaring sunlight.

We didn't bother to look around the outside camp

area again and ran straight back the short distance to the ford where we had enjoyed our lunches.

As we emerged from the bushes, we were shocked to discover our backpacks were gone!

CHAPTER FOURTEEN

'What the hell has happened to our gear?' yelled Mike.

'Somebody must have stolen it,' answered Colin.

'But there's nobody here,' I exclaimed, anxiously.

'Could it be an animal?' suggested Fred.

'Don't be bloody stupid, Fred. What animal is going to pick up all our bags and run off with them? Do you think there's a kangaroo hopping around here wearing all four of our back packs on its back?' Mike's attempt at humour did little to lighten the mood.

'Our packs were still here when I came back only a few minutes ago to collect my torch.'

'It can't be an animal then. It has to be a person and it must have only just happened. Perhaps we can chase them?' I reasoned.

My suggestion fell on deaf ears.

'There's nobody going back up the four-wheel drive track which means whoever has pinched our bags must be going back along the track we came down, or, they're still here,' posited Colin.

We all turned to look at the rough road that snaked its way up the steep hill. As we did so, a rock crashed between Fred and Mike narrowly missing them both. We swivelled around in the opposite direction to see who had thrown it, but there was no sign of anyone.

'Shit,' said Mike, 'that rock only just missed me.' The stone was about the size of a tennis ball and would have really hurt had it hit anybody.

'What are we going to do?' asked Colin in a panicky voice.

'I'm getting out of here,' shouted Fred, and he set off back in the direction of the cave.

'No point going in the cave,' I yelled, 'You could be trapped in there.'

Fred stopped in his tracks. As we all hesitated for a moment wondering what to do, another stone, a bit larger this time, bounced off the rocky surface close to where I was standing and ended up in the scrub. It had come from the same direction as the first one. We were all really scared by now and our instincts told us to run for it back along the track we had come from. We were sitting ducks standing out here at the ford, dithering.

'Bugger our backpacks, let's run for it,' Colin called out, 'Come on ...'

'Oh, no you don't!' a voice boomed at us from where the stones had been coming from.

Standing on top of a large rock, some thirty yards away, was a well-built man who must have been hiding in the thick scrub until this moment. He was dressed like a typical bushman, hob-nailed boots, long-sleeved check shirt, Hard Yakka working trousers and a knock-about hat. His face was rugged, tanned and sported a substantial black beard. Most alarming, however, he was holding a rifle in one hand, probably a 202.

'What the hell are you twits doing down here?' the stranger demanded.

'Just exploring,' I called back.

'Well, this is my patch down here and you're not welcome, see,' the stranger asserted.

'Sorry sir,' stammered Fred.

'We didn't know there was anyone living down here,' offered Colin.

'We just wanted to see where the track was going,' Mike added.

'I've been watching you. You found my camp and then you went into my cave. I could shoot you for that; trespassing on a man's property.' As the stranger spoke, he jumped from his rock and began to approach. Instinctively, the four of us huddled closer together as if there was safety in numbers.

'Lie on yer backs. Come on, move it,' he barked.

The four of us were truly terrified. This man had a gun and we four were stranded at the bottom of Paddy's Gorge with nobody around for miles to help us. He was clearly angry that we had found his hide-out. He could shoot us any moment and nobody would even hear the shots. Our parents wouldn't start to get worried until after five o'clock; the time we had said we expected to be home.

We hastily spreadeagled ourselves on the warm rock and squinted as we were obliged to look up into the sky. We lay there, motionless, each with our own fears for what seemed ages. The birds went completely silent, as if waiting to see what was going to happen. The only sound was the man walking closer.

Then there was a violent explosion. The man had fired his rifle. I felt no pain, so I knew he hadn't aimed at me. But the others ...? My ears were ringing sharply for he had been so close when he fired. Next, I heard the man laughing out loud.

'Get up yer bastards.'

We scrambled to our feet, a pathetic looking foursome, trembling with fear. I was relieved to see that the four of us were standing, the stranger must have fired in the air. There was no need for any shooting; we could hardly have been more frightened.

'Now, what am I going to do with you four idiots?' he asked.

Nobody was brave enough to reply.

'Eh? What do you think I should do? Here I am, in me quiet little spot on the river, doing a bit of huntin' and fishin' on me own, and camping, and then you idiots show up. Uninvited, I might add. Can't a man get a bit of privacy these days? Well, 'ave yer lost yer bloody tongues or what?'

'No sir,' someone stuttered.

'Well, what are me options? I could arrest you and then hand you over to the police for trespassing. It's called citizen's arrest. Or, I could just shoot the lot of yer,' and he laughed again, 'or, I suppose, I could let you off with a warning, so long as you promise never to come back?'

We knew which option we wanted. At least there seemed a glimmer of hope now that we were going to get out of this alive.

'You, what's yer name?' he was staring at me.

'Graham, sir.'

'Okay Graham, which option would you suggest, then?'

'The last one, sir.'

'Yeh, I thought you might pick that one,' and he laughed again. 'And what about the rest of yous? Has Graham 'ere, picked the one you'd all like?'

There was a chorus of affirming sounds.

'Well then, what 'ave yer got to promise me?'

Obediently, we all mumbled the answer he was anticipating.

'Now, see that big rock over there with a tree starting to grow out of the top? Yer packs are behind it. I'm going to count to twenty out real loud and when I get to twenty, I'll start firing at yer. Now scram!'

I'll never forget the mad rush to get out of there. Colin and I headed for the rock to collect our packs and then raced on frantically up to the track. Mike and Fred abandoned their packs totally and made straight for the track. All the while, the man's voice boomed out threateningly and counting down.

'FIFTEEN ... SIXTEEN ...'

By now, Mike and Fred had reached the track safely and were disappearing in amongst the bush. There was no way Colin and I would be there in time.

'SEVENTEEN ... EIGHTEEN ...'

We were still ten yards from the safety of the trees and struggling uphill over horribly rough ground.

'Keep running,' I yelled, 'He can't shoot us both.'

'NINETEEN ...'

Hanging on to our back packs we scrambled desperately on up the loose scree-like rocks. My water bottle fell out but that was the least of my worries. On the stony surface we seemed to be taking two steps forward and then slipping back. The safety of the trees was so close now, but we were easy to hit if he was going to shoot.

'TWENTY ...'

There was another shot from the rifle but we were both still upright and running. Before the sound of the shot had finished echoing around the gorge, we reached the track and scrambled on as fast as we could to be sure to be as far away as possible if the stranger fired again. The track was relatively smooth now and we could run much faster. I don't know how long we kept on running but away in the distance we could see Mike and Fred collapsed on the ground. In a moment or two, we reached them and exhausted from fear and exertion, we too collapsed. We lay there, panting, furtively looking back down the track to make sure the man wasn't following us.

Nobody spoke for a couple of minutes. Inside we were thanking God, or our lucky stars, or anything else we could think of, that the four of us were still alive and unhurt. We were sweating profusely. Colin dived into his backpack and pulled out an unopened drink canister. He took a generous swig and passed it around. It was the only water left between the four of us.

There was still no sign of the lunatic with the gun. After five more minutes resting, we wearily got to our feet and made our way slowly back to the start of the track where we were much relieved to find our bikes awaiting us. Fred and Mike knew they were in trouble when they arrived home for losing their backpacks. As we cycled home, the four of us made a pact to tell our parents every detail about our terrifying experiences.

I guess the only good thing about the day's events was that it had taken my mind off my other worries.

CHAPTER FIFTEEN

Keen to get home and tell the story of our encounter with the madman in Paddy's Gorge, I opened and closed the gate to our place well before five o'clock. I quickly stowed my bike away in the shed, patted Dee and Dum and raced indoors. Mum and Mary were there, but no sign of Dad. I had hoped to be able to tell both Mum and Dad my dramatic tale at the same time, but considering their sad circumstances, I realised that that might be asking too much. I opened up to Mum though and told her everything. She listened intently, asking a couple of questions along the way, until I had finished.

'Well, Graham dear, you sure have had an unexpected adventure. I'm just glad you're back safely to tell the tale.'

'The others are going to tell their parents too Mum. Was that man really allowed to arrest us?'

'No, of course not. He was bluffing, just trying to scare you. There is something called "citizen's arrest" but he couldn't arrest you for being in a Conservation Park which is open to the public.'

'But he said we were trespassing?'

'He may have thought you were trespassing, but in a court of law, I'm sure he would be found to be out of order. He doesn't own that land like we own this farm. You can't trespass on land that nobody owns.'

'He sure scared us Mum.'

'I wouldn't have been scared,' piped up Mary.

'Yes, you would've Mary. You'd have wet your pants!'

'Tell me more about this man you met, dear. How old do you think he was?'

'I dunno. Probably about Dad's age, perhaps a bit older.'

'How tall was he?'

'I dunno.'

'Well, was he as tall as Dad?'

'About the same I reckon.'

'Dad's six foot, so he was quite tall then?'

'Yup I suppose so.'

The phone rang. While Mum answered the call, I raided the fridge, found a Mars bar and went and sat with Mary, who was colouring in. Mary always tried to do things properly and today she was taking great care to stay within the lines and use the best colours. It was a picture of Snow White and the Seven Dwarfs.

A few minutes later Mum put down the phone and

informed me that Constable Andrew Gorton, the local copper, wanted me and the other three in the gang, to go down to the Sandalwood Police Station immediately. He wanted full details about our encounter with the man in the Conservation Park.

There was still no sign of Dad so Mum left a note on the kitchen table, and the three of us climbed into the car and set off to meet Constable Gorton. I had often seen Constable Gorton about town, but had never spoken to him. We only had the one policeman in Sandalwood and there were rumours floating about town that our police station was going to be closed before the end of the year. Nobody in town seemed pleased about that. Constable Gorton and his wife were well liked and had two kids at my school, both in infants. Constable Gorton was also a star player in the Sandalwood Taipans, our local footy team.

Sandalwood Police Station is in High Street, squeezed in between the Bank of New South Wales and "Thommo and Sons", the family butcher. I felt nervous, never having been in a police station before or even been questioned by a policeman. Mum hurried us in.

We were the last to arrive and there was quite a gathering of folk chattering away. The whole gang was present and we each had one, or two, of our parents there as well. Constable Gorton stood behind a high wooden counter but was not wearing his police uniform.

Mum explained to me later that he was "off duty" at weekends and so could wear his ordinary clothes like everyone else. I didn't think he looked as important when not in his uniform.

There were only four seats, so most of us had to stand. Colin's dad offered Mum his seat and Mum accepted gratefully because she needed to place Mary on her lap. The Police Station was one of the oldest buildings in town and was gloomy and poorly lit. The walls were covered in posters but I only had time to glance at them. There was one poster that had "WANTED" in large letters and the photograph of a rough looking man underneath. It wasn't the madman from Paddy's Gorge though.

'Thank you everybody, can we have a bit of quiet please.' It was Constable Gorton speaking, and he wasn't asking a question! He spoke with authority.

We all went silent and looked towards the policeman, except Mary, who had happily snuggled into Mum.

'It's been brought to my attention that there was an unfortunate incident this afternoon down in Paddy's Gorge. From what I can gather, the four young lads present were accosted by a man and a rifle was fired twice. The man threatened the boys and, not surprisingly, succeeded in scaring the wits out of them. Now, Paddy's Gorge is a Conservation Park. There is no law against camping in the park, provided the place is kept tidy and the campers clean up after them. However, it *is* against the law to take in a firearm. Shooting in the park, unless expressly authorised, is strictly forbidden. I intend to follow this matter up, but first I want to speak with the four young lads here to make sure I have the facts correct. Is that okay with everyone?'

There was a chorus of grunts and nods and the two fathers present spoke strongly in support of Constable Gorton's proposed action. They were particularly angry that a firearm had been involved.

We spent well over an hour at the police station. Constable Gorton took each member of the gang, one by one together with our parents, into his smaller room out the back of the office where he questioned us carefully. I was the third to be called. I had to tell him what had happened and then he asked me heaps of questions. Constable Gorton was particularly interested to hear what the man had said to us and what he made us do. The policeman told us he was going to collate what we had told him and then type it all up as an "Incident Report". Next, we were instructed to return to the police station at 10 am tomorrow when Constable Gorton would read his statement aloud to us and we would have to sign it, if we all agreed with what he had written. I was pleased about the timing of the return visit because it meant I could skip Sunday school for once.

It was getting dark when we finally arrived home. Mary, after sitting about in the police station for so long, was tired and cranky so Mum gave her something to eat and popped her straight into bed. Dad was indoors, but seemed to be sulking. He remained in his office until Mum served the evening meal when he came out somewhat grudgingly. There was little talk at the table. Mum and I tried to tell Dad what had been happening in Paddy's Gorge and at the police station, but he didn't seem interested. I could feel the tension in the room. It reminded me of another of Miss Tully's expressions we had discussed in class, "we were walking on egg-shells". At least a cold silence was better than an out and out argument. I had also noticed that Mum was sleeping now in the spare bedroom.

On Sunday Dad surprised us by offering to drive me down to the police station for my ten o'clock appointment with Constable Gorton. For the first time ever the four gang members all arrived a few minutes early. Fred and his Dad rode in on horseback and Mike came with his fancy new golden coloured yoyo with flashy decorations. He had ample time to show off his latest trick before Constable Gorton opened the front door for us to troop back into his office. Constable Gorton explained he was playing footy in Goulburn in the pre-season comp that afternoon and needed to get things wrapped up quick smart. He sat us boys down on the four seats he still had, while everyone else remained standing, and carefully read out the Incident

Statement he had compiled from our previous evening's accounts.

Everything sounded fine so the four of us signed the papers he gave us. This was the first time I had ever been asked to "sign a document". I should have practised at home beforehand. I ended up writing my name in my best modified cursive writing. I was so pleased Miss Tully had taught us how to form the letters correctly. The only trouble was that my signature looked incredibly neat and tidy, whereas grown-ups always did their signatures fast and with a flourish. You could seldom decipher a grown-up's signature but mine was dead easy to read. The constable remarked that we needed to practise our signatures as they were too easy to forge. Anyway, we were done at last and free to go.

On the way home Dad asked me several question about the man who had held us up in Paddy's Gorge. What was the colour of his beard? His eyes? Did he have a slight limp? Did he sound like an Aussie, or did he speak with an accent? To be honest, I was so petrified at the time that I didn't take in many details except to get an idea of his size and his clothing. I wondered why Dad was suddenly so interested.

'Do you think you know who he was Dad?'

'Nah, no, definitely not.'

But I thought it odd that Dad was after so much

detail and I think he was annoyed that I couldn't help him more.

The clouds had been gradually thickening since yesterday afternoon and shortly after we arrived home it began to rain. Dad was excited because he reckoned it was a substantial low-pressure system moving in and we were likely to receive as much as two inches of rain over the next twenty-four hours. It was going to help fill the dams and the creeks would rise, although flash flooding was only forecast overnight. By this time tomorrow the weather was expected to ease and the rain would peter out. The barometer had dropped to 980 hectopascals, Dad claimed, so we should be in for a decent downpour.

Steady rain fell the rest of the day and throughout the night. By morning it appeared to be easing off though, and Dad announced at the breakfast table that he was taking the ute into Goulburn; he needed more fencing wire and some bags of laying pellets for the chooks. Mum and I exchanged looks, for we both knew what a trip to Goulburn might also mean.

Dad offered to drop Mary and I off at school on his way to Goulburn which was fine for Mary, but I preferred to ride my bike. When I told Dad this, he shrugged his shoulders and merely remarked that the Timboola Creek might be up. Since getting my new bike a few weeks ago, I had not yet had a chance to ride it in the rain and I was keen to see what it was like to ride in rainy, slippery conditions.

Ten minutes later Dad left with Mary on board and I left on my bike wearing a hat and raincoat. The raincoat wouldn't fit over my backpack, so it had to get wet. Mum had thoughtfully wrapped my books and lunch up in linen bags in case the rain penetrated my backpack.

It was great fun riding my bike in the wet weather. I quickly learnt that the sediments that build up on the edge of the road become lethal in slippery conditions and I almost came to grief a couple of times. It was still raining lightly and I was getting a bit wet but it wasn't too bad. Soon I swung around the corner at the edge of our property and headed on down to the Timboola Creek. Water was up over the concrete culvert although it didn't look to be very deep. Dad, in his ute, would have sailed through without any problems. I skidded to a halt just before the flood depth sign which I then studied carefully. According to my reckoning, the water was only six inches deep so I decided to take my shoes and socks off and wade through. My feet would probably dry off on the other side of the creek in time for me to put my shoes and socks on again before arriving at school.

So, I laid my bike down on the side of the road and started to remove my shoes and socks. It was a difficult procedure because I had to stand on one leg at a time. I was barely half way through this delicate operation when, at the top of the hill, a ute appeared travelling at speed. I couldn't believe what I was seeing, it was mad old Jake careering down towards me. I had nowhere to escape to and only had enough time to hop clumsily out of the way as Jake belatedly applied the brakes, having finally seen the water lapping over the culvert. There was no way he could stop in time so he passed me travelling far too fast and hit the water hard. There was no problem for old Jake and his ute which simply whooshed its way across and sped off again on the other side. However, I was doused in a torrent of filthy muddy water. I stood there forlornly, dripping from head to toe, holding onto my saturated shoes and socks.

There was no point trying to stay dry anymore. I picked up my bike, and barefoot, pushed through the flood waters which swirled angrily around my calves. Reaching the other side safely, I wrung the water out of my socks and only put my wet shoes back on to help with the pedalling. To cap things off I reached school, looking like a totally drowned rat, at exactly the same time as the beautiful Lynda jumped out of her Dad's lovely warm, dry car and ran in to school under a pretty pink umbrella.

'What happened to you? Did you swim along Timboola Creek to get here?'

I could see from her dancing eyes that she thought my appearance enormously funny. As I squelched off to park my bike in the allotted space, she called out, 'Don't you dare sit next to me today Graham.'

I was too cold and wet to think of an appropriately rude response.

Miss Tully took pity on me though. She handed me a towel and told me to try on some of the clothes that had been left in the "Lost Property" cupboard. She's was a gem. Five minutes later I emerged from the storeroom dressed in a weird assortment of ill-fitting garments, but at least they were dry. I put up with a few corny comments from my mates and could see Lynda was watching me closely with her lovely twinkling eyes.

Steady rain continued throughout the school day. Nobody was allowed outdoors, and we stayed cooped up in the classrooms and passageways at morning recess and lunchtime. Classes were okay though. During the afternoon we had a quiz on Social Studies and I came top; Lynda was second, only one mark behind. I turned around to catch her eye, and when I did, I stuck out my tongue. She coloured prettily and looked down at her work. This time I had got away with it.

It was still raining when the bell went and I was faced with another wet ride home. Miss Tully told me to wear home the clothes I had borrowed from "Lost Property", get them washed, and bring them back when dry. My school clothes were nearly dry but still filthy, thanks to old Jake. I found Mary and assured her that Mum would arrive soon.

Mr Marsden, the Principal, kept popping out of his office to pass on messages from parents or the bus company about delays due to flooding. One message was from Mum. The Timboola Creek was up higher and she couldn't risk driving through the water as it was now too deep for the car. One of our neighbours had volunteered though to come in with his covered truck to pick up all the kids who lived along our road. We would be allowed to climb in the back to stay dry and he reckoned he had sufficient clearance to manage the flooded Timboola Creek. There was no problem putting my bike in the back as well.

Things remained chaotic at school for quite some time. The town kids were okay and could easily get home; it was the "out-of-towners" who had problems. Three buses would have to negotiate swollen creeks or drive a long way round to avoid the worst of the flooding. All this uncertainty meant the kids were getting over-excited and a few were behaving stupidly. Miss Tully and the infant's teacher, Mrs Kircudbright, were doing their best to keep everybody calm, whilst Mr Marsden stayed in his office to handle calls from anxious parents.

Mary and I as well as the other four kids who lived

along our road, only had to wait about twenty minutes before Bob Wiley and his truck pulled up outside the school playground. I held Mary's hand and led her out. Bob lifted her up into the back of his truck where she was under cover and told her to sit down. The others piled in behind her. I dashed off to collect my bike but had to ask Bob to lift it up for me. I was strong, but not that strong.

It was still raining as we moved off. A few minutes later Bob stopped his truck before the dreaded Timboola Creek crossing. I took a look at the flood height sign and noticed it was now indicating more than a foot deep.

'No problem kids,' Bob yelled out, confidently.

He engaged second gear and moved into the water at a slow, steady pace. We could feel the swirling waters tugging and heaving angrily against the side of the truck. When we reached the deepest part, I felt the truck sliding gradually sideways from the force of the fast-flowing water. I held my breath. Next, the vehicle spluttered but to everyone's relief slowly started to grind its way out on the other side of the culvert.

'All good kids,' Bob hollered, 'First stop is the two Granger nippers.'

A few minutes later we shuddered to a halt outside our gate and Bob came around the back to help Mary disembark. I jumped down and waited for Bob to get my bike down.

Holding Mary's hand and wheeling my bike with the other, we moved as fast as her little legs would allow, trying to miss the worst of the puddles. By the time we reached the front door where Mum was waiting, Mary was clearly exhausted and she virtually collapsed into Mum's waiting arms.

At least we were home safely.

After Mum had comforted Mary and settled her down on the settee, she told me that Dad had rung. The river between Goulburn and Sandalwood was flooded and the road closed to traffic until further notice. Dad was stuck in town. Mum and I just looked at each other, we both knew this did not auger well.

CHAPTER SIXTEEN

That evening the rain cleared and the sun broke through. The world looked refreshed, and apart from the inconvenience of flash flooding, everyone rejoiced that the pastures were drenched. Dams were full to overflowing and farmers could turn their attention to sowing winter crops. The air smelt fresh and cleansed.

It's a sad thing to have to say but the three of us felt far more relaxed without Dad around. Ever since Mum had returned from Sydney with Mary, the house had been tense. It was as if we lived in a pressure pot, expecting an explosion at any moment. I wondered if this is what it must have been like during the second world war when you were half-expecting to be bombed, or if you lived on the edge of an active volcano predicted to erupt at any time. Perhaps this tension was what you would feel as an ANZAC waiting to leave your trench to attack the Turks.

Then another worrying thought struck me. Whatever had happened, in all this flooding rain, to the man in Paddy's Gorge? Had he drowned? There must have been widespread flooding down there too. Did he retreat to his cave? If so, was he trapped in there by rising waters? Perhaps he had escaped up the rough road, or up the trail we boys had used? He didn't have a vehicle, so he couldn't have gone too far. Despite the shocking way he had treated the four of us; he was still a human being. Somebody should go and check on him. Perhaps Constable Gorton had already done so?

'Mum, do you think Constable Gorton has been down Paddy's Gorge to arrest the man who lives down there?'

'I very much doubt it dear. He would have been too busy handling problems with flooded rivers and road closures. When the floods subside, he might be free to do something.'

'I hope that man is okay.'

'You're a funny lad. That man scared the living daylights out of you boys, threatened you with his rifle, and here you are, worrying about whether or not he's okay.'

'I felt a bit sorry for him living alone in that gorge. I don't think he camps down there; I think he actually lives there.'

'Well, I strongly advise you to avoid going to Paddy's Gorge in future. Next time the man might actually shoot you!'

Our conversation was interrupted by Mary who was groaning about a pain in her back. She had been getting these pains more frequently in the last couple of weeks. Mum went to the cupboard to get Mary an aspirin and sat with her as she swallowed it down with a glass of milk. Mum had told me that we must expect this and that the doctors had explained it was likely to happen as Mary's kidneys continued to deteriorate. The doctors had also told Mum that after a time aspirin may not work anymore as the pain intensified and Mary would need to take stronger medication. I was so sorry for my little sister and spent the next half an hour helping her to dress and redress her dolls. I felt a bit of a sissy and Dad certainly wouldn't approve, but I knew Mary liked me playing with her.

Most children don't want to go to bed when told its bedtime, but Mary was so exhausted by the end of the day that she longed to collapse into her comfy bed. Again, the doctors had said this was to be expected. When kidneys are not functioning properly the patients feel lethargic and lack energy. Mary usually fell asleep in a matter of minutes after Mum had tucked her in.

I helped Mum with the dishes and then knocked over the homework Miss Tully had given us. It was Arithmetic and I was one of the best in the class at Arithmetic. Tonight, we had to do addition of pounds, shillings and pence. By eight o'clock I was in bed waiting for Mum to come in and read to me but I had other plans for her. I wanted to get to the bottom of this adoption business. Particularly, I wanted to know why I had been adopted and who were my biological parents. A few minutes elapsed before Mum appeared with a book she wanted to read to me, but I swung into action.

'Mum ...you know how Dad told me that I was adopted?'

'Yes, dear.'

'I really want to ask you some more questions about it?' I could see Mum was not comfortable about discussing this topic tonight, but I was determined. With Dad away, this was an ideal opportunity.

'When Dad told me I was adopted, he said he believed both my parents were still alive, but he wasn't allowed to tell me who they are. But I would really like to meet them, Mum. Please can you tell me more about them and why they didn't want me?'

Mum looked even more uncomfortable now. She shifted her position on my bed, and seemed to be thinking.

'Come on, Mum, it's not fair if I don't know these things. You can trust me. I promise, with all my heart, I won't tell anyone else. It's been really worrying me ever since Dad mentioned it. Please Mum, I need to know why they gave me away and who they are?'

Still Mum hesitated.

'Well, I guess if it's really worrying you, I could tell you a little bit more, but it's illegal for me to tell you your parents' names. When we adopted you, we signed a document agreeing not to disclose the names of your parents, or even where they live. Once an adoption has been agreed to it is essential to keep these matters confidential.'

'Please then, tell me what you can, Mum.' I sat up, expectantly.

'Okay. As you know, you were born in May, 1950. You were handed over for adoption a few days after you were born because your father and mother were not married, so you were born "out of wedlock". That's just the official way of saying your parents were unmarried.'

'Why weren't they married?'

'Well. Your mother was only sixteen when she had you, which is too young to get married in Australia. Your father was about twenty-five but he was deemed medically unfit to be able to look after you.'

'Why?'

'Your father had served in the war for a couple of years and, although he wasn't actually physically wounded, he suffered from what is called "shell shock". When he came back to Australia, he couldn't settle down and he suffered all kinds of mental problems. The doctors were trying to help him, but he couldn't get a job and he used to get drunk often. A few times he even ended up being thrown into prison. He would not have been capable of looking after a baby. So, it was decided that as an illegitimate child, that's a child born out of wedlock, you needed to be adopted by parents who could look after you properly.'

It took me a minute or two to digest this new information, nevertheless I still had a strong urge to meet my real parents.

'So, where are my parents now?'

'I have no idea. We are forbidden to even stay in contact with them. Your mother would now be about twenty-six and your father thirty-five.'

I reached over and gave my mum a big cuddle, 'Thanks for taking me, Mum.'

'Just remember dear, that we are your legal parents and are very proud of you and love you both very much.'

Mum was sniffling and when I looked at her face, I could see she was fighting to hold back tears.

'Why didn't you and Dad have children of your own?'

'We tried for six years but nothing happened. So, we went to get checked out. After a whole lot of tests, the doctors determined we would probably never be able to conceive and told us that if we wanted a family, we might have to adopt children. So, that's exactly what we did.'

'Why couldn't you conceive?'

'Things were not quite right inside me. The doctors

said that having a baby was not impossible but very unlikely.'

'What was wrong? Is it fixed up now? Can you have children now?'

'I think you have heard quite enough for tonight dear. One day, when you are a bit older, we can go into more details. All you need to know for now is that I will never be able to have children because the doctors can't fix my problem.'

'That's sad, Mum. Is Dad angry about it?'

'I don't think he's angry, just disappointed.'

'Is this why he's having an affair with Mrs Davies? Does he want to have a baby with her because you can't?'

Mum began crying. 'That's quite enough, you are upsetting me. Good night.' And Mum walked out, forgetting to take her book with her.

I didn't mean to upset Mum and felt bad about it. I considered going out to say sorry, but in the end, decided I had indeed asked more than enough questions, and it would be better if I stayed put. I had so much more to think about now. The trouble was, the more I found out about my parents and this adoption business, the more questions I wanted to ask. Mary's parents had been killed so she could never find them even if she wanted to. It was different for me, though. My real mum and dad were out there somewhere. Perhaps I would find them one day? I really hoped so.

CHAPTER SEVENTEEN

The next day the weather was fine apart from a couple of brief clearing showers. Dad rang up at breakfast time to say the river between Goulburn and Sandalwood could be crossed now and he would be back later in the day. Mum took the call but was not very enthusiastic about the news. I reckoned Dad had been round at Mrs Davies's place again. I wondered how Dad had the audacity to stay there, when Mrs Davies still had a husband and at least one child. Why didn't Davies's husband do something about "the affair"?

As usual, I rode my bike to school and Mary went in with Mum. I met up with the gang and we enjoyed another lively game of soccer on the rough bit of ground out the back that called itself "the oval". We had only just reached the classroom for the first of the morning's lessons when the Principal, Mr Marsden, stuck his head in.

'Excuse me a moment, Miss Tully. Graham, Mike, Colin and Fred I want you four to come with me please.'

We exchanged worried looks wondering what this was all about. Were we four in trouble? I tried, unsuccessfully, to think of anything I may have done that was against the school's rules. Mr Marsden took us straight to his office where we were surprised to find Constable Gorton.

'Morning boys, I'm about to drive down to Paddy's Gorge to check out the problems you reported having there last Saturday. If that man is still there, I may bring him back here for further questioning. Now, if I do that, and I decide to take this nasty matter to court, I need to know that you four boys are prepared to appear in court as witnesses.'

None of us had expected anything like this to happen and we just stood there dumbly and looking confused. Mr Marsden rescued us.

'I think the best thing you four boys can do is to chat to your parents about what Constable Gorton has just requested. If this matter has to go to court, it will only be successfully prosecuted if you four lads are prepared to stand up in a court of law and tell the judge exactly what happened to you. You will have to spend a whole day in Goulburn and your parents will need to agree that you should go and participate. One of your parents will also need to take you into Goulburn and bring you home.'

There was still no response from any of us. To be honest, I think we were totally shocked that this might happen. Appearing in a court, in front of a judge, was a terrifying thought!

Mr Marsden came to the rescue again, 'How about you chat to Mum and Dad tonight and let me know your answer first thing tomorrow morning?'

We found our tongues this time and muttered our agreement.

'Good on you lads,' said Constable Gorton, as we left and headed back to class.

'Wow, what do you think?' asked Colin, bubbling with excitement, when we were safely out of earshot.

'All right by me,' Mike replied, 'as long as I can take my yoyo.'

Fred and I were both happy about the idea too, so we were all in agreement. Tonight, we had to check it out with our parents.

❧

It was another good day at school and I cycled back home anxious to get the permission I needed to go to Goulburn to appear in front of the judge, if this was what was required. The four of us were thrilled about the possibility. Fred had heard that if you go to court as a witness, they give you a free lunch, and Colin said they paid your expenses, so we might all get some extra pocket money. We'll have to get dressed up in our Sunday best clobber asserted Colin. Whatever happened, we agreed it could be a bit of fun. By now the whole school knew about the possibility of us four appearing in court and it was quite the topic of conversation about the playground.

Dad was home when I rode in and I went out to give him a bit of a hand for a couple of hours before tea. I figured this would get me into his good books before I raised the matter of going to Goulburn later at teatime. It was a strategy that usually worked. I didn't anticipate Mum objecting.

Mum had cooked up one of my favourites for tea, crumbed veal with roast vegetables, mostly from the garden. Even Mary seemed to be enjoying her small helping. I had thought long and hard about how I was going to ask for permission. When we were half way through the main course, and everything seemed peaceful, I pitched in with my carefully prepared speech.

'Oh, Mum and Dad, Mr Marsden wants me to ask you something important.'

Everyone stopped mid-mouthful and gawped at me. To receive a special question from Mr Marsden, the School Principal, was a highly unusual happening.

Mary was the one to break the silence. Jumping up and down in her seat like a throw-down cracker, she just couldn't contain herself, and with one quick comment, totally stuffed up my brilliant speech-to-be.

'I know what it is, I know what it is. Graham has been very naughty and the policeman has told him he has to go and see a judge in Goulburn. Graham's in big, big trouble!'

I saw a look of alarm appear on my parents' faces and their eyes changed from looking curious to looking concerned. As so often happened with Mary, she had it totally wrong and now Mum and Dad had their backs up expecting trouble.

I rounded on Mary, 'That's not right, Mary. Keep your mouth shut when you don't know what you're talking about,' and I gave her one of my nastiest glares.

'Yes, I do, everybody at school knows about it. Four naughty boys have to go to Goulburn with the policeman. Graham's one of them ...'

'That's enough, Mary be quiet!' Dad had joined the fray with an angry put down of little Mary, who, in her delicate state, broke into a flood of tears and ran from the room screaming. Mum, distressed at this sudden turn of affairs, followed her out.

'So, what the hell is this all about Graham?'

I abandoned my prepared spiel and apologised in an

attempt to calm the situation. 'Sorry Dad, Mary's got it completely wrong, it's nothing like what she's saying.'

I had really wanted both my parents to be present, because with Mum there, things were discussed sensibly. Dad, on his own, usually made up his mind immediately, and once his mind was made up, it was almost impossible to get him to reconsider. With Mum out of the room trying to console Mary, it was now between Dad and me, a far trickier situation.

But I was in luck today. Dad actually listened as I did my best to fill him in about what had eventuated at school.

'It sounds good mate. You can't have idiots running around threatening to kill people. It's good for you to go in to Goulburn. I'll take you in.'

'Thanks Dad.' It was a rare moment of agreement with father and son stuff.

A couple of minutes later Mum returned without Mary. Dad did the job of explaining for me and, hey presto, everything was agreed. I could go to Goulburn and the court.

It was only later that it occurred to me that Dad might have ulterior motives. A legitimate trip, taking me into Goulburn to appear in a court of law, might also necessitate a quick visit to see Mrs Davies.

–•–

I cycled to school in record time the next day, anxious to discover whether we had all received parental approval for our possible trip to Goulburn to appear before the judge. No problems! Not only had we been given parental blessing, there were diverse offers to escort us from various mums and dads. Together we fronted up outside Mr Marsden's office to give him the good news and then it was down to the oval for a quick kick about.

Every Wednesday, Miss Tully started the day's lessons with what she called a "News Session". This was an opportunity for us kids to go out the front and tell the rest of the class about anything we had been doing in the last week that was interesting. On the way in to class "the gang" had decided we would go out the front as a foursome to update everyone. It was an unusual news item and certainly created considerable interest. The only trouble was, we didn't know the answers to most of the questions the class fired at us.

'Will the prisoner be handcuffed?' 'Will the judge be wearing one of those wigs?' Do you have to swear on the Bible?' Then Miss Tully surprised us by promising she would prepare a special lesson about law and order and how the criminal courts worked. She was great that way.

The very next day, Constable Gorton's police car was sitting outside our school at morning recess, and shortly after we had resumed our lessons, Mr Marsden sent for the four of us again. We filed into his small office feeling somewhat apprehensive. Mr Marsden was short and podgy with a balding pate and heavy rimmed glasses. He was nice enough in a homely sort of a way and he smiled as we entered.

'Come in boys.'

Mr Marsden's desk was strewn with forms, attendance registers and a copy of the blue covered "Curriculum for Primary Schools" 1960 edition. Miss Tully also had one of these books and was often looking in it. Three trays sat on Mr Marsden's desk labelled "IN", "OUT" and "PENDING". I noted there was a heap of stuff in the "IN" and the "PENDING" trays but nothing in the "OUT" tray. The principal taught a composite fifth/sixth class and his pupils reported he was always popping back into his office to deal with paper work.

Mr Marsden cleared his throat, and looking over the top of his glasses, proceeded to tell us about Constable Gorton's visit.

'I expect you saw Constable Gorton's car out the front at recess?'

'Yes sir,' we replied in unison.

'As the constable explained yesterday, he went to look for the man who you met down in Paddy's Gorge and found him there safe and well. The man's name is Mr

Donald Smithton. Mr Smithton has been living there for about three weeks and is of "no fixed abode".'

'What does that mean, sir?' asked Colin.

'It means he doesn't have a proper house or a home to live in.'

'Why's that, sir?' asked Mike.

'It's because Mr Smithton's fallen on hard times.'

'How come, sir?'

'I understand he's a returned serviceman. Many of our soldiers who returned from the second world war suffered mental problems from the strain of fighting and have not been able to settle down or earn a living since they came back.'

'But the war ended fifteen years ago sir?' I queried.

'Yes, you're right Graham. Soldiers usually overcome any physical wounds but mental wounds can stay with them for a long time.'

'Is he nuts then sir?' I asked.

'Graham, that is a most disrespectful comment. Many of our men went through a terrible time and still have awful nightmares and simply can't get over their mental problems. You have no understanding of what it must have been like in the war.'

I blushed feeling appropriately chastened.

'Were you there too sir?' Fred followed up.

'No Fred, I was fortunate. I was still just too young to go to the war when it ended in 1945.'

'Would you like to have gone sir?' Colin inquired.

'That's quite enough about me boys, now, let's get back to Mr Smithton. When Constable Gorton tracked him down, he had just ridden back in to the campsite on his horse, with his shopping for the week. Apparently, he rides all the way into Crookwell for his shopping, he doesn't possess a car. Constable Gorton interviewed him for half an hour, and came to the conclusion that he should let him off with a caution.'

'What's that mean sir?' It was Mike again.

'It means that Mr Smithton is allowed to continue living in Paddy's Gorge as long as he behaves himself. No more shooting or threatening people who use the Conservation Park, though. So, he hasn't arrested him and he won't be going to court. Mr Smithton has been told to keep the area clean and tidy and also had to surrender his rifle. Constable Gorton is going to see if he can find some cheap accommodation for Mr Smithton somewhere in Crookwell. There are sometimes special shelters and places for folk who are homeless.'

'That's a bit sad sir,' I added, anxious to make a better impression.

'I agree,' Mr Marsden replied. 'I understand he lived in these parts before the war and went to school in a one-teacher school somewhere on the other side of Crookwell.'

'Doesn't he have any family he can stay with?' asked Colin.

'Apparently not,' Mr Marsden responded. 'Now, it's time for you boys to get back to Miss Tully. When you get home this evening be sure to tell your parents that you will not be appearing in front of the judge after all. Off you go.'

We filed out, greatly disappointed that our day in Goulburn was not to be.

CHAPTER EIGHTEEN

Conversation around the dining room table that night was going surprisingly well, probably because Mum had cooked Dad's favourite meal, lamb chops. Dealings between my parents were still frosty, but at least they sat together for the evening meal. I don't think Mary had a clue about Mrs Davies and "the affair". If she did, she was too young to understand. Mum and Dad, I noted, continued to sleep in different bedrooms.

When Dad was halfway through a second helping of roast potatoes and parsnips, I broached the subject that Mr Marsden had asked the gang to raise with their parents.

'I have another message to pass on to you from Mr Marsden,' I announced. This time Mary remained silent.

Making mention of the School Principal, I knew, usually received their undivided attention.

'Oh yeah what's that then?' Dad responded, wiping

the last of the gravy from his mouth with the back of his hand. Mum, however, looked at me alert and attentive.

'We boys had to go and see Mr Marsden again today to find out what happened when Constable Gorton went down Paddy's Gorge to find the man who shot at us.'

'About bloody time too,' Dad remarked.

'He found the man. He had just ridden back in from Crookwell with his week's supplies of shopping.'

'Ridden in? You mean on horseback?' queried Mum.

'Yes, he doesn't own a car. He doesn't have much money, he can't afford a house, but he's got a horse.'

'Sounds like another bloody dole-bludger if you ask me,' Dad commented.

'Well, the policeman just gave him a warning and told him to stop shooting in the conservation park. He has to keep the place clean and tidy. So, we don't have to go to Goulburn after all.'

'Oh, that's good,' said Mum, realising immediately that one excuse for Dad to visit Mrs Davies had been closed off.

'That's not good enough,' grumbled Dad. 'He should have arrested the bugger. Going around scaring kids and shooting off a bloody rifle is not okay. Police these days are getting far too bloody soft.'

'Did Mr Marsden tell you what this man's name was, Graham?'

'Yes, he did. It was Mr Donald Smith, or something like that. I remember the Donald bit because I once saw a Donald Duck movie in Goulburn.'

My parents had gone quiet and I saw them exchange looks. It was one of those meaningful looks that parents give each other when they are sharing a secret they don't want the kids to know about.

'Was the name Donald Smithton by any chance?' Mum asked.

'Yup, that's it,' I replied. 'Do you know him?'

Both my parents quickly denied knowing Donald Smithton, but I knew they were telling porkies. When you are nearly ten you can tell these things.

'Mr Marsden told us that the man wasn't well in the head, because he had been in the war and had been mentally wounded,' I added, knowingly.

Mary, who had been pushing her food about inside her bunny plate with a look of bored disinterest, broke-up our conversation by announcing loudly she needed to go to the toilet. Mum escorted her down the hallway.

I was about to ask Dad if he was in the war but I was too late. He was already collecting up our plates and plonking things down on the side of the sink. 'You're on wash-up tonight mate,' he said, and headed off to find the newspaper.

—•—

That night, as usual, as I lay in bed waiting for Mum to come in and read to me, I decided to try to quiz her a bit more about Mr Donald Smithton. I was sure they both knew him because of the strange way they had reacted when I first mentioned his name. I was aware that Mr Smithton had been to school the other side of Crookwell somewhere so he was almost a local. Mum though, had been brought up a very long way away up near Tamworth. How then, I wondered, had she ever come across Mr Smithton?

It was getting late when Mum finally turned up. She had been chatting to Uncle Christopher and Auntie Mollie in Bondi. She sat on my bed and sighed.

'Are you tired Mum?'

'A bit but not too tired to have a quick read,' she smiled.

'Before you read Mum, can you tell me how you know Mr Donald Smithton?'

Mum was surprised by my forthright and unexpected question, but she regained her composure quickly. She paused before answering, and then tried to brush my question aside.

'Oh, Dad and I met him a long time ago, just the once.'

'What to do with Mum?'

'I don't remember now ... it was many years ago. Come on, let's finish that book that we were reading yesterday.'

My chance was lost. Mum had successfully avoided answering and I was left to ponder what the connection was between Mum, Dad and the mysterious Mr Donald Smithton.

—•—

As soon as I jumped out of bed next morning, I sensed something in the house was wrong, some sort of a sixth sense had kicked in. I used the bathroom, dressed and went to the kitchen. Arriving in the kitchen it soon became apparent what had happened. My dear little sister had had a relapse during the night and was too sick to get out of bed; the ambulance was already on its way to take her to the Goulburn Base Hospital. Mum told me it was her kidneys playing up again.

'Can I go and see her Mum?'

'Yes of course, but don't wake her if she's sleeping please.'

Mary was awake, but she was a yellowy-greyish colour and her hands felt clammy. She was almost three years younger than me, nevertheless we got along pretty well most of the time. She could be irritating sometimes, but then, I was probably irritating for her too. There was a large enamel bowl sitting on the side of her bed in case she vomited. Her favourite doll, Susan, lay next to her on the pillow. Mum had already packed a small suitcase with the things that Mary would need in hospital and was busily assembling a few things for herself as she expected to have to stay with Mary for a night or two again.

'How are you going sis?'

She gave me a brave little smile and told me that Susan was sick with bad kidneys and had to go to the big Goulburn Hospital to get fixed up. Looking at Mary lying there so still and pale, I couldn't forget what the doctors had said earlier about her illness. Essentially, they had admitted they had no way of making her better; all they could do was make her last few months pain-free and comfortable. It all seemed so unfair. Why should this sweet little girl surrender her beautiful life at the age of only six. What had she done to deserve this? And what was God doing about it? If God was so powerful why was he not making Mary better? There were all these miracles in the Bible, surely another one wasn't a problem? As the ambulance drove into our driveway, I promised Mary that I would say some prayers for her tonight. She looked at me with those gorgeous blue eyes and said, 'Say some for Susan too.'

An ambulance man entered the room with Mum and Dad and I was asked to go and collect the eggs and then wait outside. Ten minutes later I returned with my container holding eight grubby-looking eggs. Placing them on the kitchen table, I was just in time to see the ambulance man wheel Mary out on a sort of stretcher thing.

'It's all those toxins building up in her little body,' he was saying. 'If only they could get rid of them, she would feel so much better, poor little mite.'

The stretcher thing was slid into the back of the ambulance and Mum climbed in so she could look after Mary along the way. Dad handed up the two small suitcases and looked close to tears. I could never figure him out; tough and gruff most of the time and then a bit weepy on rare occasions like this.

'We'll be at least an hour getting to the hospital. I'm going to drive gently and steadily to give her a more comfortable journey. It's possible she will have to be moved to Sydney's Women's and Children's though.' And with that, the ambulance man closed the double doors and climbed into his driver's seat.

As they pulled out onto the road, I realised it was just Dad and me once again. Was it going to be lamb chops and affairs a second time round?

CHAPTER NINETEEN

As I rode to school, the awful thought struck me that Mary might never come home. It was two months ago that the Sydney doctors had said she probably had only months to live. Months seemed such a long way away then, but now I realised that two months had already elapsed. How many months did the doctors mean? Mum had told me that the doctors never really know; you cannot accurately predict when someone is going to die. So, when they say "months" it could be as few as two months or perhaps as many as eighteen. Nobody ever knows. For the first time I was now seriously facing up to the fact that my beautiful sister was going to die soon.

The first thing I did, after I parked my bike, was seek out Mrs Kircudbright, Mary's teacher. I told her Mary had been taken away in an ambulance and would be away from school for at least a few days. I was surprised, and rather ashamed to find I was crying as

I passed on this information to Mrs Kircudbright. She crossed herself and in a kindly way put a large, but comforting, arm around my shoulder. I wiped my tears away and raced off down to the oval. A good kick around might help me forget Mary for a little while.

My tears came back again when Miss Tully greeted me when I entered the classroom. I felt really embarrassed this time because my mates saw me blubbing. I don't think I had ever cried in class before and I didn't know what to do, or where to look. I just wanted the floor to open up and swallow me. But then, Miss Tully did a surprising thing, she put an arm around my shoulder and spoke to the class.

'Boys and girls Graham's cute little sister, Mary, was taken back to hospital in Goulburn early this morning. As some of you already know, she has renal disease, which means her kidneys don't work properly. It's a horrible illness and Graham is being very brave and loving because the doctors don't think they can make her better. When someone in your family is so very ill, it's a good thing to have a cry sometimes. So, if Graham has a cry occasionally you know why. Do your best to cheer him up and look after him please. If you say prayers at night, perhaps you can include little Mary, Graham and his family?'

The class was so moved by what Miss Tully had said that they gave an impromptu round of applause and there were even a few call outs such as, 'Keep yer pecker up Graham,' and 'Good on ya mate.' I noticed Lynda looking at me and she gave me the sweetest of smiles. I didn't quite know how to respond. In the end, I just wiped a couple of tears away with my sleeve, sniffed, and gave Miss Tully a sort of smile and went to my desk. Afterwards I realised how much I appreciated what Miss Tully had done. She had stepped in when I really needed some help. She was great and I worked hard all day to pay her back.

It felt strange at the end of the school day when I would usually go and check that little Mary was ready for Mum or Dad to pick her up in the car. Instead, Colin invited me back to his place along with Mike and Fred. The thought of the yummy tucker that Colin's mum always produced meant I couldn't possibly refuse. Fred had come to school riding his pony today so we were a strange bunch heading back to the Post Office. Colin and I on our bikes, Mike riding no hands so he could practise his latest tricks on his yoyo and Fred trotting along beside us on his pony.

Colin's mum, Mrs Trent, did not disappoint. She knocked up fresh vegemite and cheese sandwiches and opened a new packet of assorted chocolate biscuits. Beaming with pleasure, she announced that if that was not enough, she thought she might be able to find a jam sponge cake in the cupboard somewhere. Today,

Mrs Trent was wearing red. Apart from a large apron covered in enormous red apples and tomatoes, she had bright red lipstick and a striking crimson ribbon in her hair. Her redness even included scarlet shoes, bangles and ruby earrings.

Pouring out cordial into four large glasses, Mrs Trent looked around the four of us and inquired, 'And what might you boys be getting up to this weekend?' I had the distinct feeling she considered our gang of four to be a healthy, worthwhile group and certainly good for her son, Colin, to be involved with.

'You're always welcome here. Nobody has yet succeeded in eating me out of house and home, but sometimes I have to admit, you do get close,' she guffawed. Mrs Trent's podgy hands were busy pushing plates of food towards us as we sat around the sturdy wooden kitchen table, complete with its tablecloth that displayed giant crimson strawberries all around the edge.

Mike paused from eating for a moment or two to bring his yoyo back into action. His latest trick was the "Reverse Sleeper" and Mrs Trent, who had not yet had the pleasure of witnessing this particular trick, was persuaded to watch. Whilst this was happening, Colin threw out a challenge.

'How about we go back down to Paddy's Gorge to see if the ratty character down there has changed his ways?'

'Are you serious?' I asked.

'Yes, why not? He's not allowed to use his rifle anymore, so it'll be safer.'

'Hey, that could be exciting,' Fred agreed. 'If he's short of money and food, we could take something with us, like some apples, or a cake or something.'

Mike took a break from his yoyo, 'Sounds like a great idea, I'm in.'

Personally, I was in an awkward predicament. Dad had instructed me to stay away from Donald Smithton, although I wasn't sure just why. If I went with the gang, it would be against his wishes, and I could be in big trouble if he ever found out. However, if I pulled out of the trip my mates would think I was a sook. I hadn't actually said I would go, but already they were assuming I was coming. Mrs Trent even lent her support by promising to provide something to take down to Mr Smithton in a container. Before I had time to fully sort out my thoughts everything was arranged; meet at ten at Colin's place on Saturday morning and bring a picnic lunch.

I rode home to an empty house. Dad was somewhere out on the farm and had taken Dee and Dum. A couple of hours giving him a hand was always a wise move, particularly when I needed his permission to go out with the boys tomorrow. I would certainly volunteer to cook lamb chops tonight and wash up everything afterwards, anything to put him in a pleasant mood. I found him out on the tractor ripping up another rabbit warren he had discovered in the back paddock.

With the job done, we rode home together with the dogs as our escorts. Dad told me that Mum had rung at lunchtime to say that Mary had been transferred immediately to the Women's and Children's Hospital in Sydney. Apparently, Mary was comfortable and wanted us to know that Susan was going to get better in the big Sydney Hospital. On hearing this, I felt the tears welling up again. Fortunately, Dad never noticed.

Everything went beautifully to plan that evening. Dad showered while I cooked tea. The chops were a bit burnt, however, Dad assured me he liked them that way. I even found a new bottle of tomato ketchup which Dad liked to splosh about extravagantly. I served it all up with potatoes in their jackets, some butter and a pile of Brussel sprouts, another vegetable Dad was partial to. We had leftover apple pie and ice cream to finish.

I didn't have to worry about asking permission to go to see Donald Smithton because Dad announced that he was going into Goulburn tomorrow. He didn't say why, but I knew! Consequently, he was delighted to hear I had arranged to team up with "the gang" on Saturday. This was a far better option than leaving me at home all day alone. He didn't even ask what we were going to do, or where we planned to go, so I was spared any difficult explanations.

Mum rang again that evening and the news about Mary was not good. She was described by the hospital as "comfortable and stable". Mum was allowed to sleep in Mary's room and the doctors and nurses had run another series of tests on Mary and had been very kind and understanding. It would be a couple of days before they knew the results of the tests. After Mum's call, Dad shocked me by hinting that the two of us may be called to Sydney to say goodbye to Mary soon. This last comment really hit home. Sadness and my love for my little sister, kept me awake for hours.

CHAPTER TWENTY

I had no idea how to deal with grief and there was nobody I could easily turn to. Mum was far away in Sydney and she was the person I naturally would go to when I needed comforting. I didn't relate well to Dad; he had some kind of an impenetrable wall that went up around him whenever feelings or emotions were floating about. He simply clammed up. He didn't even notice that I was worried and anxious when I joined him for breakfast on Saturday morning.

'Bacon and eggs, mate?'

'Yes, please Dad.'

'One or two?'

'Two.'

'Any toast?'

'Just one thanks.'

Dad rammed my slice of bread down into the toaster, broke my eggs into the pan and grabbed a plate from the rack.

'When are you kids going to get back?'

'I don't know Dad. We might spend some time at Colin's.' I was petrified he was about to ask me where we were going, but he was distracted by the kettle that obligingly began singing loudly.

'Just make sure you're back here before dark. It's getting dark around six now. Understand?'

'Sure Dad. What time do you expect to be home, Dad? I asked, nervously.

'When I'm ready,' was his blunt and unhelpful reply.

My meal was ready and Dad plonked my plate down in front of me. Not long afterwards he popped his head round the door to say farewell and left hastily in the car, leaving a plume of dust spraying out the back as he drove down the road. It was nine o'clock. I still had enough time to do the dishes, pack something for lunch and be down at Colin's by ten. In the middle of cutting a couple of slices of bread, the telephone rang. It was Mum.

'Hi darling, how are things at home?'

I didn't say I had been feeling miserable all night, and wanted to have my mum around, but she sensed it all the same. Mums are like that, they must have extra powerful sensors.

We had a little chat and I could tell she was trying to cheer me up. Then she asked to speak to Dad.

'Dad's not here.'

'Then I'll try again at lunchtime.'

'I don't think he'll be back by then Mum.'

'Oh … where's he gone then?'

'Goulburn.'

There was a long pause and I knew what must have been going through Mum's mind.

'Did he say why he's gone to Goulburn?'

'No, sorry Mum.'

I'm sure we were both thinking that it was Mrs Davies who had tempted Dad back into Goulburn but neither of us wanted to say it. We pretended it was something else, something quite legitimate.

'Oh well, I'll try again tonight then,' said Mum, trying to sound cheerful and carefree.

'How's Mary?'

'She's okay dear. She sleeps a lot, I think it's the drugs they give her to stop the pain.'

I didn't dare ask if Mary was coming home soon because I was afraid of the answer. I feared she may never be coming home and I didn't know if I could handle such devastating news. So, I let the matter drop.

'Give Mary my love and kisses please,' I said meekly. 'And you had better include Susan as well.'

'I certainly will, darling. I know she sends you her love too. Now be good, help Dad as much as possible and I'll talk to you again soon.'

'Love you Mum,' and she was gone.

I still had time to collect the eggs and feed and water Dee and Dum. In his haste to get away, Dad had forgotten to feed them. Then I grabbed my water bottle, picnic lunch and hat and cycled off for what I hoped might end up as a really interesting adventure.

The gang were there ahead of me enjoying a morning snack provided by Colin's mum, undoubtedly the best cook in town. Mrs Trent had been making sausage rolls this time and as soon as I arrived, she thrust a plate under my nose containing three hot sausage rolls accompanied by a generous splosh of tomato sauce.

'Here you are Graham, you have a bit of catching up to do.' She gave me a warm hug and then sidled off to the fridge, where, as if by magic, she produced a sponge cake with two lavish layers of jam and cream. This magnificent offering, she then proceeded to cut into handsome slices and leave invitingly in the centre of the table. Irresistible!

'Help yourselves boys. I need you to eat at least half of it before you leave. Then I'll know you won't starve before you get there,' and she broke into peals of laughter.

We did our best. By the time we left, we were overfed with sausage rolls and luscious sponge cake, which was washed down with green lime cordial. It was no surprise that shortly after leaving Sandalwood, we had to pull over to the side of the road to have a pee. In fact, I'd eaten so much, I doubted I would need any of my hastily assembled picnic lunch.

We made good progress along the rough dirt road that wound its way to the Conservation Park's car park. At one point we were nearly collected by a couple of large grey kangaroos that suddenly broke cover and bounded frantically across the road in front of us. Mike, who was leading at the time, hit the brakes hard and left an impressive set of skid marks in the sandy dirt. On another occasion we encountered a koala wandering aimlessly along the road, presumably seeking a tastier eucalyptus tree to satisfy its appetite.

There was a bright red sporty-looking car in the car park when we arrived. We screeched to a halt directly behind the vehicle, in a cloud of dust, much to the annoyance of the young couple within. The pair scrambled apart and the young woman glanced at us in the rear vision mirror fumbling with her blouse, embarrassed.

'Canoodling,' announced Fred, in a knowing voice.

'More than canoodling,' replied Colin.

'What's canoodling anyway?' asked Mike.

'It's sloppy kissing,' I declared, 'they were only kissing.'

'How do you know?' challenged Colin.

'Because they still have their clothes on, stupid,' I responded.

Our discussion was abruptly interrupted by the young man in the red car who stuck his head out of the window and yelled, 'Bugger off you kids, or I'll get my gun out. Fuck off!'

We didn't want another nasty experience with a man with a firearm, so we cleared off as directed, and found the same spot we had selected last time to hide our bikes.

'Hey, why don't we hide here for a bit and watch what they do?' suggested Mike, 'it might be interesting.'

'Yuk,' Colin reacted.

'Well, you might learn something,' Mike persisted.

'I've seen my parents doing it,' Fred chimed in. 'Who wants to watch that?'

In the end we decided not to hang around. I didn't tell them I had seen my Dad doing it with Mrs Davies. That was my horrid little private secret.

We set off down the same bush track with backpacks shouldered and in high spirits. Now that we were well into autumn there was a crispness in the air and recent showers had washed the vegetation clean. The track seemed a bit more overgrown and in places we had to navigate our way carefully around blackberry fronds all too anxious to grab at us as we passed. A couple of rabbits scurried for cover and we disturbed a flock of black cockatoos that set up an angry din to tell us they were unimpressed. Rainbow lorikeets were gorging on the blossoms of a grey box tree.

'What's the plan then boys? I asked.

'Caution, I reckon,' responded Colin. 'He might be trigger-happy still.'

'I agree,' added Mike. 'There are no police about today so he can do what he likes. If he wants to be a bastard and shoot one of us, nobody can stop him.'

'What did the copper say his name was?' inquired Fred.

'Donald, Donald Smithton,' I replied.

'Wow, you've got a good memory,' remarked Colin.

I didn't let on that my parents had reacted rather strangely to the man's name when I had mentioned it to them a couple of weeks back.

'When we get closer, let's stalk him. I saw soldiers doing it in a film I watched. We go silently through the bush, keeping out of sight until we get really close to him,' I suggested.

'And what then?' queried Mike.

'We observe,' I said rather lamely.

'We've got to talk to him,' insisted Fred.

'Why? He didn't like us coming to his campsite before, so we can't expect him to be friendly this time,' warned Colin.

'What about a peace offering?' I suggested.

'Good idea, but what have we got that he would want?' Mike asked.

'I've got four extra slices of Mum's creamy sponge cake that we didn't finish this morning. There's supposed to be a piece for each one of us for lunch,' volunteered Colin.

There was general agreement that four pieces of Mrs Trent's creamy sponge cake should do the trick and prove irresistible. It was a small but tasty sacrifice we were each prepared to make.

We were now nearing the campsite and stopped before a sharp bend to talk final tactics.

'So, do we all front up as a group, or will just one of us go into the camp with the four slices of cake clearly visible so we are seen to be friendly?' asked Fred.

It was not easy to decide. Eventually, Colin was selected as the person to go into the campsite alone, after all, it was his Mum's cake. Colin was not comfortable with this idea and wished he'd never offered his mum's creamy sponge cake as the peace offering.

In silence, we slipped stealthily around the final sharp bend just before the campsite. Three of us then hid in the bushes and waved Colin on. He retrieved his four pieces of creamy sponge cake, which he arranged neatly on top of his picnic box, but then faltered. It took nearly five minutes of nudging, cajoling, threats and much laughter before Colin was finally persuaded to break cover and make his entrance to the campsite.

Looking furtively about, he left the safety of the bushes and went out into the open where he stood still on some red coloured rocks by the edge of the creek. There were no signs of life.

'Go on, go on …' we hissed, from the safety of our bushes, 'go a bit further.'

Colin looked back and signalled us to follow him.

'Come on, we have to support him,' and I made my way out quietly down to the rocks followed reluctantly by the others. Still no signs of life.

We caught up with Colin and stopped briefly to discuss what to do next, staying as quiet as possible. We spoke in whispers.

'Perhaps he's left?' wondered Mike.

'It's strangely quiet,' I agreed.

'This cake's going to dry out if we don't give it to him soon,' warned Colin, standing on his rock like a lost waiter.

'Let's eat it while we're planning,' urged Fred.

'Hold on, it's our peace offering. We might need it still. I vote we go on slowly, really quietly, and see if he's in his cave,' I hissed.

My suggestion earned affirmative nods, so we formed a single line behind Colin and crept slowly forward, a miniature Conga line.

As we neared the mouth of the cave, there were clear

signs that someone had been cooking on the fire place in the last day or so but there was no smoke. The fire was totally out. Cigarette butts lay randomly on the ground and a few open cans lay discarded on their sides. A couple of dirty plates with knives and forks lay abandoned on a stump. A fishing rod had been left propped up against a tree.

'Where is he?' hissed Colin.

'He's not gone shopping because his horse is still tethered to that tree over there,' Fred pointed out.

'Perhaps he's gone walk-about?' I suggested.

'Or he's asleep in his cave,' Mike commented.

'Shall we take a look in the cave?' inquired Colin.

'Why not? replied Mike. 'He's had his rifle confiscated so he's unarmed.'

'He might have a knife or something though,' I cautioned.

'Quiet, listen!' commanded Fred, raising his hands.

We stood still. There it was again; the unmistakable sound of groaning coming from inside the cave. We all heard it this time.

'Watch out, it could be a trick,' said Colin. 'He's in there but he may be pretending. What if it's a trap to get us to go in and then he'll kill us?'

'Those groans sound real enough to me,' I responded, 'Listen again.'

If the man was play-acting it was a masterful

performance. We stood motionless for fully another minute.

Fred broke the silence, 'He's hurt I reckon; he sounds really bad.'

'I'm going in,' said Mike being always the decisive one. 'Anyone coming with me?'

By now we were convinced that this was a genuine emergency and we nodded. One by one we filed in behind Mike and stood inside waiting for our eyes to adjust to the near darkness. Sure enough, the man was there, lying on his stretcher bed. He looked to be in a bad way. We watched fascinated as he thrashed about groaning and mumbling incoherently. He had thrown his blankets on the ground and was bare to the waist. Sweat glistened on his face and torso.

'He's got a fever,' Colin declared, 'he needs a doctor, urgently.'

'Get him some water,' ordered Mike.

I left the cave and raced down to the creek with a billy which I filled and hurried back, spilling much of it on the way. Arriving back in the cave, I placed it down next to Mr Smithton and told him there was some water there for him. He suddenly sat bolt upright and looked at me with wild, glazed eyes, but he had understood, because he reached out and poured the water down his throat and all over his face and the top of his bed. Slumping back down again he threw the empty billy to the floor and resumed his ghastly groaning. This time Fred picked the billy up and refilled it.

There was no doubt in our minds now that Donald Smithton was seriously ill and needed urgent medical attention. None of us had seen anyone with a severe fever like this before and it was frightening to witness. It was decided that Colin and I, who were the fastest runners, and the quickest on our bikes, would race back to Sandalwood and bring the doctor. If Dr Zegalski wasn't about, we would go on to find Constable Gorton. Mike and Fred would stay with Mr Smithton to keep him supplied with water and try to calm him down. We were grateful to our cub master who had instructed us recently on what to do in emergencies. He had stressed that people with a high fever must be kept hydrated. People could die if they didn't drink enough, he had said.

CHAPTER TWENTY-ONE

Colin and I were glad to be doing something to help. As we left the cave, we grabbed a piece of Colin's mum's sponge cake that had been left on a rock when we entered Mr Smithton's dark abode. Trying to run fast and stuff soft cake into your mouth at the same time is hardly a pretty sight. Much of it never reached its planned destination.

We had a tad over a mile to run uphill to reach our bikes and this soon proved more than a good test of our fitness. After only a few minutes I felt a painful stitch in my left side and had to pull up. Colin was exhausted too and was glad of the chance to rest for a moment. We used the pause to have a drink and then resumed our uphill dash. There was no time to enjoy the scenery, we were on a mercy mission.

Arriving at the carpark, we were relieved to find the canoodling couple had moved off, and our bikes were untouched. We were hot and sweaty from our exertions and swigged down more water before jumping on our bikes for the four-mile ride back into Sandalwood. The ride was uneventful and we virtually raced each other to help maintain a good speed. We reached Sandalwood in quick time and pulled up outside the doctor's surgery. We dropped our bikes down on the footpath and ran, breathlessly, into the small waiting room.

Three people were sitting around the room waiting for their appointments. They looked up in surprise to see two dirty, sweaty little boys fly through the door and run to the receptionist's desk blabbering as they did so. We were so anxious to get a rescue mission underway, that we both spouted a string of sentences off to the unfortunate receptionist, who must have found our jabbering totally incomprehensible.

'Be quiet, both of you,' she demanded, putting her hands to her ears to indicate she couldn't abide the cacophony of noise. We stopped.

'Now, one at a time, calm down, and stop yelling at me.'

Colin and I looked at each other and then both started to speak again at precisely the same moment. I'm sure the three waiting patients found this little bit of drama entertaining.

'Graham, will you explain to me quietly and calmly what the problem is, and maybe I can then help you?'

I had been so agitated that I had forgotten that the receptionist, who was smiling sweetly at me by now, was none other than Mrs Thompson, the lovely Lynda's mother.

'I'm sorry. Us boys have been down in Paddy's Gorge and we found this man there who's really ill. He needs help urgently. He looks like he might die!'

Colin couldn't contain himself and added a few more lurid details to further emphasise the need for action. 'He's sweating like a pig, and tossing about like a madman, he can't talk properly and he's throwing things about.'

At this point a little old lady emerged from Dr Zegalski's consulting room and wobbled her way slowly over to the receptionist's desk.

'Could you take a seat for a minute please, Mrs Chandler. I just need to pop in to see the doctor for a moment. I'll be straight back.' Giving Mrs Chandler another of her delightful smiles, Mrs Thompson disappeared into the consulting room. We two boys were left standing there at the desk feeling and looking rather stupid.

'Argh, yer don't wanna be going down into Paddy's Gorge yer know,' a gravelly voice rasped. We turned to see a wrinkled old man eying us suspiciously. 'Paddy, the wild Irishman, 'e died down there of 'is wounds and they say 'e still 'aunts the gorge. Yer sure yer did'na see 'im? It might 'ave been 'is ghost yer saw?'

'No sir this wasn't a ghost, it was Donald Smithton,' I replied.

The door of the consulting room flew open and Dr Zegalski and Mrs Thompson came over to speak to us.

'Hello boys, tell more to me please?'

We knew that Dr Zegalski's English was less than perfect, but that did not worry us as we provided as much detail as we could and answered several questions to the best of our ability. After a few minutes, convinced that urgent medical assistance was indeed required, Dr Zegalski moved into action.

'Dora, please ring policeman. Tell him urgent. Come to surgery now. I, the policeman, and boys, all go to gorge very pronto. Surgery must close early. One more patient I see now but only one.'

Mrs Thompson rang Constable Gorton and then explained to the two unfortunate patients who would miss their consultations that this was an emergency. Constable Gorton apparently was going to be another ten minutes before he could reach the surgery. In the meantime, Mrs Thompson kindly handed us the remains of a packet of biscuits together with a glass of water.

True to his word, Constable Gorton arrived in ten minutes, just as the wizened old man completed his consultation with Dr Zegalski. A moment later the doctor emerged with his portable medical kit and a stethoscope around his neck. The old man, who was settling his account, couldn't resist one last comment.

'Watch it down there, constable, that gorge is

spooked. Some of us old timers 'ave been fishin' down them parts but we gave it away. Too bloody creepy if yer ask me. Paddy were a nasty bit o' work and 'e ain't any better now 'e's gone. Wouldn't be surprised if this geyser what's sick, was cursed. Watch out that Paddy's ghost don't get yer too, constable!'

Constable Gorton politely thanked the old timer for his warning and ordered everyone into his jeep. Dr Zegalski sat in the front and we two boys climbed in the back. Mrs Thompson promised to take our bikes back to her place for when we returned. That was particularly pleasing because I now had the perfect excuse to go and see Lynda again.

Having visited Donald Smithton only a couple of weeks earlier, Constable Gorton knew the back roads that eventually would lead down to the gorge, using the same track Mr Smithton and his horse would have to traverse when he journeyed to Crookwell to do his shopping. The policeman's route was shorter but certainly rougher. We boys could never have ridden our bikes this way. Coming down the last section into the gorge itself was particularly difficult as the gradient was so steep; there were no fences and we came frighteningly close to numerous precipitous drops down to the river far below. When we finally pulled up at the campsite there was the pungent smell of burning rubber from our frequent braking and I was feeling horribly carsick. We scrambled out and headed the short distance to the cave.

Mike and Fred must have heard us approaching and were already standing outside the cave to meet us. They were both looking stressed.

'He's unconscious doctor,' was Fred's opening comment.

We trailed back into the cave, all six of us now, plus Mr Smithton. The doctor took one look at the patient and promptly ordered everyone outside. 'Maybe infectious,' he cautioned. We didn't need a second warning so we hastily retreated back into the fresh air.

Constable Gorton was already thinking ahead.

'I will need to drive him out of here in the back of my jeep with the doc sitting with him. Graham and Colin, you can come with me and you other two fellows will have to make your own way home on your bikes. That okay?'

We all concurred.

'Bloody good effort lads. Couldn't have done better myself,' and with that he strolled over to the jeep and tidied up the back. He had an old sleeping bag there which would come in handy for Mr Smithton to lie on. Next, he backed the jeep up as close to the front of the cave as possible leaving it open ready to receive the unconscious man.

A few minutes later Dr Zegalski exited the cave. He

had hastily examined Mr Smithton and administered an injection. We all wanted to know what was wrong with Mr Smithton but the doctor simply shrugged his shoulders and suggested, 'Viral infection, perhaps? Big fever, very ill. We put in da car at back. Can you ring please for ambulance to meet us and take patient to Goulburn Hospital?' he asked, looking at Constable Gorton.

'No problem doctor, but there's no reception till we get out of this bloody gorge.'

Constable Gorton went back into the cave with the doctor to bring Mr Smithton out on his stretcher. This was no easy task as Mr Smithton was heavily built and, being unconscious, was no help to them at all. Manoeuvring through the small cave entrance was another challenge. It was another five minutes before they finally came staggering out with Mr Smithton tied onto his flimsy bed stretcher by a dirty sheet. With a big effort and much grunting, they heaved the stretcher up onto the back of the jeep and slid Mr Smithton in. Dr Zegalski then clambered into the cramped space next to his patient and Colin and I jumped into the passenger's seat.

Fred and Mike offered us their bikes in the vain hope that we might exchange places with them, but we scoffed at the idea. 'See you at school,' we yelled out of the open window. Our cheerful farewell was returned with a couple of rude signs.

The jeep laboured torturously back up the rough track now carrying the weight of three adults and two boys. At one stage, when we came to a nasty hairpin bend, I thought we might have to jump out and push as the jeep lost traction in the loose sand and pebbles. Once we crested the ridge, however, Constable Gorton tried to make contact with the Ambulance Service in Goulburn but without success. So, he called Mrs Thompson at the doctor's surgery and asked her to order an ambulance to meet us somewhere along the Sandalwood to Goulburn Road.

Mr Smithton seemed to be travelling well enough and Dr Zegalski would, from time to time, say just one word from the back of the jeep, 'Stable.' Colin and I bounced about in the front seat like rubber balls but felt really chuffed to be now sitting in the front of a police vehicle. We left every window open to lessen the chance of infection but were feeling seriously cold by the time we pulled up at the doctor's surgery. Mrs Thompson had already locked up and left for home, hopefully wheeling our two bikes with her. Donald was starting to moan again and the doctor jumped out to get something else from his surgery to further sedate him. Colin and I said our farewells and the policeman thanked us again for our help, 'You probably saved this poor bugger's life,' he called after us, as we set off walking to Mrs Thompson's and Lynda's place.

Sandalwood is only a small town and it takes merely ten minutes to walk from one end of the main street to the other. Lynda, and her parents and younger sister, Jasmine, lived in a large rambling Federation house set well back from the road. An assortment of trees surrounded the house making it a shady cool place in summer. Now that we were half way through autumn, the deciduous trees had shed most of their foliage leaving a multi-coloured leaf-carpet that rustled as we walked up the driveway. I rang the bell, apprehensively.

The front door swung open to reveal a laughing Lynda with a blob of something white on her cheek and hands covered in flour.

'Hi boys, come on in. Want a scone?' and she skipped down the hallway leading us along to the kitchen at the rear of the house. It was a huge room with an enormous wooden bench in the centre on which sat everything that was necessary for making and serving batches of scones. The first batch was already in the oven and the warm soft aroma of scones cooking flooded the room. Mrs Thompson stood by the oven with oven gloves poised waiting for the right moment to remove the scones.

'Here you are,' squealed Lynda and she passed us both a plate and a knife and placed large bowls of butter, cream and strawberry jam tantalisingly close. 'They'll be ready in a jiff.'

Lynda's little sister was already sitting at the table waiting for her plate to be filled. No such luck for Lynda's dad, who was a stock and station agent and had rung to say he would not be home until later.

The timer buzzed and Mrs Thompson gingerly removed the first lightly browned batch of scones which Lynda then took around the table for everyone to enjoy. I'm sure she gave me an extra special smile. Lynda was not just beautiful to look at but really talented, clever at school and so athletic. But what I liked most about Lynda was her open, happy disposition. She was so genuine, kind and considerate. I had determined long ago that I was going to marry Lynda. The only problem was that most of the other boys in our school had the same idea.

Mrs Thompson had already briefed Lynda and her sister about what had been happening during the afternoon and had painted a colourful picture of us four brave boys doing everything we could to help an ill man down in Paddy's Gorge. Lynda was clearly impressed and wanted to hear more. Colin and I then spent a delightful ten minutes filling in some of the details and naturally embellishing the story as we went. We took it in turns to relate our adventures though, so we didn't miss out on eating scones.

Three scones later, and with jam-sticky fingers, I realised that it was already past five o'clock and that I should head for home. We thanked Mrs Thompson and Lynda for the yummy scones and for looking after our bikes. Lynda then volunteered to take us out through the back door to collect our bikes.

'See you boys,' and she was gone.

I was back home by half-past-five, well before dark, but there was no sign of Dad.

I couldn't help comparing my family with Lynda's. At Lynda's I was a bit of a hero, but if Dad was to find out that I had been down Paddy's Gorge again and had helped rescue Donald Smithton, I was in for the high jump.

If only I could discover why my parents didn't want me to have anything to do with Donald Smithton. Was he a criminal? Had my parents fallen out with Mr Smithton sometime in the past? Did they owe him money? I felt sorry for the man ...

CHAPTER TWENTY-TWO

As soon as I arrived home, I busied myself with the chores. I let Dum and Dee have a run and topped up their water before giving them a meal. I struggled in with some wood for the fire, set it, and had it blazing away well before Dad turned up. I didn't dare ask where he had been and he offered no explanation. When he asked what I had been up to, I was able to truthfully say I had been out riding with the gang and had ended up at Lynda's for scones.

Dad was moody during our evening meal and said little. Whilst I was washing up, Mum rang again from Sydney. I did my best to listen in on their conversation but it was difficult. It was only a short call.

'Things are not good with Mary,' Dad remarked, as he collected a cold beer from the fridge and sat down with his feet up on the table.

'Is she going to get better?' I asked, knowing all along that I was being stupidly optimistic.

'Nah, don't think so mate. Mum said it will only be a day or two now. To say our goodbyes, we had better drive down to Sydney tomorrow. We can stay with Uncle Christopher and Auntie Mollie for a few days.'

I tried to imagine little Mary in a big white hospital bed with her favourite dolly, Susan, sleeping next to her. I had never had to go into hospital myself. Apart from a couple of times when Mary had been in Goulburn Base Hospital, I had never even set foot in one. They were scary places. The nurses all looked starchy clean, business-like and unfriendly. The wards had a strange smell and everyone looked tense and worried. I hated the quietness and everyone whispering. People were seriously ill, or badly injured, so you could only creep about so as not to disturb them. I shivered at the thought of ever having to stay in a hospital. My heart went out to Mary lying there in such a joyless place.

Sleep was horribly difficult that night. I would manage to drift off only to wake up terrified by a hospital nightmare. In my dreams, I witnessed doctors running about with strangely shaped bloodied instruments and patients screaming for help but nobody coming to them. In another dream a lengthy line of hospital beds with patients in them was being pushed past me along a long hospital corridor. The patients had their eyes wide open, unblinking, and were dead. The worst dream was seeing little Mary screaming because a stern looking nurse was trying to take Susan from her. If only Mum was home, I could climb into bed with her and the bad dreams might go away.

I was tired and feeling miserable again when dawn finally arrived and it was time to get up on this Sunday morning. I felt numb and went about my early morning jobs in a sort of a trance, barely aware I was even doing them. Dad told me to put the eggs in a container and we would take a dozen down to Sydney with us. We rang the neighbours to let them know we were going to be away for a few days and asked them to feed the dogs and keep an eye on the place. When I went to my bedroom to pack a few things, I think Dad made a quick call to Mrs Davies. He looked embarrassed and put the phone down hastily when I returned to the kitchen.

We left Sandalwood around nine o'clock for Goulburn and then the long drive down the Hume Highway to Sydney. I wondered who would tell Miss Tully that I would be absent for a few days. I also wanted to know what had happened to Donald Smithton. Was he recovering well in hospital? It was disappointing to be missing school where I was sure news about Mr Smithton would be shared. But I desperately wanted to see Mum and Mary so this trip to Sydney would be worthwhile.

Dad seemed preoccupied with his own private thoughts on the journey and seldom spoke. He should have been worrying about Mum and little Mary but Mrs Davies was very likely to be uppermost in his thoughts. I found it extraordinary that adults could "fall in love", as Dad had put it, and become so obsessed with the one person they loved. Had my mum and dad been like this once? These days it was hard to believe it had ever happened for them. And why do people fall out of love? Clearly, Mum and Dad had fallen out of love, although perhaps Mum still loved Dad? So many questions and no satisfactory answers.

We stopped in Picton and went into a Greek café called "The Acropolis". For lunch, Dad bought hot pies and tomato sauce with a bag of chips to share. I had a strawberry milkshake and Dad a chocolate one. Dad reckoned we would be at the Women's and Children's Hospital in about another two hours.

Around three o'clock we pulled into the visitors' car park at the hospital and I followed Dad in through the main entrance. We walked over to an office window with a sign saying "Inquiries" where we were greeted by a young woman who smiled and asked if she could assist us. Dad asked where we could find Mary Granger. The lady opened a large folder and looked for the section listed under the letter "G". Running her finger down the page she came to the names starting with "Gr".

'Granger, you said?'

'Yes, Mary Granger, she's my daughter.'

'Yes, I've found her. She's in a private room and is only permitted visits from family members. Is this lad your son?'

'Yes, he is.'

'Please take the lift to the seventh floor. When you get out, turn to the right and walk down the corridor until you come to the Janet Jones Wing at the end of the corridor. Mary is in room five but you must first check with the matron, or the nurse in charge, before you go to her room. Ask please at the reception desk.'

'Thank you.'

Dad looked a bit out of place here I thought. His gnarled, sunburnt hands with dirt engrained in the fingernails and rugged facial features contrasted wildly with the manicured hands of this young lady and her delicate make-up and hairdo. Come to think of it, we probably both looked and spoke like country bumpkins. Sandalwood, I suppose, doesn't have quite the same level of sophistication as a Sydney hospital.

It took us a minute or two to find the lifts. I had only been in a lift a couple of times before at one of the largest department stores in Goulburn that went up three floors. This lift was going up an incredible seven floors! The lift seemed to take an age to come down to the ground floor to meet us and finally, when it did arrive, we had to allow an orderly with a hospital bed to have the lift. There was no room for us and another gentleman who was also waiting. A minute later the other lift arrived and we were finally on our way.

We stop-started our way slowly upwards as people came and went and eventually arrived at the seventh floor. It must have been a hundred yards to walk along to the Janet Jones Wing. As soon as we exited the lift, I could smell the horrid all-pervasive hospital disinfectant. The long corridor had pictures along the inside walls and windows on the other side overlooking a park. We met a few nurses in their smart uniforms and a boy about my age being pushed in a wheelchair with what looked like two broken legs.

The door to the Janet Jones Wing was beautifully decorated with Winnie the Pooh characters. I recognised Christopher Robin, Eeyore, Piglet, Tigger, Kanga, and of course, Pooh himself, with his head stuck in a bowl of honey. The Winnie the Pooh books have long been favourites of mine and to a lesser extent Mary. Often, when Mary was feeling low, and wanting company, I would grab one of AA Milne's books and read stories to her. She would giggle away and I'm sure the stories lifted her spirits. She would have been so happy to see the Winnie the Pooh characters here at the entrance to her ward.

We opened the door to the Janet Jones Wing and I was amazed to see the splendour of the ward we had entered. It was full of fun children's things and was more like some kind of a giant playroom than a hospital ward. There were paintings on the walls of scenes from famous nursery stories and I immediately recognised Cinderella, Goldilocks and the three bears, Jack and the beanstalk and the seven dwarfs. Some very talented artists had been busy. Even the ceiling was decorated in places and mobiles hung down and rotated with the slight breezes in the ward. Best of all, the unpleasant disinfectant odours were absent from the Janet Jones Wing. I think Dad was impressed with the ward too.

We advanced to the reception desk that was decorated with a cacophony of Australian animals in a kind of a bush setting. Sitting, seemingly in the midst of all these animals, was a pleasant looking lady with a large badge on her front that simply said, "Nurse Rebecca". She looked up from her notes and gave us a warm smile.

'Welcome to the Janet Jones Wing. Who have you come to see, please?'

'We have come to see Mary Granger.'

'Ah, such a sweetie. Are you her father?'

'Yes, I am.'

'And this is Mary's brother?'

'Yes,' I piped up.

'Lovely to meet you both. Have you just driven down from the country?'

'Yup, drove down from Sandalwood today.'

'Sandalwood? Whereabouts is that?' I was amazed

that this pleasant lady, a nurse, didn't know Sandalwood. I suppose it had never occurred to me before that some people might not have heard of our town.

'Near Goulburn,' added Dad.

'Oh, I know Goulburn. Such a cold place and so windy!'

'That's for sure.' Dad seemed to be warming to this kindly soul.

'Now your wife is with Mary and has been sleeping in her room for the last two nights. But there is only one bed available for family visitors I'm afraid.' Nurse Rebecca seemed almost apologetic.

'Mary has been in and out of consciousness today, so you may have to stay for a while to be able to speak to her. She is having regular doses of morphine to control the pain and the sweet girl seems very peaceful. She is in room five. There is a small waiting room in the middle of the ward where you can retire if you wish, and you can have a cup of tea or coffee there too.' Nurse Rebecca gave us both another warm smile, 'Room five is down on your left.'

As we walked to room five, I asked Dad what morphine was. He didn't seem to know and just said it was a drug that doctors gave to people who were suffering with a lot of pain.

When we reached room five, we found the door ajar and a notice saying "Mary Granger" in large pink lettering. Underneath Mary's name was the doctor's which was a horribly long, unpronounceable name. The rest of the door was adorned with pictures of things from the sea like seaweed, crabs, fish and even a cute mermaid with a large number 5 lodged in her long wispy hair. This marine theme was continued inside, however, the room was in semi-darkness which made it harder to pick out things until our eyes adjusted.

As we entered, Mum stood up and I ran over and gave her the biggest of hugs and didn't let go of her for a long time. I couldn't help it but I started crying again. I think I was craving love and had missed it badly during the last few days. Mum was so warm and comforting and I instantly felt safer and less frightened of the world when in her embrace. Sadly, there was no such warmth showing between Mum and Dad. They just nodded curtly at each other and seemed reluctant to even speak.

Mary looked angelic, lying with her eyes closed on two fluffed-up pillows. Even her bedspread was a watery scene. Susan had slipped out of position and was lying on the bedspread next to a blue-ringed octopus. How appropriate that Mary was in this room, decorated like the sea, with her gorgeous blue eyes. I so hoped she would open them again for me. Nobody else I knew had such lovely blue eyes. I tucked Susan back in where she belonged.

A nurse popped her head round the door and asked if we would like another couple of chairs.

'How is she?' asked Dad.

'She's doing okay,' replied Mum. 'She drifts in and out of consciousness, but, thankfully, is asleep most of the time. Apparently, it's the morphine. When she's awake she's quite lucid though.'

'What's lucid mean, Mum?'

'Clear, thinking straight, able to talk sensibly,' Mum replied.

'Is she going to be lucid soon?' I asked.

'You can never tell when she will next wake up Graham; sometimes it's in the middle of the night.'

Two chairs arrived and Dad sat on one, but I sat on Mary's bed; on top of a large patch of coral to be precise.

'She's got even thinner, Mum,' I declared. 'Is she eating her meals?'

'No sweetheart. When you are very ill like Mary, you don't really want to eat anything, but she drinks lots of water.'

Mum looked across at Dad. 'I need to talk to you for a few minutes. There's a waiting room across the way, we can go in there and get a coffee at the same time. Graham could you stay here with Mary, please? I think she will sleep a while longer but if she wakes up come and get us please.'

'Sure Mum,' and they left the room together. I wondered if they were going to have another fight. How could they possibly go on living together when Dad now loved Mrs Davies? If they were going to split up, I had decided long ago that I wanted to stay with Mum.

There was nothing to do in Mary's room, so I just sat there looking at my cute sister and wanting her to stay with me.

Another nurse came in and very pleasantly asked me to move off the bed. She went over to Mary and took her temperature and then held her wrist.

'Why are you doing that?' I inquired.

'Just checking that Mary's okay. We do this every half-hour or so. Would you like something to do while Mary is asleep?'

'Oh yes please.'

'Wait there and I'll see what I can find for you in the playroom.'

A few minutes later she was back with an armful of rather battered looking books, a couple of puzzles and a yoyo. I thanked her and began thumbing through one of the books.

Mum and Dad were back a few minutes later both looking sour, no doubt they had been arguing about Mrs Davies again. How I hated this bitterness. I could feel the tension between them, the glares, the refusal to even look at each other. The coldness was catching.

I sided with Mum but wasn't game to get involved. If Dad ever thought I was supporting Mum he would be furious. He must surely realise though, that all this ill-feeling was entirely his fault. It was his affair with Mrs Davies that had changed everything for the worse in our small once-happy family.

Sometimes I wondered where this was all going to end. If Mum and Dad decided to split up what would happen to me? Would Dad kick us both out and keep the farm? Would Mrs Davies come and live with him in Sandalwood? Where would Mum and I go? What about school, Miss Tully, and all my friends there? And Lynda, would I ever see her again? I was distressed by the uncertainties, the unknowns. And now it looked as though Mary would be spared all this unpleasantness and soon leave us.

This was the first time I had faced losing someone I dearly loved, and I was far too young to have to manage such a trauma. My Scripture teacher had told me that when good people die, they go to heaven which is a wonderful, beautiful place, far better than living here on the earth. But was Mary good enough to make it to heaven? If not, she was destined for hell, a terrible place full of fire and ruled over by the devil. Looking at her now, so lovely and calm, it was difficult to believe she wouldn't be going to heaven.

I went over to Mum who was sitting at the head of the bed again where she must have been for most of the last couple of days and nights. She was gently caressing Mary's limp hand. I whispered, because I didn't want Mary to hear.

'Mum, will Mary go to heaven?'

'Of course, she will.'

'But, how do you know?'

'Mary hasn't got a nasty bone in her body. She's sweet and kind and usually does what we ask her to do. She tries hard at school too.'

'Is that enough?'

'Certainly,' and Mum put her spare arm around me and gave me another warm hug. I looked into her face and thought I could see a small tear.

'What about me? Am I good enough to get to heaven?' I asked.

Quite suddenly, Mary gave a small grunt and opened her eyes. For a moment she seemed to be confused, but then she looked around her room and everything seemed to fall into place for her.

'Mummy?'

'Yes, darling?'

'Are Daddy and Graham here yet?'

Dad and I moved closer so Mary could see us. Then Dad bent over and gave Mary a kiss on the forehead. I did the same. We didn't say anything, somehow the kisses said it all. Best of all, Mary looked straight at me with her gorgeous blue eyes and smiled.

Chapter Twenty-two

We didn't know it then, but that was the last time Mary opened her eyes.

CHAPTER TWENTY-THREE

Around five o'clock it was agreed that Dad and I would leave the hospital and drive over to Bondi to stay the night with Uncle Christopher and Auntie Mollie. They were expecting us. Mum would kip down for a third night with Mary and give us an update around eight o'clock in the morning. Uncle Christopher and Auntie Mollie had been in to visit Mary earlier this morning.

Uncle Christopher was Mum's oldest brother; she said he was forty-five which sounded old to me. I remembered Uncle Christopher from a couple of years back when we all stayed with them and had a terrific time. I had fond memories of a fun-loving man, rather rotund and a keen surfer, in fact, he was a member of the Bondi Beach Surf Life Saving Club. He used to do silly things to keep us kids amused and was always telling jokes. He worked in a bank.

Auntie Mollie was a couple of years younger than

her husband and amazingly fit. Every year she ran the famous City to Surf race and always finished amongst the first one hundred women. Auntie Mollie was a language teacher and taught French and Latin at a large state high school. She still ran marathons occasionally and went regularly to the local gym. My aunt had been to Sydney University so I knew she was clever. When we had visited before she was always challenging me with questions about all sorts of things. Usually, I couldn't get the answers quite right but then she would spend time explaining everything. I found her really interesting.

My aunt and uncle had two teenagers. Mum told me that Janine was now nineteen and studying Law at the University of Sydney and Tom was seventeen and doing his final year at high school. They were nice enough but they didn't spend much time with Mary and I because the last time we visited we were too young for them. I could understand that.

Dad became hopelessly lost trying to find the way to their suburb and kept stopping on the side of the road to look at his out-of-date Sydney UBD maps. To make things worse, the traffic was crazy busy because it was the "rush hour" and everybody was madly heading home. Dad was getting more and more irritated and soon began swearing. I cowered in my seat holding the map for Dad but unable to help. Finally, we joined the long lines of traffic approaching the Sydney Harbour

Bridge and Dad relaxed a bit, realising he knew the way from there. We finally pulled into Uncle Christopher and Auntie Mollie's driveway at nearly eight o'clock. We were starving and I was dead tired.

As soon as Uncle Christopher saw the lights of our car, he came bounding out of the house to greet us, followed closely by their pet spaniel, Bonzo.

'Welcome guys. Come on in and eat, you must be bloody starving. We'll get your bags and things later.' He grabbed Dad's hand and shook it vigorously and then came over to me and gave me a bear-hug. 'Hey, Graham, you're quite the young man, strong and solid like your Dad. But we had better get some good tucker into you.' Bonzo, was jumping up and down barking demanding at least a pat and a cuddle, which I was happy to give him.

We all trooped indoors where we were welcomed by the rest of the family. Auntie Mollie gave me a hug and a couple of kisses, 'Lovely to see you Graham. You are better looking than your Dad already. Sit down here and I'll get your tea, pronto.' They had all had their tea much earlier so it was just Dad and me to eat.

'How does a chunk of steak sound, Graham? This one will put hairs on your chest,' Uncle Christopher said, placing a large juicy steak in front of me which smelt divine. 'Help yourself to veggies.' A large container arrived with roast potatoes, parsnips, onions and Brussel sprouts. 'Grab the veggies first Graham otherwise your Dad will hog the lot.' Everyone laughed and I was more than happy to oblige. Next, Auntie Mollie was at my shoulder holding a steaming gravy boat which she poured generously onto my steak. I felt truly welcome already and realised just how hungry I was.

Auntie Mollie and Uncle Christopher kept up a constant flow of interesting chatter while Dad and I did justice to the hearty meal set before us. Janine and Tom quietly and discretely left the room.

'Make sure you leave a little space in that tummy of yours,' laughed Uncle Christopher, 'there's sticky-date pudding and ice cream to follow.'

'Do you mind if I leave the parsnips then, Uncle Christopher?'

'Of course not, although I expect your aunt will serve them up again for your breakfast tomorrow morning,' he beamed, but I could tell he was joking.

After the meal I was dispatched to the spare bedroom to sleep on a camp bed. Auntie Mollie came in and stayed for a bit, in case I wanted to chat, but I was exhausted and fell asleep as soon as I climbed in under the blanket. Dad was going to come in later and sleep in the proper bed. I slept soundly and didn't hear him come in.

Dad was snoring gently when I awoke. I crept out and went to the bathroom. I could hear voices downstairs, so I dressed quickly and went down. The whole family were there having breakfast. Uncle Christopher was all dressed up in a suit, looking smart, and ready to go to work at his bank. Auntie Mollie was dressed in a tracksuit, she had been out for her morning jog she said.

'Now, what's it to be for breaky young Graham?' asked Uncle Christopher. 'We kept the parsnips but the walrus is tasty, the snails are delightful, though the shark is a trifle tough.' I looked at him questioningly, wondering if he was serious.

'Don't worry about him, I'll get you some decent breaky,' interrupted Auntie Mollie, who proceeded to serve out eggs and bacon with tomato and mushrooms.

'Now, your Dad is still asleep and your Mum said she would give us a ring at eight. It's nearly eight now and I can stay another fifteen minutes or so to take the call if you like? Or, we can wake up Dad? Everybody else has to get going.' As she spoke there was a flurry of people leaving, calling out their farewells followed by the sound of their car exiting the garage.

'Could you take the call, please?' I replied through a mouthful of crispy bacon.

Mum rang right on eight and Auntie Mollie grabbed the phone quickly. As I watched Auntie Mollie, Bonzo scuppered about under the table looking for breakfast scraps. Auntie Mollie looked serious and glanced across at me a couple of times as I was finishing off my meal with a tasty piece of buttered toast.

'Yes, of course, we'll sit down and have a talk. I'm not teaching the first period at school today … I'm so sorry … get a taxi … I'm happy to pay for it … see you later Betty, dear. Bye.'

As soon as Auntie Mollie turned to look at me, I knew what the news was from the look on her face. She came straight over and took me in her arms. There was no need to say anything. After a moment or two, she surprised me by asking if the two of us might take Bonzo for a short walk. I agreed, and we collected Bonzo's leash, and set off.

There was a park across the road from their place so we went there. I don't know how long we walked about and threw sticks for Bonzo, but I'm sure it helped. Auntie Mollie told me Mary had died around two in the morning, very peacefully in her sleep. It was the best way to go, she said. I cried a bit and held Auntie Mollie's hand. I was glad it was Auntie Mollie who had told me because I could have a good cry without Dad knowing.

When we returned, Dad was up and showered. Auntie Mollie broke the news to him gently. He didn't say much. Auntie Mollie had to leave for work so she showed Dad where the food was for him to cook up his own breakfast, apologising she couldn't cook it for him. Grabbing her bag, she left to catch her bus.

Dad had just sat down to breakfast when there was a knock at the front door. I opened it to find Mum standing there with her suitcase. We had a big cuddle and I could see Mum had been crying. She said she had had some breakfast at the hospital.

Mum and Dad told me they had to discuss a lot of things about Mary's funeral and left me in the kitchen to wash up.

At around eleven o'clock the three of us departed for Sandalwood. Mum left a card with a 'thank you' note. I was sorry to be leaving the welcoming home of Uncle Christopher and Auntie Mollie and wondered when I might be back again.

CHAPTER TWENTY-FOUR

It was a relief to be able to jump on my bike and escape to school on Tuesday morning. I had had more than enough of the tension between my parents both at home and during the long and tedious drive home from Bondi.

I had never seen a volcano, but Miss Tully was teaching my class about volcanoes last term and was describing how volcanoes can rumble and grumble for years with small eruptions from time to time, while everyone was holding their breath awaiting the massive explosion that eventually came. Recently, living on our farm felt as though it was a volcanic zone and that at any moment everything was going to blow up. Nobody was happy waiting for the inevitable final explosive showdown.

Mum quickly took charge of the funeral arrangements. Mary was to be buried on Sunday at St Ninian's Church, Sandalwood. Sunday school would be cancelled because many of the Sunday school children would want to say goodbye to my sister. Fortunately, Dad spent his days out on the farm and left Mum to make the funeral decisions. It was only in the evenings that he was about in the house. Mum told me that Dad had even started to stay out on the farm at lunchtime so as to avoid her. After breakfast he would grab half a loaf of bread, a lump of cheese, a couple of pieces of fruit, and then boil the billy somewhere out around the farm for his lunch.

During the morning, news filtered through that Donald Smithton was recovering well in the Goulburn Base Hospital. Mr Marsden told us he had suffered from pneumonia which was so serious he would probably have died from it if we hadn't found him and called for assistance. Our gang became famous overnight and everyone about town congratulated us whenever we were out and about on our bikes. But it didn't stop there. The Sandalwood Bakery gave the four of us a free cream bun and the Newsagent gifted us a bar of chocolate each. One morning a lady turned up at school from *The Sandalwood Snippets*. She interviewed us, took our photographs and promised to put an article about us in the next week's edition.

We had our school assembly on Wednesday mornings and the entire school attended. This particular assembly was bittersweet for me because Mr Marsden made out that we four boys were heroes for helping Mr Smithton.

He held us up as pupils that the whole school should be proud about and congratulated us. But then he spoke about Mary's passing and Mrs Kircudbright read a lovely poem and many of the kids in the infants' class started crying. For many pupils this was the first time they had to grieve for a person they knew well.

It didn't take long however for Mum and Dad to learn about our adventures. Mum went into Sandalwood that Wednesday morning to get groceries and as soon as she parked the car people came over and started congratulating her for having such a wonderful son. At first, she had no idea what they were talking about because I hadn't dared tell my parents I had disobeyed them and re-visited Donald Smithton in Paddy's Gorge. It must have been a difficult time for Mum and her friends because they were full of the story of my exploits and then she had to deflate them by telling them about Mary's sad passing. Poor Mum.

When she saw Dad that evening, she broke the news about what we boys had done on the weekend. He wasn't pleased but there was little he could do about it. Later that evening, a couple of his farming buddies actually rang him up to tell him what a great dad he was to have brought up such a fine son who was so sensible and capable. Consequently, my act of disobedience was largely ignored and for a short time I even enjoyed praise from them both.

It was a weird week with my moods swinging wildly all over the place. One moment someone would be praising me for helping Donald Smithton and the next moment I would be sadly remembering my beautiful little sister. Miss Tully was wonderful. She sat me down after school a couple of times to talk things through. She explained about grieving, a sadness that would gradually lessen but never go away completely. She knew because she had lost a close friend in a car accident three years ago when she was at Teachers' College in Newcastle. I was so tempted to open up to her about my other problems at home. I think the only reason I didn't, was because I still held on to the slight hope that Dad would end his affair with Mrs Davies and start to love Mum again.

One morning, a week or so later, something unexpected happened. We were enjoying our weekly music lesson when Mr Marsden knocked on the door and walked in. He complimented the class on its singing and then asked for the four members of our gang to accompany him back to his office. We assembled there to find two men standing by the principal's desk, one was a clergyman and the other, surprisingly, was Mr Donald Smithton.

'Now boys I want you to meet these two gentlemen. They have driven over from Crookwell specially to meet you. This is the Reverend Cameron and you may remember, Mr Smithton?'

We all agreed that we knew Donald Smithton, although it was not easy to recognise that this was the same man we had encountered twice before. The wild bushman, who was living deep in Paddy's Gorge, had somehow transformed himself into a well-dressed respectable looking man. He was clean-shaven, dressed in casual about-town clothes and appeared to be scrubbed clean.

'Mr Smithton is living at the Presbyterian Manse in Crookwell with Reverend Cameron and his family and was discharged from hospital a few days ago. He has come here today to thank you for rescuing him.'

'Do you mind if I sit down please? I'm still weak after being in hospital for over a week.'

'Of course,' Mr Marsden offered Donald Smithton one of the two seats he had squeezed into his office for visitors. Mr Smithton sat down with a look of relief and I noticed how thin and unsteady he was still.

'Boys, I wanted to come and thank you personally for probably saving my life when you came down to Paddy's Gorge. As you know, when you found me, I was gravely ill. It was pneumonia. The doctors have told me that if you had not found me when you did, and helped to get me urgent medical attention, I would most likely have died by the next day. What you did was particularly generous because I did not make you very welcome the first time you turned up in the gorge a couple of weeks earlier.'

'That's okay, sir.' Mike responded rather cheekily.

'Coming here is the first thing I've done since getting out of hospital. Reverend Cameron here, has been very kind to take me in and bring me over to meet you four boys today. Now, I want to write a letter to your parents to tell them how grateful I am for your help and will be enclosing a small reward for each of you. Does that sound a good idea?'

'Sure does.' Once again Mike had jumped in as the unofficial gang's spokesman.

'I hope to write the letters this weekend, so you will get your rewards on Monday or Tuesday at the latest.' Mr Smithton smiled broadly revealing a couple of missing teeth.

'With Mr Marsden's permission, I'd like each of you to write your name and address on a piece of paper for me please?'

'No problem, here's a pen and paper. Best modified cursive writing now boys.'

I remember wondering at the time, how a man who was homeless could afford to give us each a reward A man with no job and no home could hardly be flush with money. Anyway, I wasn't going to ask Mr Smithton any such awkward questions. One by one we carefully and neatly wrote down our names and addresses on the piece of paper the principal had provided. While we were thus occupied, the three grown-ups chatted about what it was like being a patient in the Goulburn Base Hospital.

When the job was done, Donald Smithton picked up the piece of paper to make sure he could read everything correctly.

'Thank you, boys. Incidentally, which one of you is Graham Granger?'

'I am, sir.'

Donald Smithton looked at me searchingly for a moment and then turned to Mr Marsden.

'Thank you so much for your time, I really appreciate having the chance to meet the boys face to face. You can be very proud of them.'

'Would you like a cup of tea or coffee before you drive back to Crookwell?'

'I'd rather not, thanks all the same,' Reverend Cameron spoke for the first time. 'I have a sermon to prepare for Sunday.'

At this point, we boys were dispatched back to our classroom. On the way, we chatted excitedly about the letter and the reward Donald had promised us. Ideas flew about like confetti.

'Hey what do you reckon the reward will be?' asked Colin.

'Won't be much, a stick of chewing gum, probably,' Fred suggested, cynically.

'Nah,' Mike interjected, 'I reckon it will be a lottery

ticket. Can't go wrong with a lottery ticket and then we might win something.'

'Perhaps he won't even get around to it,' I said, not feeling optimistic.

'He might surprise us and send us a ten-shilling note,' Colin suggested.

'That would be more than welcome … I would put it towards paying off my bike,' I remarked.

This sudden appearance of Donald Smithton at school had presented me with another problem, although this time not of my making. I would have to tell my parents about Mr Smithton's visit and warn them to expect a letter containing a reward for me. I decided to break the news to them when I arrived home this afternoon.

As it turned out everything was crazy busy at home. Uncle Christopher and Auntie Mollie were arriving by car on Saturday afternoon and would stay Saturday night in readiness for Mary's funeral at eleven o'clock on Sunday morning. This necessitated Mum moving back into Mum and Dad's bedroom again so that our visitors could have the spare double-bed. I wondered how Mum would feel about that!

Mum had been flat-out all day organising food and beverages to be served in the Church Hall after the burial. She had mustered up a band of loyal church ladies to help her with preparing and serving the lunch. She spent most of Friday afternoon and evening discussing the arrangements with numerous people. My meagre piece of news, about meeting Donald Smithton, barely registered with Mum, as she had so many other more important matters on her mind. I didn't even mention the matter to Dad.

Dad had been roped in to go around several shops in town early on Saturday morning to collect items required for the lunch. It was quite a list, bread and cakes from the bakery, sausage rolls, ham and frankfurters from the butcher and sugar, milk, salad ingredients and an assortment of fruits from the general store. Everything had been pre-ordered. It was considered wise to have me out of the house on Saturday and I was encouraged to get together with the gang and make myself scarce. I had no problem with this idea.

Saturday dawned damp and foggy. A thick mist hung over the countryside blotting out the sun and creating a cold, eerie world. I rather liked these mornings. The moisture in the air dulled any sounds and the birds, usually noisy around our place, were silent. Millions of tiny droplets clung to fence wires, grasses and cobwebs. I shivered as I went out to collect the eggs and I could barely make out Dum and Dee lying quietly in front of their kennels.

After breakfast I rode down to Colin's place. He had invited me to work with him on a new meccano set he had been given for his birthday. We spent a happy day together. When we grew tired of the meccano set, we set off with our bug-catchers to see what we could find out the back of Colin's yard. As always, Colin's mum kept us more than well fed. I returned home about five o'clock to find Uncle Christopher and Auntie Mollie had arrived. Mum and Dad were on their best behaviour and refrained from exchanging any snide comments the whole evening.

There was a decent frost Saturday night and everything was white when I looked out of my bedroom window on the day of the funeral. We were rather subdued over breakfast; it was going to be a difficult day. The five of us left for St Ninians's at ten-thirty and, as family, were asked to sit in the very front pew. Mum had a few extra handkerchiefs on hand, she assured me.

The service was a bit of a blur. The church, I remember, was packed, and some folk had to stand at the back of the church because there were no more seats left. Sitting in the front row meant I couldn't see who was there but my mates reckoned almost every kid in the school and one or both of their parents had turned up. During the service there was frequent sniffling and nose blowing. I held onto Mum's hand.

I found it hard to believe that Mary was lying inside the small wooden coffin sitting in front of us. So close yet so far. There was a large bunch of flowers lying on the coffin and at one end, propped up for all to see, was the well-worn, much adored, Susan. She had a bandage around her middle to help with the kidney disease.

The minister conducted the service and was supported by the organist and choir. There were prayers, sombre hymns and four people went out the front to talk about my sister and said lovely things about her. Mum was first but she broke down several times and I felt desperately sorry for her. When she resumed her seat, I held her hand again. Dad was sitting on the other side of Mum but he didn't hold her hand, perhaps because Mum was still using her handkerchief. Uncle Christopher spoke next and told a couple of funny stories about Mary. Mary's teacher, Mrs Kircudbright read the same poem she had read at School Assembly and finally Mary's Sunday school teacher spoke briefly.

This was my first funeral so I didn't know what to expect. At the end of the service only family members were invited to follow the coffin around to the back of the church where Mary was to be "laid to rest". Everyone else was asked to move to the Church Hall to start lunch.

The family stood around the grave weeping. Like everyone else, I was invited to throw some soil over the coffin which I did. Then we left the grave-diggers to it and joined everyone else for lunch in the Church Hall.

The gang was there and their parents made a pleasant fuss of me. I think all my class were there too. Lynda was so sweet; she gave me a little peck on the cheek and pressed something into my hand. It was a spare handkerchief. I think she must have nicked it out of her dad's drawer because it was not one of those pretty ones that the ladies have.

CHAPTER TWENTY-FIVE

It was late in the afternoon when we finally left the Church Hall. Everyone who had stayed for lunch and wanted to offer their condolences to Mum and Dad disappeared, except for Mum's trusted band of church helpers who stayed on to clean up. Mum was emotionally exhausted and cried again on the way home. Uncle Christopher and Auntie Mollie were so understanding and sympathetic promising to help Mum prepare the tea later. Mum, however, said she found it easier to stay busy; sitting about doing nothing gave her more time to think sad thoughts. Dad made some excuse about wanting to do a couple of jobs, changed out of his good clothes as soon as we were home, and went out. It was going to get dark by six o'clock, so he must have headed off to the shed where he had electric light.

Mum offered drinks: beer, sherry or whisky? Uncle Christopher opted for whisky, while the ladies both chose a sweet sherry. Offering alcoholic drinks to visitors rarely happened in our house and it was soon made clear to me that the three grown-ups wanted to be left alone and I was unceremoniously dispatched to my bedroom to play. The last thing I wanted right now was to be left alone. It was cold in my room and I felt I needed cheering-up. I fiddled about for a few minutes bored and yearning for company. It was most unusual for Mum to send me off to my room as normally I was allowed to stay wherever the action was. Perhaps, I mused, grown-ups don't want to have kids about when they are drinking? That's what happens in pubs. Alternatively, the grown-ups might be talking about something private that they don't want me to hear? The more I thought about that, the more I was convinced that something secret was being discussed.

I took off my shoes and padded silently up the hallway to the door to the lounge that had been left slightly ajar. I could hear earnest conversation. It sounded serious, but I had no difficulty eavesdropping. Uncle Christopher was speaking.

'Betty, I know you've had a hell of a day, but Mollie and I have to leave early in the morning and this is an excellent opportunity to have some frank discussion whilst John and Graham are out.'

'Spot on Chris. We are both very worried about you Betty. I don't know how you have put up with John and this dreadful floosy for so long? It's been going on for many weeks now, and shows no sign of calming down. If Chris had carried on like this, I would have ended our relationship long ago.'

'I know, I know. Forgive me crying, but I've lost my most beautiful daughter and a husband of fifteen years all in the space of a few months.'

'Betty, I know this is an awful thing to be talking about, but seriously, is it in your best interest to struggle on like this? If there is no love left in your relationship, then for your sake, and for Graham's, you are both best out of it.'

'That's how I've been feeling too but I couldn't bring all this to a head when I had my dearest Mary to look after. A dying daughter takes precedence over everything. I could only deal with one thing at a time.' Mum, I could hear, was sobbing until interrupted by my aunt.

'Of course, Betty, dear. Every mother would have done just what you have done and you have been a tower of strength. But now the situation has drastically changed. Dear Mary has left us, God bless her, and there is only you and Graham left, with a husband who has completely lost interest in you, and probably, Graham. I'm sure, given half a chance, John will end your relationship and go and shack up with this other woman. Face it Betty your marriage is on the rocks, something has to give.'

There was the sound of more subdued sobbing. Mum

seemed unable to respond. Suddenly I heard someone push back their chair. Was someone coming into the hallway to go to the toilet? I held my breath and stood back flat against the wall terrified I was going to be caught.

'Another drink anyone?' It was Uncle Christopher, who must have walked over to the drinks cabinet to top up his glass. Both the ladies accepted his offer, and there was a moment or two of quietness as drinks were dispensed. I relaxed a little.

'If John and I separate, he will surely kick Graham and I off the farm, and then what do we do?' wailed Mum. 'We barely have enough money to get by now. I'll have to find work and God knows where we would live. I need more time to think all this through.' My aunt was quick to respond.

'Betty, you and Graham can come and live with us for a time until you get a job and find somewhere else to live. Isn't that right, Chris?'

'Yes of course. Janine and Tom are virtually grown-up now and I suspect that Janine will want to move out on her own soon anyway. That would mean Betty, you can have the spare bedroom and Graham can have Janine's room if she leaves us. In the meantime, we have a camp bed he can sleep on. Plenty of fine schools nearby. If you're looking for work, you are far more likely to find it in Sydney.'

'That is so, so kind of you both. I don't know how to thank you. I would, of course, pay you for our board.'

'No need to worry about the details right now Betty. As my sister, it is the least I can do. I guess you will need a little time to think this through, and if you do decide to separate, you will need also to talk about your decision with John and young Graham.'

'I think I can hear John coming in the back door,' warned Mum. 'Please don't say anything to him about all this. I'll approach him when the time is right … Oh, hello John, would you like a drink?'

'A beer would go down well, thanks.'

It was time for me to scarper. I had heard more than I could ever have imagined. Without a sound I crept back along the corridor and re-entered my cold, cheerless bedroom, closing the door quietly behind me. Now, I had so much more to think about.

It sounded as though Mum was definitely going to leave Dad, and if that happened, we would be off to Bondi to live with Uncle Christopher and Auntie Mollie. Living in Sydney would be exciting and I really liked Uncle Christopher and Auntie Mollie. They were both good fun and I think I would enjoy staying with them, near the beach and all those ice cream parlours. But going to a big city school would be terrifying. Here in Sandalwood, I was in a composite third/fourth grade class with only twenty-four kids all up. I had heard of large schools in Sydney where there were as many as four fourth grade classes, each with over thirty children in them. Miss Tully had told us that the classes were sometimes "streamed" with the cleverest kids in the top class and the dumbos all together in the bottom class. How scary was that! Would I be put in with the dumbos?

Next, I began thinking about what I would miss most if I had to move to Sydney. Top of the list was the gang, Mike, Fred and my best buddy, Colin. Not far behind was the lovely Lynda, who I was going to marry. How could we get married if we lived so far apart? And then there was Miss Tully, my favourite teacher. The teachers in Sydney probably wouldn't be a patch on her. Plenty of other enjoyable things associated with Sandalwood came to mind, the friendly folk in town, Sunday school, cubs, Dee and Dum, the farm, Colin's mother's cooking, even mad old Jake careering down our dirt road at a hundred miles an hour. Then I thought about Dad. I guess I loved him in a weird distant sort of way, but I was also frightened of him too. It was a love-hate relationship.

Mum was at the door. 'Come and join us darling. Sorry I had to ask you to leave but we had to discuss something important and confidential. Wow, it's cold down here, you must be frozen? Come and get warm, tea will be ready soon.'

'What were you talking about Mum?' I asked, rather mischievously.

'Oh, just something confidential, dear. Nothing for you to worry about.'

That was hard to believe!

CHAPTER TWENTY-SIX

As expected, Uncle Christopher and Auntie Mollie left for Sydney after an early breakfast before I wheeled the bike out to ride to school. I wondered when I would be seeing them again. It all depended on Mum and Dad coming to an agreement to separate and, so far, they had not even had that conversation. My uncle and aunt have always been affectionate, but they seemed even more so this morning when they said their goodbyes. Living with them in Bondi could be great, as long as Mum was there too.

Everyone went seriously out of their way to be nice to me at school. I was invited to join in with games during recess and lunch and a couple of kids offered me biscuits or lollies from their lunch-boxes. The gang was particularly protective and Colin invited me back to his place again after school. Miss Tully quietly checked with me a couple of times to see if I was bearing up okay during the day's lessons, even Mr Marsden had a little chat with me during recess.

After school I no longer needed to wait around for Mary, which was a sad moment, but it meant that Colin and I were back at his place in record time. As always, Mrs Trent was most welcoming and announced that she had an interesting surprise for Colin. She went over to the sideboard and returned with a letter addressed to Mr and Mrs Trent.

'The letter is actually written to us, dear, but you can read it if you like. While you are reading it, I'll see if there is anything left in the cupboard.'

We both knew who the letter was from and I watched enthusiastically as Colin dived his hand into the envelope. Two pieces of paper came flying out, a letter and a one-pound note which fell to the floor. Together we dived down to pick up the money to check it was real and not some kind of Monopoly currency. Colin fingered the note and examined it closely.

'Wow, it's a genuine one-pound note, I'm rich!'

'Hey, that's fantastic! If Mr Smithton has also sent me a pound, I can pay off my bike debts.'

'This Mr Smithton fellow is certainly very grateful for the help you boys gave him.'

'People reckon he might have died, Mrs Trent, if we hadn't found him and had him rescued,' I replied.

'Well, here you are, something to help you celebrate,'

and Mrs Trent placed a plate stacked with chocolate biscuits on the table.

'Read the letter out loud Colin,' I urged.

Colin fumbled with the letter, which was upside down, and then cleared his throat.

Dear Mr and Mrs Trent,

I am writing to tell you how grateful I am for the assistance that your son, Colin, gave me recently, when I was very sick with pneumonia. As I am sure Colin has told you, the boys discovered me camping in Paddy's Gorge, and, realising how ill I was, raced back into Sandalwood to raise the alarm.

Thanks to the help of Dr Zegalski, Constable Gorton and the excellent staff at Goulburn Base Hospital, I am now home and recovering well.

The least I can do is to offer a small reward to the four boys who probably saved my life. To this end, I hope you will accept this monetary award of a pound for Colin for him to make use of as he wishes.

Congratulations to you too, Mr and Mrs Trent, for raising a son with so much common sense and resilience. You should be proud of him and I'm sure Colin will do well in the future.

Yours faithfully,

Donald Smithton (Ex-serviceman)

'What's an "Ex-serviceman"? I asked.

Mrs Trent answered after she had swallowed her second chocolate biscuit. 'It's someone who has served their country during war.'

'What are you going to do with your money, Colin?' I inquired.

'I don't know. I'm going to put it in the bank for now and keep it safe there until I think of something.'

I was anxious to get home to see if my pound, together with a letter for my parents, had arrived. I thanked Mrs Trent and was off.

As I rode home, I wondered whether Mum had already broached the tricky question of a separation with Dad. It was hard to believe that soon I might be moving to Bondi and away from my good mates. It was so tempting to say something to Colin, Mike and Fred, but because I only knew about the possibility of my parents' separation as a consequence of listening at the door, it was too dangerous a thing to do. Who knows, perhaps it will never happen. Perhaps Mrs Davies will call a stop to the affair, or her husband will find out. Maybe Dad will see the error of his ways and decide to stay with Mum after all. There were heaps of possibilities. Anyway, right now I only wanted to discover whether my pound had arrived.

I circled the house and parked the bike up in the shed. Dad and the dogs were still out so I ran across the yard and into the house through the back door.

'Hi Mum, any letters today?'

'Hello Graham, dear. To be honest, I've been too busy to have a look. Why are you so interested in the mail all of a sudden anyway?'

I flew out the front door without answering, jumped the three steps and raced to the letter box. There were two letters, one looked like a bill, but the second one had the same hand-writing as the letter Mr and Mrs Trent had received today. Grabbing them both I charged back in doors and pleaded with Mum to open the one I was interested in.

'Why are you in such a rush? This letter is not for you, it's for me and Dad.'

'Yes, but it's from Mr Smithton and there's a reward in it for me. A pound note! It means I can pay off my debt for the bike and start getting my weekly pocket money again. Open it up Mum, open it.'

'How do you know all this?'

'Because Colin got one. Please Mum, open it up!'

Mum finished drying her hands and took the letter from me. Then she collected the silver letter-opener, that had once been her Dad's, and sat down at the kitchen table. She slit the envelope open and withdrew a letter, but no money. My heart stopped. Where was my pound? Had Mr Smithton forgotten to put my money in? Had he, for some reason, decided I didn't deserve the reward?

Mum read the letter through and then read it out loud to me. It was exactly the same letter the Trent family had received. The letter clearly said that I was to get a reward. I grabbed the envelope and peered inside. What a relief, there it was, a beautiful crisp, clean one-pound note. This was the first pound note I had ever owned and I felt so proud. Sadly, I now had to hand it over to Dad to pay for the last instalment for my bike. There was some change to come back to me though, as I had been paying sixpence a week for the last four months or so. On my reckoning, I should get about eight bob back.

'Well, aren't you a lucky lad, Graham.'

'Will you give it to Dad please, Mum, and give me back whatever I have already paid?'

'No problem darling. I have been keeping a record of all your weekly payments. Give me the pound and we will need to give you back eight and six. I'll go and get it for you right now.'

Dad came in after dark, tired and grumpy. Mum and I knew to keep well clear of him until he had showered and downed a beer or two. A hearty cooked evening meal nearly always improved his mood noticeably, so that after tea was the time to raise any delicate matters with him.

'We received a really nice letter today, dear.' Mum had decided to put her toe in the water.

'Oh yes, what was that then?'

Mum handed Dad the letter.

'This is from bloody Smithton,' exclaimed Dad, looking first at the name at the bottom of the page. 'For Christ's sake, why's he writing to us. It's not bloody allowed.'

'Just read it dear. The parents of all four boys received the same letter,' Mum added hastily.

Dad didn't seem to know quite what to make of the letter. While he was thinking about it, Mum placed the crisp clean pound note down on the table in front of him. Finally, Dad reacted.

'Well, good on ya son. Mum, have we got some change to give Graham?'

'Already got it thanks Dad.'

'Now listen to me Graham, I don't want you trying to make bloody contact with this Smithton bloke. Is that understood? That man's half crazy, so you, and your mates, should keep well away from him. He's given you a pound as a reward and that's the end of the matter. Do I make myself clear? No writing letters or any of that bullshit!'

'Yes Dad.'

'He probably flogged the bloody money from somewhere anyway.'

I really couldn't understand why there was this strong antagonism towards Mr Smithton. For some strange reason, neither Mum nor Dad wanted our family to have anything to do with him. To my parents, Donald Smithton seemed to be some kind of an outcast. Now Dad had even said that a letter from Donald Smithton was not allowed.

But why? Why was contact not allowed?

CHAPTER TWENTY-SEVEN

I slept well because, for a very short time, I had been the proud owner of my first one-pound note. Everything at breakfast next morning seemed calm so I presumed that the topic of separation had not yet been discussed. It was a totally different situation when I returned from school that afternoon.

I was always starving when I got home and my first move was to head straight for the fridge. Mum appreciates my need for urgent sustenance and sees to it that there is always something tasty there for me. As long as I limit myself to two or three biscuits, or one large slice of cake, or some fruit, she's happy. Often, Mum will sit down with me at the kitchen table and we chat about the day's events or tackle some homework together. It's mother and son quality time and I valued the time we share.

Today, as soon as I charged through the door and made my way towards the fridge, I sensed things were not right. Mum had not heard me arrive until I barged in suddenly, but one look showed me she had been crying. Now Mum is a tough nut, and I don't think I have ever seen her crying before, except at Mary's passing, not even when she nearly sliced a finger off one night when cutting up quinces. Instinctively, I ran over and gave her a hug and we held each other for what seemed a long time before Mum fumbled for a handkerchief and wiped her eyes. I reckoned I knew what had happened but of course I had to pretend that I had no idea.

'What's up Mum?'

'There's some of that cake you like in the fridge, dear. Grab a bit and I'll tell you.'

I wasn't sure I was still hungry, however, I cut myself a decent slice of chocolate cake and sat at the table.

'Want some Mum?'

'No thanks.'

As I tucked into the cake with its substantial layer of dark oozie chocolate icing, I noticed something on the table I had never seen there before, a packet of cigarettes and a lighter.

'Are you smoking Mum?'

'Oh ... I meant to put the packet away before you came home.'

'Why are you starting to smoke Mum? Miss Tully told us it's bad for our health.'

'It's something adults do when they are feeling stressed, dear.'

Mum reached out a hand and placed it gently on my arm. 'Graham dear, I have some very sad news. We have had all the unhappiness with Mary and now something else has happened.'

Mum looked at me through tear-stained eyes. I kept up the pretence of ignorance and took another mouthful.

'Dad and I had a terrible row this afternoon,' and Mum got out her handkerchief again, 'I don't think we can go on living in the same house anymore.'

'Why Mum?'

'Well dear, it has to do with Dad and this other lady that he likes in Goulburn. He's infatuated with her.'

'What does that mean?'

'It means he thinks she's wonderful. He thinks he's in love with her and he wants her to leave her husband and come and live here on the farm with him.'

I couldn't think of anything useful or helpful to say, so I took another mouthful of cake.

'Dad has driven into Goulburn to talk to Mrs Davies about leaving her husband and their son and coming here to live.' Mum started to cry again and fished around for her elusive handkerchief. 'If Mrs Davies agrees, then you and I will have to move out and go and live for a time in Bondi with Uncle Christopher and Auntie Mollie.'

Mum was looking straight at me to see how I was coping with this dramatic news and expecting me to take it hard. I think she was surprised at how nonchalantly I accepted it. I'm sure my sneaky eavesdropping had really helped me to prepare mentally and emotionally.

'So, when's all this going to happen Mum?'

Mum reached for a cigarette and went through the lighting up procedure, rather clumsily, unlike other more practised smokers I had watched. Once she had the cigarette alight, she blew out some smoke in a cloud and answered.

'Graham, I'm dreadfully sorry this has happened. I know you love it here and have all your mates at school. Today is Tuesday. I think we should go by the weekend.'

'That quick Mum!' This revelation came as a shock. Somehow, I had been thinking of our departure as being something that would happen way into the future, in a few months perhaps, or even next year. Suddenly, I also felt panicked, under pressure, stressed. Mum wanted us to leave in four or five days! It was hard to take in.

'But Mum, it may never happen. Dad may change his mind; you might change your mind. And what about Mrs Davies? She may not be prepared to give up her house, her husband, and her son just to come and live on our farm.'

'That's true dear. We will know more when Dad gets home. Now, have you any homework tonight?'

'Only my spelling words.'

'Okay have a go at learning them for ten minutes, then I'll test you before I get tea.'

My mind was too full of worries to concentrate. When Mum tested me later, I could only get half my spelling words correct, but I still had until Friday to perfect them. I was one of the best spellers in the class, only Lynda sometimes beat me.

—•—

Dad always listened to the seven o'clock news on the radio, but tonight he was not home in time. Mum put his meal in the fridge and we ate ours. I felt I wanted company so I helped Mum to get the vegetables peeled and cut up, laid the table and generally just hung around. I guess I was feeling insecure and anxious and being around Mum seemed to help.

It was after eight when the lights of Dad's car finally flashed across my bedroom window. Mum had told me to go to bed because she and Dad would want to discuss things before speaking to me about anything in the morning. I had been left entirely out of the conversations. It was as if what I felt, what I wanted, was not really important. But it was *my* future that was being decided. None of this was my fault yet I was being forced to endure the outcome of Mum and Dad's falling out. What if I refused to leave Sandalwood? Perhaps I could stay with my best mate, Colin, or one of the others? Maybe Lynda would invite me to live in her house? I really wanted to stay with my class and my favourite teacher at Sandalwood Primary School.

I was becoming used to disturbed nights and finding sleep eluding me. There was so much to worry about, so much to ponder, and so many "ifs" and "buts" to my life. I envied my mates and their trouble-free lives. Mike's biggest worry was whether or not he would do well in the next yoyo competition, for Fred it was the welfare of his pony, and Colin, well he didn't appear to have anything to worry about. As for the gorgeous Lynda, it was probably whether she could beat me in spelling each Friday. They all prospered with happy parents and contented loving homes.

I must have fallen asleep eventually, because Mum had to come in to wake me up next morning.

'What's the news, Mum?'

'The news is that it has been snowing overnight and you may not be able to ride your bike to school. It's three or four inches deep already and still snowing. Mary would have loved it.'

'Wow, that's great, but I really wanted the news about you and Dad?'

'We are definitely separating, darling. Mrs Davies will leave her husband and come over here to live when you and I have left the farm. I rang Uncle Christopher early this morning and he is driving up on Sunday morning to pick us up.'

'What about Mrs Davies' son? The one who has fits?'

'He will stay in Goulburn with his Dad to look after him.'

'Is this permanent Mum? Can you change your mind if you want to?'

'Well yes, I suppose that could happen, but all four grown-ups are agreed that this is the best way to go for now. Mrs Davies and her husband barely talk to each other and, well … you know how it is between Dad and me. It's likely that both couples will divorce sometime in the future.'

'What does that mean?'

'It means we legally separate and the marriage is ended. It also entitles us to re-marry but that seems most unlikely to ever happen for me. Now, get dressed in your warmest gear for school, scarf, gloves and wear your boots. Hurry up, you slept in.'

I climbed out of bed and ran to the window. Mum was right, the snow was deep, the best fall for a couple of years. Sandalwood is high up on the Southern Highlands and we nearly always get two or three snowfalls every winter. It doesn't always settle, but this one was a beauty. The quicker I can get to school, I realised, the more fun I'll have there. So, I dressed hurriedly, rugged up, and went out to bring in the eggs and three more logs for the fire. I wolfed down my breakfast, scrambled eggs and toast, and collected my lunch box.

'See you later, Mum.'

'Now, wait a minute, Graham. It's still snowing. Is it safe to ride your bike? It's quite deep you know. Let me come out and have a look.'

'It's okay Mum, I'll manage.'

Mum donned her lambswool coat and a beanie and followed me out. The snow was fabulous, wet and perfect for snowballing but slippery too. I ran round the back to collect my bike and patted Dum and Dee who were not sure what to make of this white stuff coming out of the sky. Gingerly, I mounted and rode around the house finding it harder going than usual. Just as I approached Mum, mad old Jake came slithering and sliding down the road outside our place.

'That man's an idiot,' exclaimed Mum, 'but he's done you a favour. You can ride to school in his tracks. That way you will be safer. Off you go, and have a good day.'

'Bye Mum.'

I forgot my worries with the prospect of having fun in the snow with my mates at school. I did as Mum suggested, followed old Jake's compacted vehicle tracks and made it to school safely, just as the snow eased and the skies brightened. Mr Marsden waived the first half hour of lessons so the primary school kids could have a massive snowball fight.

CHAPTER TWENTY-EIGHT

I had found it difficult at school. After the terrific snowball fight, we were wet through and through and were pleased, in the end, to get back to our well heated classrooms to dry out and get warm. When it was time for recess we were told to stay in our classrooms because it had started snowing again and the teachers didn't want us to get wet again. Our gang assembled in one corner of the classroom to play Heads, Bodies and Tails, a really fun game, but we never really started because I broke the news to them of my imminent departure to Bondi. It takes something big to surprise the gang but my news stopped them in their tracks.

'You're kidding us,' exclaimed Michael.

'Pull the other leg, it plays Beethoven,' was Fred's reaction.

Colin knew me best of all, and I could see he believed me. 'Shit,' was all he said. I think he and his mother had somehow sensed that things were not good out on the farm.

'When do you leave?' he asked.

'Sunday morning.'

'That soon?' exclaimed Mike.

'But why are you leaving?' Fred demanded.

'Because Mum and Dad are separating and don't want to live together anymore,' I answered simply.

'Let's have a special farewell party for Graham on Saturday,' suggested Colin, 'I'll ask Mum if we can have it at our place. She's a whiz at organising parties. Invite whoever you want Graham.'

'Thanks Colin. Just the gang and Lynda, I reckon.'

'No, invite the whole class and Miss Tully too,' urged Colin, 'that would be about twenty all up. Mum can manage, the more the merrier.'

'The more the sadder,' Fred corrected.

The bell went. Time for maths and Miss Tully was already calling for quiet.

I told Miss Tully my news at lunchtime. I could see she was quite shocked and saddened. She put her arm around my shoulders and told me how sorry she would be to see me leave. She repeated her offer to chat with me anytime I felt I needed to talk to someone. I thanked her and told her she would be receiving an invitation to my farewell party on Saturday. She thanked me and then apologised; she would be out on Saturday with her boyfriend.

On Thursday morning Colin announced to the class that his mum and dad would be hosting a farewell party for me at 2p.m. on Saturday afternoon and everybody in the class was invited. The party would end by five o'clock so everyone could get home before dark. Colin then asked everybody to be sure to let him know on Friday morning whether they could come so his Mum would know how many to cater for.

On Friday morning, before school, Mum showed me a small, pretty box, with three delicate bars of soap inside. They smelt sweet, like candy.

'Would you like to give these soaps to Miss Tully, Graham? She has been a lovely teacher and this would be a good way to thank her.'

'Wow, that's great Mum, thanks.'

'And here's a card if you would like to write in it. Then we can wrap up the present.'

I sat down at the table and took great care with my writing. I wrote: 'To dear Miss Tully, the best teacher in the world, with love from Graham.'

For the last time, I wheeled my bike out of the shed, after patting Dee and Dum more affectionately than ever, and rode off to school. In my pocket I had a few shillings of pocket money because I planned to visit the general store after school. Nobody would know why, it was a secret.

Miss Tully allowed Colin to ask for a show of hands

of those who were coming to the party. Twenty-two of my twenty-four classmates said 'yes'. One was away with a cold and little Tommy said he had to go to Crookwell for his grandmother's eightieth birthday party.

Miss Tully helped me to collect up my exercise books at the end of the day. She explained that my teachers in Bondi might be interested to look at these books to assess the standard of my school work when deciding the class in which to place me. When this was done, I gave Miss Tully my present and the card. I think she was almost crying when she thanked me and wished me luck. Before I left, she suggested that the class would love to receive a letter from me when I felt settled and she would make sure that the class sent me a letter in return.

Next, it was off to the only general store in Sandalwood. The Jones Family Store was in prime position in the middle of the main street and had a so-called window display that, as far as I knew, had never changed. There was a cob-webby swaggie sitting in the corner of the window with a big smile on his face holding a sign that said, "Come on in folks and get your goodies here." The rest of the window contained a pile of things that looked as though they had been there forever. There were a few gardening tools, some pieces of wooden furniture, a grandfather clock that had stopped years ago, several pairs of work boots and a faded dining set, so covered in dust you couldn't tell what colour it had been originally.

Mr and Mrs Jones were just as ancient as the items in their window. Little Mrs Ivy Jones was, however, still quite energetic and welcomed everyone with a partly toothless smile. Her grey hair was thinning and the veins stuck out on her hands like networks of blue rivers. She still managed, most of the time, without any glasses, which explained why her customers were wise to check their change carefully for she was prone to making errors. 'It's me eyes dearie,' she would always claim.

Even more elderly Mr Alfred Jones suffered from a plethora of ailments. Customers could never escape without a lengthy update of the most serious malady that was troubling him on that particular day. It might be the arthritic knees caused by the wet weather, the frozen shoulder from heaving too many heavy boxes about, a sore back from digging in the garden, or private problems with his "you-know-what". Customers, more often than not, had to be rescued by Ivy, who would come bustling around and make some statement along the lines of, 'Fiddlesticks, he's as fit as an ox, it's just laziness.'

Alfred and Ivy had been threatening to retire for years but somehow managed to struggle on. Everybody in Sandalwood, and the surrounding countryside, was prepared to put up with their eccentricities because the alternative was to travel thirty-five miles on the dirt road to Goulburn to get their groceries and other necessities. Besides, there was something satisfying about having a friendly yarn with the Jones' and whoever else happened to be in the shop. If you were after the latest gossip, the Jones Family Store was usually a good bet.

With my few shillings and pence rattling about in my trouser pocket, I cycled down the main street, then mounted the footpath and leant my bike up against one of the pillars outside the Jones Family Store. Shopping on my own was a bit nerve-racking; normally I would be accompanying Mum, and I would just have to stand about while she did everything. I sauntered in, feeling self-conscious, and had to wait a moment or two for my eyes to adjust to the gloom. The store was long and narrow and seemed to go on out the back for ever. I had come to buy a farewell gift for the lovely Lynda.

'Hello, dearie. What yer after then?' It was the ever-enthusiastic Ivy who had swooped down on me from some dark recess.

'Urr ... umm, I'd like some soap please.'

'What kind love? There's 'eaps of 'em yer know.'

'I'm not sure.'

'Well, who's it for dearie?'

I blushed. 'It's for a girl.'

'Oh my, you *are* starting young, love. Well, you want the pretty, nice smelling kinds then.'

I followed Ivy to a part of the shop that was slightly better lit, and there, under the scratched glass, was an array of small boxes containing a variety of coloured soaps.

'Ow much money 'ave yer got to spend on this 'eart throb then dearie?'

I rummaged around in my pocket and eventually assembled six shillings and threepence halfpenny that I placed on the scratched glass.

'That's okay, dearie. You've got plenty there,' and Ivy's eyes lit up for she was sure of a sale.

A few minutes later and two shillings and sixpence worse off, I escaped Ivy's attentions with a nice smelling round box, neatly wrapped, and containing four different coloured soaps each a different shape. One of the soaps was heart-shaped so that one said it all. Pleased with my purchase, I stuck it in my school bag and headed for home. Instead of racing first to the fridge, I broke with my routine and trotted down to my bedroom to hide Lynda's present under my pillow. Then it was back to the kitchen for something to eat. Mum had noticed the change in my routine but, fortunately, said nothing.

Dad was around and seemed to be making a special effort to be pleasant. Normally, it was my job to struggle in with the logs of wood for the fire each evening. They are too heavy for me to manage more than two at a time. As we can go through seven or eight logs every night, I'm usually traipsing back and forth several times and letting blasts of cold air into the house because the outside door needs to be left open. Tonight, for once, Dad said he would help, and because he could carry six logs at a time, I only had to make one trip.

Mum was also making a great effort to avoid any nastiness and had cooked Dad's favourite lamb chops with mashed potatoes and Brussel sprouts. Sitting at the table that night it was almost as if everything was okay. There was a bit of chatting about this and that, a fly on the wall would never have believed that Mum and Dad were separating the day after tomorrow. I enthusiastically told them about my farewell party but not about my special gift for Lynda. Dad even offered to drive me to Colin's house for the party and pick me up afterwards, because there might be some presents for me to bring home and it would be difficult riding back with them when it was getting dark.

Most of Saturday morning was spent packing. By lunchtime, five suitcases were sitting in the hallway ready, but there were still some boxes to be added. Uncle Christopher had hired a small truck to collect everything, including my precious bike. My clothes had fitted into two of the suitcases and my toys were to go into some of the boxes. I had grown out of a number of toys and these were left in Mary's room along with her toys, books and dolls. Dad promised to look after them. Mum instructed him to take everything to the Salvos when next in Goulburn, but he seemed reluctant. Mum told me later that Dad wanted to keep them, just in case he and Mrs Davies started a family!

CHAPTER TWENTY-NINE

Shortly after two o'clock, Dad dropped me off at Colin's place. It was drizzling, so I held Lynda's gift close against my chest to keep it dry. I had torn a page out of my spelling exercise book and written Lynda a short letter. Miss Tully had taught us about letter writing and how to do the address and the date at the top of the page, but that seemed unnecessary when writing to Lynda, so I left those bits out. Apart from some brief "thank you" letters for presents received for my birthday and at Christmas, I had never written a personal letter to anyone before, so this was a "first". This is what I wrote.

<u>*PRIVATE*</u>

Dear Lynda,

I am sorry to be going away and leaving you. I like you a lot.

I would like to write to you when I am in Bondi. Will you write back please?

These soaps are for you. I hope you like them.
Yours sincerely,
Graham

I folded the paper over twice and shoved it in under a flap on the parcel. I wondered if writing to a girl meant I was having an affair. I was nearly ten, so perhaps it was not an affair until I was grown-up? Next, I wondered what Lynda would make of my present. Would she think I was a stupid idiot? Perhaps she would just laugh at me. More importantly, I wondered how I was going to give Lynda the present? I didn't want to be seen handing it to her because that would be embarrassing for both of us. As I was climbing the stairs, I hit on a brilliant idea, I would give it to Mrs Trent and ask her to give it to Lynda when Lynda was leaving the party.

My plan worked perfectly. Mrs Trent was at the top of the stairs welcoming everyone so I was able to have a quiet word to her as I handed the parcel over. As soon as Mrs Trent and I walked together into the large lounge a big cheer went up followed by clapping. I think everyone had arrived early and they were waiting for me to make my entrance. Mrs Trent had excelled, as I knew she would. She had put a couple of large sheets on the floor to protect the carpet and moved their dining room table into the middle. It was positively groaning with food. We spent the first part of the afternoon eating and drinking from the spectacular range of tasty items on offer.

Once we had had our fill, Mr Trent asked us all to follow him down to the garage where he had some games organised. He had parked his car out on the driveway, closed the garage door, and heated the place up. For the next hour or so we had heaps of fun. We played Pin the Tail on the Donkey, Pass the Parcel, What's the Time Mr Wolf? and a couple of other games. Finally, we trooped back upstairs to the lounge room for what Mrs Trent called a "top-up".

Just as the first mums and dads were arriving to pick up their party-goers, Mrs Trent clapped her hands and called for quiet.

Quiet please everyone. Come on, quieten down. We have an important duty to perform.' Once she had everyone's attention, she called me and Colin out to join her at the end of the table. 'Colin wants to say a few words on behalf of the class.'

'Graham is my best mate and I know he is good friends to everyone else in our class. We don't want you to leave our school, Graham, and we don't want to lose you as a friend. So, we are all coming down to Bondi for another party next year (laughter). We have passed the hat around and bought this for you.' There was an awkward moment while the gift was looked for, apparently it had been there a minute ago. Finally,

Tubby Norman was discovered to be sitting on it. Safely retrieved, a net containing a Stanley Matthew's soccer ball was presented to me by Colin and then, shock horror, I was called upon to make a speech.

Making speeches terrified me. I was all right answering questions in class but having to stand up and talk about something made me tongue-tied and nervous. I was not expecting to get a combined present from the class so had given no thought to what I might say in a situation like this. I can't recollect what I actually said. I do remember looking at the floor and saying thanks, but that was all. Colin told me later that I had also thanked Mr and Mrs Trent for organising the party which had been well received and the right thing to do.

The final farewells were a chaotic flurry of kindly words, smiles, good luck wishes, laughs and slaps on the back. There was a huge "Good Luck" card that everyone had signed, including Miss Tully. Even some of the parents came over and gave me a kind word and wished me well. Nobody mentioned anything about why I was leaving but I'm sure the story was all about Sandalwood by now.

When almost everybody had left, I noticed there was only Colin, Lynda and me still in the room. Mrs Trent had passed my gift to Lynda who had opened it and read my letter. Lynda and I walked slowly down the stairs together, it was just enough time for her to thank me for the present and to promise that if I wrote to her first, she would write back.

CHAPTER THIRTY

Mum and I moved to Bondi in late June 1960. As planned, we stayed with Mum's brother, Uncle Christopher, and his wife, Auntie Mollie. We settled in surprisingly well and our hosts were wonderful. Nothing was too much trouble for them and they did everything they could to help us adapt to our new surroundings.

Mum found work within a few days as a junior receptionist at Dr Morcom's practice. Dr Morcom was easy walking distance away and employed two receptionists. Although Mum had had no previous experience, she was a fast learner and soon was thoroughly enjoying the work. Dr Morcom was pleasant to work for and even offered to provide free consultations for Mum and I whilst Mum worked there. Now that Mum was earning a reasonable income, we were able to contribute regularly towards our upkeep.

Auntie Mollie, being a high school teacher, had

an excellent understanding of the standards of the four public schools that were feeder schools for her institution. One school, she felt, was superior academically. Consequently, I was enrolled at this school, even though it was not the closest one but it could be reached easily on the bus. I was tested on arrival and placed in 4B with Mr Thompson as my teacher. Mum was told that I was borderline 4A material, and that if I worked hard and settled in easily, the school would reconsider my placement at the end of the year. There were four classes in fourth year and I was most surprised to discover that about half the kids in the school came from overseas, mostly Poms, Greeks and Italians but also a sprinkling of other nationalities. Mr Thompson was a good teacher and I was soon doing well, making new friends and really enjoying school.

Weekends were great. Uncle Christopher took me surfing, Auntie Mollie introduced me to long distance running, and once a week, Mum took me to a tennis club that she had joined for me to have tennis lessons. Wonderful as all these things were, I still missed little Sandalwood and all my classmates. One day, Miss Tully sent me a wad of letters from my classmates that were a scream and I wrote back a long happy letter.

After a few weeks, I disappeared into my bedroom to write a letter to Lynda. There was so much to tell her. Mum had bought a packet of envelopes but I didn't think

I could ask her for a stamp, so I went to the Post Office nearby and bought a few with my pocket money. Mum thought I was writing to my class at Sandalwood and I didn't dare mention that I was secretly writing to Lynda. About a week after I had dispatched my first letter to Lynda one came back from her and landed in Uncle Christopher and Auntie Mollie's letter box. Fortunately, Auntie Mollie arrived home first so she found the letter and gave it to me without comment. She probably thought it was from one of the boys at Sandalwood.

Lynda and I exchanged letters every fortnight or so from thereon and she sent me a birthday card for when I turned ten on July 27th while Mum remained blissfully unaware that I was writing regularly to her. I even remembered Lynda's birthday on November 8th and sent her a silly card.

As the months slipped by, I gradually lost some interest in my previous life at Sandalwood. Mum told me that Mrs Davies had moved in with Dad and by the end of the year she was pregnant with their first child. There had been excellent rains in the district and Dad had received a handsome wool cheque some of which he had to pay to Mum. Mum mentioned that now she had a decent steady job, and money would soon be coming from Dad, it was time to seriously consider finding our own place somewhere nearby so I could stay at the same school. Mum had some Christmas leave coming up during January and she promised she would take me house-hunting with her.

Lynda kept me in touch with some other snippets of Sandalwood news. Mad old Jake had sped down our road once too often and crashed into Timboola Creek one night in the middle of a storm. He had died at the scene. Miss Tully was engaged to a young man from one of the wealthiest farming families in the district and planned to marry next year. Mike had won a junior yoyo competition with a prize of fifty pounds, and Fred had fallen off his horse at a gymkhana and broken his leg. Finally, Mr Trent had been given a promotion and was going to be the Postmaster at the Goulburn Post Office in 1961.

Christmas was a happy time. Mum seemed so much more relaxed nowadays and entered into the spirit of the season with terrific enthusiasm. Best of all she had given up smoking! I think I received the finest Christmas presents ever, including a surprise gift from Dad and Mrs Davies, a remote-controlled car. Fred, Mike and Colin exchanged Christmas cards with me and Lynda sent me a fountain-pen with a photo.

Everybody seemed to get a bit tipsy on Christmas Day, except me. Uncle Christopher and Auntie Mollie had "lashed out" and now proudly displayed their very first television set. We sat down and watched the Queen's Christmas address from Buckingham Palace.

During the afternoon, we played cricket in the backyard and I smashed a tennis ball through a window in the garden shed. Everybody thought that was very funny and I didn't even have to pay for it. By evening I was whacked because on Christmas Eve we had all gone to the midnight service and sung heaps of carols so I was well down on sleep. I went to bed tired but happy whilst everyone else stayed up quietly drinking.

The long January holiday was hot and humid. Sandalwood used to get hot in summer but it was a dry heat and didn't bother me. I was allowed to go down to Bondi Beach on my own where I would meet up with some mates from school. A few had joined the Bondi Junior Surf Club and I was allowed to join up too. We would spend most of our days on the beach and I was soon as brown as a berry. The simple rule was to be home before dark. One day, Uncle Christopher took me down to get fitted up for my first surfboard and he gave me lessons on the days when he wasn't working. He took a couple of photos of me with my new board and I sent one to Lynda. When she wrote back, she said I looked very handsome and included another photo of herself with her family on Christmas Day. She was wearing a lovely dress and looked happy. She was still the best-looking girl I had ever met and none of the girls at my new school even came near for looks or personality.

Sundays were very different. We all went to Matins

at the Anglican church at ten o'clock and I attended Sunday school. Sunday school in Bondi was far better than at Sandalwood and I had a male teacher. After church we would come home for the Sunday roast cooked by Auntie Mollie with Mum usually helping. It was always a big family affair with Uncle Christopher doing the carving and looking after the drinks and Auntie Mollie making everyone feel welcome. Their two children usually were there too together with whoever was their current boyfriend or girlfriend. Often there were ten of us to feed. The roasts were great. It was usually lamb or beef but we also had pork which soon became my favourite. Just when I felt I couldn't eat any more, Auntie Mollie would disappear into the kitchen with Mum and return with some yummy desserts. Pavlova, ice cream, fruit salad, cream, Fruit of the Forest, brandy snaps, sticky-date pudding and apple, rhubarb or apricot crumble were often served.

Sunday afternoons were a bit of a bore though. The grown-ups would sit about and chat whilst Mum and I did most of the washing up. Mum said it was the least we could do since they were providing us with a home. Sometimes we would watch the test match on TV or have a game of touch-cricket in the backyard.

When school resumed in the last week of January, I was thrilled to discover that I had been put up to 5A. Two of the kids who had been in 4A last year had gone overseas so there were two vacancies. My new teacher was Mrs Shaw and she was terrific. She really pushed us hard and had heaps of creative ways for us to learn. I was down towards the bottom of the class in most subjects but everyone said not to worry because I was now in the top class and was learning so much.

Every second Saturday morning Mum did not have to go to work and she would take me with her to inspect apartments that we might rent. Mum said she did not have enough money to buy a small house and explained that it would not be right to stay with Uncle Christopher and Auntie Mollie much longer. We had already been their paying guests for about eight months, so she insisted that we find our own place.

I don't know how many rental flats and apartments we visited, but it was a lot. Finally, early in May, we found what Mum was looking for. It was a neat two-bedroom place on a quiet street with a decent kitchen. Mum reckoned she could afford the rent and she liked the landlady. We took a six-month lease and moved in the very next week. Uncle Christopher helped us move our few belongings and Auntie Mollie lent us stuff for the kitchen. We had to purchase sheets and blankets but the place had a washing machine, oven and fridge together with reasonable furnishings. Most importantly, it was well-located, being walking distance to church, mum's work, shops and near my school bus route.

The worst thing about living at our new address was that there was only Mum and I there. We really missed the fun and company of Uncle Christopher, Auntie Mollie and their grown-up children. We got along famously with the landlady, Mrs Mackenzie, who hailed from Scotland and always spoke too fast and with a funny accent. Sometimes she would knock on our door and bring us something special such as shortbreads or kippers (yuck!) and on Robbie Burns Day a piece of haggis (double yuck!).

Soon we had settled in to our new home. School was great and I still met up with my mates at the Bondi Junior Surf Club when there was something special on. Mum was promoted to be the senior receptionist at the doctor's surgery with a slightly better salary because the previous lady had moved to Adelaide. We still went to church on Sundays and I was confirmed. Nearly every Sunday we were invited to enjoy the roast at Uncle Christopher and Auntie Mollie's home. But, best of all, I still corresponded with Lynda.

And then something unexpected happened!

CHAPTER THIRTY-ONE

One wet Sunday when Matins and Sunday school were over, I made a dash for the church from the Church Hall where my Sunday school was held. I didn't have a raincoat or an umbrella and it was teeming down. I splashed through several puddles and charged up the steps that led into the church. On rainy Sundays most of the congregation would stay indoors at the back of the church to chat and socialise. Somewhere amongst this sizeable congregation I knew I would find Mum or Uncle Christopher or Auntie Mollie. Usually they would be deep in conversation with another grown-up or having a laugh about something.

On this particular Sunday I found Uncle Christopher first and asked him if he knew where Mum was. He was able to tell me that she was sitting in a small lady chapel to the right of the altar talking to a man he didn't know. I walked over, still dripping rainwater wherever I went, and peered in from behind the chapel. Sure enough, there was Mum sitting in a pew with her back to me. I would recognise Mum's blue hat anywhere. She was in earnest discussion with a tallish man who looked vaguely familiar. It's annoying when you see somebody you think you know but you can't place them.

Something told me not to disturb them so I just stood and watched from behind a stone column. Behind me the congregation was starting to drift towards home but Mum and this man remained deep in conversation. What were they discussing so intently? It must have been something serious because they were not laughing or giggling. It must have been private too for them to have come over to this lady chapel where they could talk quietly without being disturbed. Then it occurred to me that they would not like it if they discovered I was eavesdropping; not that I could hear what they were saying. So, I retreated back into the main part of the church and walked down the aisle towards the main entrance. One of my mates from Sunday school was still there moaning about his parents always being the last to leave. We messed around together for another ten minutes or so.

The two duty sidesmen were collecting and stacking up the hymnals and prayer books. Uncle Christopher and Auntie Mollie had left, no doubt to attend to their roast that would still be in the oven and smelling delicious by now. The elderly minister remained still chatting to my mate's parents. Finally, I saw Mum and this strange man coming down the aisle towards me. Believe it or not, they were still talking! I studied the man carefully as he approached. I definitely knew the face and the way he walked also seemed familiar. And then it came to me. The man now standing in front of me was Mr Donald Smithton.

It was almost a year since our gang in Sandalwood had come to Donald Smithton's rescue and helped to get him to Goulburn Base Hospital. I hadn't seen him since but still had fond memories of receiving the one-pound note through the mail. He looked tanned, lean and fit now, clean-shaven and wearing a jacket and tie. His hair was dark and neatly cut and he had a confident manner that was not there when we had met him before down in Paddy's Gorge. In fact, it was hard to believe that this was the same man who previously had lived like a hermit in a cave. He flashed me a big welcoming smile.

'Hello Graham Granger. You're looking well and liking Sydney I hear?'

'I sure do.'

'Your mum has been telling me how well you are doing at school. In the top class I believe?'

'Yes, that's right. It's a good school too.'

'And a talented surfer and cricketer?'

I blushed. How do you respond to comments like

that? So, I said nothing and just nodded. It was true I was a good surfer for my age and I was scoring plenty of runs for my South Bondi under twelve cricket team. Mum joined the conversation.

'Mr Smithton played cricket a few times for New South Wales before he joined the army and went overseas. He was a fine pace bowler.'

'Wow, you must have been good. Did you play with Don Bradman?'

'A couple of times,' he grinned and then turned to Mum. 'Must be off Betty, I'm umpiring this afternoon if the weather improves. Hope to see you next week?'

'Yes, I hope so.'

'Catch you next week Tiger,' he said, winking at me.

With that, he nodded at the minister, trotted down the stairs and disappeared from sight.

Mum had brought an umbrella so the two of us huddled underneath it and set off for our apartment. Along the way I quizzed Mum as I had heaps of questions.

'What's Mr Smithton doing here Mum?'

'He's working for the council as a surveyor.'

'What do surveyors do?'

'They plan out roads and buildings and things.'

'So, he's got a proper job now?'

'Yes, a good one. He learnt surveying when he was in the army.'

'Then he must be well again? I remember being told that he was mentally sick after the war which is why he wanted to live by himself down in Paddy's Gorge.'

'He seems fine now. There are some new treatments available today that have helped him recover.'

'So does Mr Smithton live around here now?'

'Yes, he's in Bondi somewhere.'

'Is he coming to our church now?'

'Stop asking me all these questions Graham!'

'Sorry Mum.'

We were home and after we had changed out of our Sunday best clothes, we walked on to Uncle Christopher and Auntie Mollie's for another luscious Sunday roast.

We spent the afternoon with Uncle Christopher and Auntie Mollie and had a great time as always. Mum and I set off for home before dark armed with leftover lamb and pavlova. I had maths homework to finish and spent an hour or so making sure this was properly completed. Our 5A teacher set a cracking pace so that we were all challenged. So far, I was coping well and I was determined to make the standard required to get into 6A next year. Mum could help me with anything to do with English but said she was now really struggling with my maths homework.

Ever since Matins, I had been thinking on and off about our surprise meeting with Mr Smithton. I felt a strange desire to know more about him. I couldn't explain it, but I really wanted to know more. I think I liked him and he seemed friendly enough although quite different to the Mr Smithton the gang had first encountered down in Paddy's Gorge. Even though Mum had grown impatient with all my questions earlier in the day, I planned to try and squeeze some more information out of Mum at bedtime. She breezed into my bedroom around half past eight to say goodnight and sat on my bed.

'Did you get all the maths homework finished?'

'Sure Mum. Who's going to help me with my fractions and decimals when it gets too difficult for you?'

'That's no problem, Auntie Mollie is a high school teacher and Uncle Christopher is in the bank so they are both good at maths.'

'What about Mr Smithton. Could he help me?'

Mum stopped to think for a minute. 'Yes, I guess he would be good too. Surveying work needs lots of mathematics. But you can't ask him for help.'

'Why not?'

Mum appeared to be rather taken aback by this question and went on the defensive. 'Well he's not family for a start, and anyway you don't even know him.'

'How did you get to know him Mum?'

Chapter Thirty-one

'I don't know him well, Graham.'

'But you were talking to him in the lady chapel for a long time this morning. You must know him quite well Mum?'

I could see Mum was trapped and didn't know how to reply. You don't normally spend fifteen minutes alone with somebody deep in conversation unless you know them reasonably well.

'I haven't seen Mr Smithton for many years. The last time I met him was almost ten years ago, so I guess we had a bit of catching up to do.'

'What were you talking about Mum?'

'Graham that's being rude. What grown-ups discuss is their business and you are being insolent to even ask. What Mr Smithton and I were talking about is none of your business.'

'Sorry, Mum.' I knew I had overstepped the mark.

Being a reasonably intelligent child, and blessed with a high quota of curiosity, I pondered what meagre crumbs Mum had divulged before finally dropping off to sleep. I remembered that Dad had told me on several occasions not to get involved with Mr Smithton. But why? Mum had always agreed with Dad yet here she was in church today talking at length with Mr Smithton. A few half-crazy possible explanations surfaced. Was Mr Smithton once a criminal and Mum and Dad had somehow been involved in his criminal activities ten years ago? I could imagine Dad having some criminal tendencies perhaps, but certainly not Mum.

Could it be that Mum and Mr Smithton were romantically involved many years ago? They are about the same age, mid to late thirties, so ten years ago they would have been in their mid to late twenties. But Mum and Dad had been married for fifteen years before they separated a year ago so this seemed unlikely. Perhaps Mr Smithton and Mum were romantically involved more than fifteen years ago before Mum met and married Dad? This seemed a distinct possibility.

Dad had always been on the land so maybe he and Mr Smithton had met at some kind of farming activity? Another thought was that they had played rugby league together. On reflection there seemed no end to the ways whereby a connection had been forged many years ago between Mum and Dad and the mysterious Mr Smithton. I would just have to keep on gently nudging Mum to try to get to the bottom of the matter.

CHAPTER THIRTY-TWO

Mum had purchased a small desk that just fitted into the corner of my bedroom. I even had a bright-red anglepoise lamp beside it that helped me with my homework in the evenings. Unbeknown to Mum, this was where I also wrote my letters to Lynda every couple of weeks. Letters from Lynda arrived regularly and I have to admit that I had lied to Mum about the source of these letters. She believed I was receiving letters from my old gang in Sandalwood. Posting my letters secretly to Lynda was easy because I passed a letterbox on my way to school each day.

There was no new homework this Monday, but I convinced Mum that I had some to complete and so was able to retire to my desk to write two letters, one to the gang and one to sweet Lynda. I was keen to tell my friends about the unexpected meeting with Donald Smithton and to report that he seemed fit and well and had even once played cricket with Bradman. As always,

I hid the letter to Lynda in my schoolbag for posting next day but I left the letter addressed to Colin on the dining room table for Mum to see. She was delighted I was writing back at last because she had observed regular letters arriving from what she believed was the gang but rarely a letter being returned. She was so pleased, in fact, that she pasted a stamp on the envelope and promised to put my letter in the mail with her other mail at the doctor's surgery.

Every time I wrote secretly to Lynda, I felt a little bit guilty. I knew I was not being entirely honest pretending to be doing homework and then surreptitiously posting letters off to her every fortnight. Sometimes, when Lynda's letters arrived, Mum would ask me what the news was from the boys in the gang or what was happening in Sandalwood. I have to confess that on occasions I simply lied, or did something to distract Mum, in the hope she would forget she asked.

Mum came into my bedroom regularly to say goodnight, to do the cleaning or to check on some item of clothing. I couldn't risk her finding Lynda's letters lying about so I would read them carefully and then immediately hide them in my schoolbag for disposal the following day in a rubbish bin on the way to school. These covert activities had been going on for many months now and, so far, had remained undetected. I didn't feel the act of writing to Lynda was wrong, it was more the lying and covering up that was shameful. Every time another letter arrived from Lynda, or I dropped one in the letter box addressed to her, I thought about coming out into the open and ending my slightly deceitful ways. What was I afraid of? Was I worried about being teased, or laughed at, or people would think me stupid? On the other hand, perhaps Lynda and I had some kind of a secret pact that only she and I shared? This last thought I found exciting in a strange, inexplicable way. I felt Lynda and I had something special that we wanted nobody else to know about. Was that wrong? I didn't think it was, so I kept up the pretence.

I had a good week at school and on Saturday morning turned up at the local cricket ground where my under twelve team was playing. Uncle Christopher and Mum had come down to watch and had set up camp under some shady peppercorn trees with an esky and their camping chairs. Our captain won the toss and elected to bat. As always, I was batting number five. Our opponents had an exceptionally tall and fierce fast bowler who managed to hurl the ball down faster than anyone else we had ever faced. In the first ten minutes three of our batters had been removed and I was on my way out to the concrete strip in the centre to face the music. We had had a disastrous start to the innings, three down for a measly nine runs.

The first ball I faced I barely saw and it whistled past my head into the wicket-keeper's gloves. Their fast bowler glared at me in an attempt to further intimidate me. He had no need to worry, I was already dead scared of him. The second ball was right on the stumps but somehow, I managed, untidily, to get bat on ball and it rolled away harmlessly. I took a wild swing at the third ball and, to my pleasant surprise, edged it. The ball shot up in the air and sailed away over the slips to the boundary for four. In fact, it was close to a six! A big cheer went up from our supporters because this was the first boundary of the innings. I had been lucky and I could see the bowler had not appreciated my fluky swing.

A moment later he was steaming in with his fourth bowl of the over but that is all I remember!

I came round a moment or two later on the ground with a crowd of worried looking boys and adults staring down at me. Two of the adults who appeared slowly through the fog turned out to be Mum and Uncle Christopher both of whom gently helped me to my feet along with a torrent of comforting words. Mum held my head still to inspect the damage, with Uncle Christopher staring intently at my face.

'Nothing too serious, a nasty bruise and a shiner. There's no cut or bleeding.'

'Thank heavens,' added Mum, 'Come on Graham, come and have a rest. You had a nasty blow.'

Somebody must have found my bat and cap. The next thing I remember I was sitting under one of the peppercorn trees nursing a nasty headache. My right eye had started to swell and I felt nauseous. Mum rolled my sweater up to make a pillow so I could lie back. Someone else placed a cloth and an ice pack over my right eye. There were mutterings from nearby spectators that such body-liners should not be allowed in the under twelves. My teammates were told to keep away from me. After about ten minutes, Uncle Christopher and Mum took me home. They were worried, they said, about something called a "concussion". Later, I was to find out that the ball had clipped the top of my bat and shot straight up into my face. Apparently, I fell like a sack of potatoes. I appeared in the scorebook as, "G. Granger, Retired hurt, 4".

Mum put me to bed as soon as we arrived home after giving me a couple of aspirins to stop the headache. I slept soundly. A few hours later I surfaced and was pleased to find the headache had passed and I was left with an eye that I could hardly see out of and a very sympathetic mother who couldn't do enough to fuss over me. Uncle Christopher rang later to see how I was feeling. I told him I was fine and thanked him for driving me home.

Next morning, Mum gave me the opportunity to stay home from school if I didn't feel well enough but

I was keen to go. On Mondays our 5A teacher always gave us our spelling words for the week, started us on the next story in "The School Magazine" and on this particular Monday was going to introduce us to area and perimeters. I certainly didn't want to fall behind.

My eye was still swollen allowing me to only see partially out of it. A deep blue-red bruise had developed beneath the eye which Mum now described as a "shiner". When I looked in the mirror, I was surprised at how bad it looked. Everybody at school was going to notice it and I could expect to get comments galore. The injury was extremely tender to the touch. Before I left for school, I asked Mum to take a photo of my face. I told her I wanted to send the photo, when she had had it developed, to the gang in Sandalwood, which was another lie, because it was actually destined for Lynda's eyes only.

I put up with all the comments at school without much trouble and remained pain-free as long as I didn't run or do anything too energetic. Fortunately, there is no sport or PE on Mondays. I sat about during recess and lunch, something I would never normally do. I was pleased I had gone to school but have to admit I was glad to get home that afternoon to be fussed over again by Mum when she arrived home from the surgery at five o'clock.

Gradually, as the week progressed, my eye opened

up and the bruise spread and changed to a more yellowish hue. By Wednesday, I was back in action in the playground and turned up for cricket training after school on Thursday afternoon. The coach refused to let me have a bat in the nets though and I was obliged to limit my activities to bowling and fielding practice.

As Sunday approached, I kept thinking more and more about Mr Donald Smithton. I asked Mum if she thought he would be at church. She was quite evasive, just shrugged her shoulders and said 'possibly.' There had not been another chance for me to explore with Mum the earlier connection between Mr Smithton and my parents, which was disappointing.

There was no cricket for my team this coming weekend, we had the bye. By Sunday, my eye was back to its normal shape but I still looked as though I had jaundice on one side of my face and the eye itself remained bloodshot. I braced myself for another round of questions and comments about my looks from members of the congregation and the kids in Sunday school.

At our church the children stayed in church for the first part of the service and didn't leave for Sunday school until instructed to do so. Mum and I sat in our usual seats about two-thirds of the way back and were soon joined by Uncle Christopher and Auntie Mollie. A few minutes before the service began the tall figure of Mr Smithton dropped into a pew two rows in front of us. I gave Mum a sharp dig in the ribs that only elicited a rather cross glare from my mother. I watched Mr Smithton closely until it was time for me to leave. He sang the hymns heartily and seemed engrossed in the service. I wondered whether I would find Mum and Mr Smithton once again locked in conversation in the lady chapel later on when I was released from Sunday school. I don't know why, but I rather hoped I would.

Forty minutes later my Sunday school class was dismissed and I promptly made my way back to the church. En route I bumped into Auntie Mollie who did a double-take at the sight of my bruised eye. Although she had seen my injury earlier, when she sat with us in church, I had to explain what had happened because she hadn't had a chance to hear the gory details. She was full of sympathy but I was anxious to escape from my aunt and find out what was happening with my mum and Mr Smithton.

There was no sign of them outside so I headed up the steps and discovered that there was some sort of a morning tea happening. Tables with urns had been set up at the back of the church and for sixpence you could get yourself a cup of tea and a couple of biscuits or a piece of cake. Mum and Mr Smithton were nearing the front of one of the tea queues and were once again engrossed in conversation. I observed them for a minute or two until they had paid their money and collected a cup of tea and something to eat. I wanted to be noticed, so I stood in a place where they would almost fall over me. It worked. Mr Smithton stopped suddenly at the sight of me, and stared.

'What the heck happened to you Graham?'

'I got too close to a cricket ball,' I replied.

'I'd say you did,' and he came over to have a closer inspection. Mr Smithton wanted to hear the whole story about my shiner from start to finish and was clearly most concerned.

'Are you playing again today?'

'No, our team has the bye this week.'

'How do you feel about facing another fast bowler next time you play?'

'Okay. It was just bad luck really but he was incredibly fast.'

'Have you got training this week to give you a chance to get your confidence back?'

'Yup on Thursday.'

'That's good. If you want someone to lob a few extra balls at you sometime let me know Tiger and I'll give you a work out in the nets. I can also give you a few tips on fast bowling if you like?'

'Wow, thanks Mr Smithton.'

I could see Mum was rather worried about Mr Smithton's offer to help with my cricket though I wasn't sure why. Knowing he had previously been a fast bowler for New South Wales she was probably fearful that he would bowl too fast at me and I could be injured again. Mr Smithton must have sensed Mum's concern too because he hastily added, 'It's okay Betty, I will only bowl gentle ones to him.'

'Look after yourself, Tiger. I must come and watch you play sometime.'

Mr Smithton gave me a playful punch on the arm as he and Mum moved off to chat some more. I looked around and saw a couple of my friends from my Sunday school class playing chasings so I went and joined them until Mum and Mr Smithton were ready to leave.

CHAPTER THIRTY-THREE

That evening, when I was helping with the dishes, Mum said something that surprised me.

'Graham, Mr Smithton and I will be going out together on Thursday evening so how would you feel if you stayed the night with Uncle Christopher and Auntie Mollie?'

It was always great fun at their place *and* they had television! So, I jumped at the opportunity and readily agreed. It was only later that evening that I started thinking about what this business of Mum and Mr Smithton going out together might mean. I still had not discovered what the connection was between Mr Smithton and my parents all those years ago and now these two were "going out together". I wondered what the term, "going out together" actually meant? Was it just two friends going somewhere together or did it mean more than that? Could it be that Mum and Mr Smithton were becoming boyfriend and girlfriend? I decided to be forthright with Mum at bedtime.

There was some maths homework to do that evening but it was quite easy and only took about twenty minutes. While I was waiting for Mum to come to my bedroom, I spent another ten minutes learning my spelling words and then grabbed a book to read. Finally, Mum appeared looking pleased with herself.

'Guess what Graham, the divorce papers have come through. It looks as though Dad and I will be able to officially get divorced in the next month or so. What do you think of that?'

I didn't know what to think. It seemed as though everyone was keen for this divorce to go ahead but I still had some misgivings. All the grown-ups involved seemed pleased, Mum, Dad and Mrs Davies, although I didn't know about Mrs Davies's husband, or her son, still living somewhere in Goulburn. In my case, I was still sorry to leave the farm, Sandalwood and my mates and, of course, there was Lynda. How was I supposed to marry her one day when she was now living so far away?

'I guess it's okay if that's what you want Mum,' I replied.

'Do you miss your dad?'

'Sometimes.'

'Well, it looks as though everything will go through soon which means we can all move on.'

'Mum, is Mr Smithton your new boyfriend?'

Mum was shocked by my confronting question and it was now her turn to look confused. She had not expected such a direct question and for a moment didn't seem to know how to answer. She fiddled with the bangle on her wrist and kept her eyes lowered. She was struggling to find the right words. I waited patiently.

'Well, I don't really know, dear. We are just good friends I suppose.'

'Do you like him?'

'Of course, I do. I wouldn't be going out with him if I didn't like him, would I?'

'Where are you going?'

'We are going to the pictures if you must know.'

'Is this an affair, Mum?'

'I don't really like that expression Graham.'

'Well, Dad told me he was having an affair with Mrs Davies.'

'He should never have said such a thing and certainly not to you.'

'Well, he had to.'

'What do you mean by that?'

'I saw them in bed together trying to make a baby.'

'You what?'

Mum was furious. I had never mentioned this to her before because Dad had sworn me to secrecy and I had kept my promise, but now that Mum and Dad were close to a divorce, it didn't seem necessary to keep it a secret any longer.

'Yes, I saw them in your bed. Dad made me promise not to tell you. I wanted to tell you but I couldn't. Sorry Mum.'

'That's okay, Graham. Anyway, that whole sad episode is over now and, as I said before, with the divorce coming through we can all move on.'

'So, are you going to marry Mr Smithton now Mum?'

'It's far too early to start talking about marriage Graham. All we are doing is going to a movie together. So, don't worry that little head of yours about such things.'

'But you have known Mr Smithton for a long time Mum. You told me so.'

'I only met him briefly about ten years ago. We certainly weren't friends then, just acquaintances.'

'Mum, why didn't you and Dad want me to meet Mr Smithton when he was living down in Paddy's Gorge?'

'Graham, that's more than enough questions for one night, it's time for you to go to sleep. So good night and I'll see you in the morning.'

Mum gave me a kiss and tucked me in as she always did and then left the room after turning the light off. It had been an interesting day and our short conversation had been most revealing! Perhaps Mr Smithton would be around much more in the future and already I had next Thursday night to look forward to.

Thursday turned out to be a bleak day with squally showers, a cool change had come rampaging through on Wednesday evening. Whilst the cooler weather was welcome, the frequent showers had resulted in the cancellation of cricket training that afternoon. Now that my eye was not looking as fearsome, I had been looking forward to padding up and having a decent batting session in the nets. There was a game on Sunday but I had hardly hit a ball for a fortnight so was feeling rusty.

I arrived home early and raided the fridge. Mum didn't usually get home until around five o'clock so I had time to get my homework finished and started another secret missive to Lynda. I had so much to tell her about the upcoming divorce and Mum and Mr Smithton. Because we didn't have a car, Mum had told me to leave the house by 5.30 pm and walk around with my overnight bag to Uncle Christopher and Auntie Mollie's house. Mr Smithton was picking Mum up at 6.00 pm.

Mum arrived shortly before I was due to leave, grumbling about having to stay late at the doctor's surgery. She wanted me out of the bathroom pronto so she could have her shower and get dressed. She told me she had a new dress to wear and that they were going to grab a bite to eat before the movie. There was no time to talk and I set off a few minutes after half-past-five. My half-written letter to Lynda lay safely in my school bag out of sight.

I loved it round at Uncle Christopher and Auntie Mollie's. They were always great fun and the food was yummy. They were strict about television though, and I was permitted to watch one program only. When it was time for bed, I showered in their classy shower with sliding glass doors and then climbed into bed under the single blanket. Auntie Mollie came in to bid me goodnight.

'Well, what do you think about Mum going out with Donald Smithton?' she asked.

'I dunno. Are they boyfriend and girlfriend, Auntie Mollie?'

'I think so Graham.'

'Is Mr Smithton well now? Last year he was very sick. Did you know my gang helped get him out of Paddy's Gorge and into Goulburn Base Hospital?'

'Yes, your Mum told me about it. You boys did a great job. Mr Smithton had a bad time in the war and it took him a very long time to recover from the terrible things he saw.'

'What sort of things?'

'I don't know the details but many men came back either physically injured or with psychological problems. Mr Smithton had psychological difficulties.'

'What were they?'

'Horrible repeating nightmares, finding it hard to get along with people, being angry, seeing things that aren't there, having panic attacks. There are lots of ways the men were affected.'

'Sounds awful.'

'It is, but Mr Smithton seems to be over it now. He's got an excellent job and seems happy, and now he's taking your Mum out!'

'Auntie Mollie, can I ask you something?'

'You can always ask Graham but I may not know the answer.'

'When I first met Mr Smithton in Paddy's Gorge, my parents didn't want me to have anything to do with him. They wouldn't tell me why. Do you know why? He's always nice to me and I really like him.'

I watched Auntie Mollie carefully and again I could see I had touched a nerve. For some reason, she too, hesitated before replying.

'I expect it was because they knew he was unwell.'

'Mum has admitted she knew Mr Smithton about ten years ago. Was he a criminal Auntie Mollie?'

Auntie Mollie laughed, 'No he wasn't a criminal.'

'Then what's the problem?

'Time for sleep young man, have a good snooze. I'll wake you up in time for a full breaky and school tomorrow.' Without another word, Auntie Mollie flicked the light switch and left the room.

For a brief moment I thought Auntie Mollie was going to open up and tell me why my parents were so reluctant to let me meet Mr Smithton, but then she had decided against it. I was convinced now, more than ever, that there was a secret that everyone was keeping from me. It had something to do with Mr Smithton's past but I was still no closer to finding out.

CHAPTER THIRTY-FOUR

Friday evening was the first opportunity I had to discover how Mum's night out with Mr Smithton had gone. Mum was always tired by the end of the week, however when she arrived home from work this Friday she seemed in a particularly good mood. I thought that was a good omen. I made her a cup of her favourite tea with a biscuit and we sat down at the dining room table to chat about the day's happenings.

'What's for tea Mum?'

'Sausages.'

'Can I help?'

'Sure, you can start peeling the spuds if you like. And there's stewed apples and ice cream for afters.'

'Great.'

'How did you go at Uncle Christopher's last night?'

'Had a good time thanks. How did your night out with Mr Smithton go?'

'We went to a Chinese restaurant and the food was

really tasty, we even tried using chopsticks but diced them quick smart. The film was a Hollywood western; it was okay but nothing special. This was the first time I have had a real night out for many years so it was just lovely to be able to go out and enjoy myself.'

'How did you get on with Mr Smithton?'

'He was excellent company thanks. Now let's get started on the tea. By the way, we thought we might go shopping together next Thursday when it's late night shopping. How would you feel about going round to Uncle Christopher and Auntie Mollie's again next week?'

'It's okay by me Mum. It's great round there.'

'Terrific! I'll give them a ring later tonight.'

And so it was that Thursday nights with Mr Smithton became a regular event for Mum. So too were my stays round at Uncle Christopher and Auntie Mollie's place. Mum never told me much about her nights out but usually it was for a meal, a movie or shopping. Mr Smithton was a member of the Returned Servicemen's League so the local RSL Club became a frequent destination. Mum reckoned they could get excellent, reasonably priced meals there and there was always some kind of entertainment available. Every Thursday afternoon after work Mum would come home excited and take considerable care over her appearance. I knew not to be in her way, or in the bathroom when she wanted to shower and spruce up. Mum started to wear more fashionable clothes and she even had a fancy pair of high-heels and a smart new handbag for Thursday evenings. Overall, I had to admit, Mum seemed so much happier. Mr Smithton was good for Mum!

Auntie Mollie told me one night that Mum and Mr Smithton, or Donald, as he was increasingly being referred to now, were "courting". I guess I knew that but I increasingly wondered how everything was going to end up. Mum allowed me to call Mr Smithton by his Christian name too and I was getting used to calling him Donald.

Donald was even coming around to our little flat sometimes at weekends. I really enjoyed his visits because he took a genuine interest in me. He wanted to know about school and cricket and introduced me to stamp collecting. One day Donald turned up with a board game called "Cluedo" and taught Mum and I how to play. After that he would often bring it around on weekends and we would spend hours playing.

When Donald came around at weekends, Mum often asked him if he would like to stay for tea, an invitation he always gratefully accepted and Mum would make a special effort to prepare something tasty she knew he liked. We would always have out the best place mats, serviettes and a tablecloth and Mum would insist I laid the table correctly.

Mum had made friends with Maud, a sweet old lady who lived next door whose greatest joy was her garden. Mum would sometimes pop round with something for Maud to eat, and in return, Maud invited Mum to pick whatever she liked from her garden. So, whenever Donald was due to visit, there was often a generous bunch of flowers on display or a tasty vegetable from Maud's productive garden on the menu. Mum still missed her veggie patch from the farm.

This pleasant lifestyle continued for months, over the long Christmas school holidays and well into 1962. I worked hard at my schoolwork and progressed to 6A and was appointed a school prefect with a special badge to wear. Auntie Mollie was excited that in another year's time I would be coming to her high school. I was popular at school and some of the girls started to try and get extra friendly but I stayed faithful to Lynda who still corresponded with me regularly. Lynda's parents knew we were writing to each other but I had still kept it a secret from everyone in Bondi.

My cricket was improving hugely. Donald had incredible knowledge of the game and was still playing grade cricket most weekends. Often, he would take me over to the park nearby and toss a ball up to me in the nets or we would have fielding practice. He reckoned I'd never make it as a fast bowler because I didn't look as though I would ever have the height to demonise batsmen. Instead, Donald encouraged me to become an off-spinner and he painstakingly showed me the basics. I was still eligible to play for the under twelve team and was way up there with my batting averages as well as being appointed vice-captain.

Uncle Christopher continued to take me surfing but this sport was taking second place to my cricket. During the winter months I played soccer. Both Mum and Auntie Mollie encouraged me to help in the kitchen so that I was gradually absorbing some cooking skills. They both reckoned I'd make a better husband one day if I was a dab hand in the culinary department. Sometimes Donald would talk about his job as a surveyor and what it entailed, it sounded interesting. Best of all, Donald was a whiz at mathematics and could help with my maths homework and any mathematical concepts with which I was struggling.

I suppose Donald gradually became a kind of father figure for me. He spent most of Christmas Day with us and gave me a quality new cricket bat together with the linseed oil to properly break it in. He gave Mum a beautiful, expensive pearl necklace and Mum reciprocated with a set of gold cuff-links and a matching tie-pin. It was clear to everyone that they were very much in love but it was not until March that the divorce papers were finally approved and they were free to marry. However, there was another problem that needed to be dealt with first and this went all the way back to when Mum first met Donald twelve years ago way back in 1950.

—•—

One Thursday, late in March, Mum and Donald elected not to go out for the evening but to dine at home instead. This was most unusual and I wondered why the change in the normal routine. I had an uneasy feeling about the evening. Mum produced a tasty meal, however, and the conversation flowed easily enough. After the evening meal when the washing up was done and put away, Mum invited me to come and join her and Donald in the lounge where they were going to have their coffee and biscuits.

'Graham darling, Donald and I want to talk to you about something.'

Naturally, I thought this was the moment I had been waiting so long for and they would tell me what I already knew, that they wanted to get married. Long ago I had anticipated this conversation so I had no qualms at all about accepting Donald as my step-father. He and I got along famously now and he had been a great help and a mentor to me in many ways. I knew the divorce had been settled and so legally they were now free to marry.

I appreciated that Mum and Donald were doing

the right thing by telling me first of their decision and hoping that I had no objections. I respected them for that. My previous Dad back in Sandalwood had well and truly faded into the background. I never heard from him anymore except when I received a present at Christmas time. He had forgotten my birthday completely. Lynda had told me in her last letter that Dad and Mrs Davies were now expecting another baby. I was so pleased that Mum and Donald had decided to marry as a future with them both promised so much.

'Fire away Mum.'

Apparently, what should have been an easy quick conversation for Mum, wasn't. She was looking down at her hands again, a sure sign she was uneasy and wouldn't look me in the eye. I was about to announce that I had no problems with them getting married when Mum finally managed to string some words together.

'Graham, we haven't been entirely honest with you. Donald and I think we should come clean, as it were, and explain some important things to you.'

I sat expectantly. How could a simple joyful occasion be made so complicated? Did they think I was some kind of a buffoon that I hadn't noticed that they were infatuated with each other? It had been obvious for months that they wanted to marry. What was there to explain? It was perfectly straightforward, just say it, I thought to myself!

But Mum continued to appear tongue-tied and awkward. She tried again.

'Graham, I expect you realise that Donald and I are in love and would like to get married?'

'Sure Mum, that's been pretty obvious for yonks.'

'And the divorce has come through, so legally, we are both now single and can marry.'

'Yes Mum, I know that.'

'Well, there's still a problem but it's difficult for me to explain.'

Donald was holding Mum's hand now I noticed as she stumbled on. I sat there, saying nothing.

'Do you remember Dad telling you that you were adopted?'

'Of course.'

'And you wanted to know who your parents were?'

'Yes, and you explained that you were not allowed to tell me.'

'Yes, that's right. We're still not legally allowed to tell you, but Donald and I have decided that we cannot remain silent any longer because a strange and most unusual thing has happened.'

I was hanging on every word now impatient to hear more.

'Well your first father, your natural, biological father, is sitting in front of you. Donald is your real Dad.'

CHAPTER THIRTY-FIVE

I shall never forget that moment when Mum broke this news to me. She told me later that I simply sat there silent and in disbelief. We laugh about it now of course, but at the time my brain simply couldn't process the information. Donald said I looked at the time like a "stunned mullet". In that instant Donald had changed from a future step-father to my father. He and I were suddenly family by birth not just through marriage.

Donald broke the silence.

'Graham, I know this has come as a huge shock to you but I hope it's a pleasant shock?'

I looked at Donald and mumbled something incoherently. A thousand questions were invading my poor brain and I didn't know where to start. Before I had a chance to answer Donald, Mum spoke again.

'I know this is wonderful news for you Graham darling but there is still just one little problem for us all.'

I switched my gaze to Mum. 'What's that?'

'When an adoption takes place, all the people involved have to agree not to divulge who the natural or biological parents are. That's why I, and your adoptive dad, could not tell you that Donald Smithton was your real father or even encourage you to have anything to do with him. It's against the law. Strictly speaking we should not be telling you even now.

'But that's crazy Mum. I've really wanted to know who my real parents are ever since you told me I was adopted. It's natural to want to know.'

'I agree,' said Donald, 'nevertheless it's the law and there are good reasons for maintaining the secrecy.'

I looked at him blankly.

'Eleven years ago, I agreed to allow you to be adopted and I signed your adoption papers. I didn't want to let you go and nor did your mother, but at the time I was too unwell to be trusted to look after you properly. Sadly, your mother was also in a bad way and would not have been able to care for you. If you had stayed with us you would have been neglected or possibly have even died. You were adopted for your own good to give you a better chance in life and you have done so brilliantly because of the love and care of your adoptive parents.'

'But why the secrecy?'

Mum started to explain. 'It's best for the adopted child, dear. Imagine what it would have been like, if over the last eleven years, you had had two mothers and two fathers. Imagine the fights we grown-ups might have had about how to best look after you. Very likely your natural mother would want you back or Donald would want you back and so you would be torn between them and us as your adopting parents. Where would your loyalties lie? It would lead to an impossible situation. Little children need love and security and this comes best from only one set of parents.'

'So, are we all breaking the law now? Are we going to get into trouble with the police because you have told me your secret?'

They both laughed at my questions and shook their heads. 'I hope not,' responded Donald. 'You see, ours is an extraordinary situation. It is extremely rare that one of the natural parents ends up wanting to marry one of the adopting parents, so we are going to a solicitor to help us sort this all out.'

'How can a solicitor help you?'

'Solicitors are especially trained to handle legal issues. We have to pay them well and they will then argue our case for us. We will be asking the solicitor to arrange for us to receive special permission to marry.'

'Will that work?'

'We think so,' said Mum. 'But it may take months. Legal matters always take a long time.'

'Donald, why were you too unwell to look after me when I was a baby?'

'Well, you were born in 1950, only five years after the end of World War II, and I still hadn't recovered.'

'Were you wounded?'

'In a way, yes.'

'I don't understand.'

'I don't want to go into gruesome details but I saw terrible things while I was serving in the army. My mates were being killed or wounded, bombs were going off all around me, two or three times I narrowly escaped being killed or badly maimed. When you witness these sorts of things for many months it starts to affect you mentally. I was having terrifying nightmares, panic attacks and suffered severe depression. I was too ill to stay in the army, so shortly after I returned to Australia after the war ended, I was invalided out of the forces on a disability pension.'

'Why couldn't my mother look after me then?'

'She wasn't well either.'

'What was wrong with her?'

'She was an alcoholic.'

'What's that?'

'An alcoholic is a person who can't manage to live without drinking too much alcohol. They are always drunk or nearly drunk. Your mother would never have been able to look after you properly. With both me and your mother incapable of caring for you as a baby we did the one sensible thing that was possible, we gave you up for adoption.'

'Why did you have a baby then? If you were both unfit to be parents why did you have a baby?'

'We didn't mean to have a baby, Graham. It just happened.'

'How?'

Mum interrupted our conversation. 'I think that's enough for today, we can talk about the details another time. The main thing for you to remember Graham dear, is that because Donald here had the good sense to have you adopted all those years ago, you have had a happy childhood and you are doing well at school and in sport. You would have had a terrible life if they hadn't put you up for adoption.'

I couldn't disagree with Mum's conclusion.

'Thanks for telling me all this.' I jumped up and went off to my bedroom, I needed time to think.

CHAPTER THIRTY-SIX

My first thought, when I reached the safety of my bedroom, was to write to Lynda to relay all that I had just learnt about my past. Then I had second thoughts. My mind was still wrestling with what I had just learnt and it was messy in there. Before writing to Lynda I wanted time to make more sense of everything. I needed to settle things down, go over some things again and think about the gaps that still remained after our conversation. I had learnt so much already. Top of the list was the amazing revelation that Donald was my real Dad! I couldn't believe it! I guess this explained why I had always felt a strange closeness with Donald even when he was living like a hermit down in Paddy's Gorge.

I grabbed a pen and a piece of paper and started to jot down some of the things that were still worrying me. This was my list:

1. What's happened to my mother?

2. Why was she an alcoholic?

3. Why did Donald marry her if she was an alcoholic?

4. Do I have any brothers or sisters?

5. When did Donald discover that one of his rescuers was his son?

6. Should I call Donald "Dad" now?

7. Is Donald/Dad completely well now?

8. What happens if the law says that Mum cannot marry Donald?

9. If Mum and Donald marry where will we live?

I was still thinking about some more questions to ask when there was a knock on the door and Mum entered. I looked up from my desk and explained what I was doing. She looked at the long list and smiled.

'Do you want to get some answers now, dear, or can it wait until another time?'

'It would be best now please, Mum.'

'Come on then …'

We returned to the lounge and I gave my hastily scribbled list of questions to Donald who read them through. 'Not too difficult,' he remarked. 'Shall I start at number one?'

Mum went into the kitchen to organise three Milos and open another packet of biscuits, leaving Donald and I to tackle the questions together.

'Your mother was a few years younger than me and,

I believe, had had a sad upbringing. I know very little about her. The last I heard she had been admitted to a special kind of a hospice as a patient. Hospices are places that try to help alcoholics to stop drinking alcohol so they can lead a decent life again. I have not seen her, or heard anything about her, since shortly after you were born and we surrendered you for adoption.'

'So, she's still alive today?'

'I certainly hope so.'

'Do you think she's cured?'

'Again, I hope so.'

'Where does she live?'

'I have no idea Graham. Sorry. Your second question asks why she was an alcoholic. People usually turn to alcohol when they are deeply unhappy and can't face normal life. I think your mother's unhappy childhood was the reason she turned to drinking. You see alcohol can help to drown out a person's unhappy memories.'

'Why was her childhood unhappy?'

'Again, I'm sorry I don't know.'

'Why did you marry her if she was an alcoholic?'

'This is a difficult one to answer.'

Donald stopped for a moment to have a first tentative sip at his freshly delivered hot Milo and took a couple of biscuits.

'We didn't get married, Graham.'

'But you had a baby?'

'Yes ... you!'

'But you're supposed to be married to have children? What you did was wrong wasn't it?'

'Yes, most people would say you're right. At the time I was unwell, I was lonely and feeling down. I met this pretty girl in the pub and, well ... you know what happened.

'Not really.'

'Well, I can explain things more when you are a bit older. Now what was your next question?'

Donald re-visited my list.

'Question four was about brothers and sisters. No, you don't have any, apart from little Mary, of course.'

Question five asks when it was that I realised who you were. That's an interesting one. I had no idea when you found me down in Paddy's Gorge and later rescued me. I just thought you were another ratty kid coming to upset my idyllic life out in the bush. It was not until I was recovering in Goulburn Base Hospital that I asked one of the nurses if she could find out who the four kids were who had raised the alarm that I'm sure saved my life. One of the other nurses working on the shift with her came from Sandalwood and she knew the names of the four kids. I wanted to reward the four of you.'

'It was great to get the pound note. It was the first one I ever owned.'

'There was a minister from Crookwell who used to

come to visit his parishioners at the hospital who helped me. I had nowhere to go when I came out of hospital and he very kindly agreed to board me at the Manse until I was better. It was he who lent me four pounds to send each of you a pound as your reward. He was a great guy. When the nurse gave me the names of you four boys, I recognised the name Graham Granger straight away. You see, I had met a Mr and Mrs Granger from Sandalwood who had applied to adopt our little boy. I had already registered you as Graham Mark Smithton at the Registry Office in Sydney.' Donald looked up at Mum who was perched on the arm of his chair and she took up the story.

'We liked the names Graham and Mark so we kept those but changed your surname from Smithton to Granger.'

I jumped in excitedly. 'So, does that mean if you get married, I can become Graham Mark Smithton again?'

'It sure does.' Mum responded.

'Hey that's great,' I exclaimed.

'Okay, question six. Should you call me Donald or Dad? They laughed and exchanged glances.

'I think it best if you use Donald for now,' said Mum. 'Later, when we are properly married, and I become Mrs Smithton, would be the appropriate time to call him Dad.'

'Once we are married you should call me whichever

name you are more comfortable with,' added Donald. Moving on, question seven asks whether I am completely well now and the answer to that is about 95%. I still have nightmares sometimes. If I feel anxious, I can take a tablet to calm me down. I take medication every day which really helps and once a month I see my psychologist for a session. I may never be quite one hundred per cent, but life is pretty good now. Having your mum for company is a Godsend.'

Mum gave Donald's shoulder a gentle massage as he mentioned her. 'Donald makes light of his nightmares dear but they are really horrible when they happen. He wakes up screaming and thrashes about like a madman. It takes me quite some time to talk to him and calm him down. Sometimes he finds it helpful to get up and walk around the house with the lights all on.'

For a moment I wondered how Mum knew all this, but then Donald was speaking again.

'Question eight is about what happens if we are not allowed to marry. I honestly don't think there will be any problems. The solicitor will explain what procedures, if any, we have to go through to get the green light. We don't anticipate any difficulties but going to a solicitor will guarantee everything is in order. Now for your last question, perhaps Mum would like to answer that one?'

'Oh yes. Where will we live? This is so exciting!

We have good jobs and are doing our best to save up for a deposit on a house. At the moment we are both renting and that is far too costly an arrangement. If we have enough for a deposit, and the bank thinks we are reliable, it will allow us to have a loan so we can purchase our own small house. It will probably be just a two-bedroom fibro place but it will be ours, our very own house!'

'In Bondi?'

'Who knows? Donald responded. 'We may have to find a suburb where the house prices are a bit cheaper. House prices around here are starting to go up. Everyone wants to be near the famous Bondi Beach.'

'Well next year I'm enrolled to go to Auntie Mollie's high school. Do you think I'll still be able to go there?'

'I don't think we can promise that dear, but it's a very important thing for us to consider. We are hoping to be married before Christmas. We are not going for a honeymoon so we can save that money. We might even find a house we all like over the long Christmas holidays.'

'I hope it has a backyard for cricket,' I remarked.

'Righto, young man, it's well and truly time for bed,' announced Donald jumping up from his seat.

And so ended one of the most amazing days of my young life.

EPILOGUE

The appointment with the solicitor was arranged for the Friday of the following week. The solicitor told Mum and Donald that he had never heard of another case where the adopting mother wished to marry the man who had put the child up for adoption. The solicitor asked them to be patient while he checked out the legalities of the proposed marriage and if there were any impediments. A fortnight later he rang them to confirm that all was in order to proceed with the wedding. A relieved Mum and Donald started planning a low-key, low-cost ceremony at their church in late November.

Meanwhile school continued to go well for the remainder of the year and my role as a prefect was not particularly demanding. On the sporting field I managed a few good innings and avoided coming into contact with the ball in my face again. I continued with surfing and soccer, but cricket remained my passion.

I did reasonably well on the athletics field too and I managed a third in the finals of the 220 yards.

My relationship with my new Dad blossomed and we soon became totally relaxed in each other's company. Mum and he were clearly devoted to each other and I felt their relationship to be far warmer than that which had existed between Mum and my adoptive father. They also went out of their way to include me in many of their decisions and we became a tight-knit family group.

Uncle Christopher or Auntie Mollie accompanied us for several days during the long summer holidays as we hunted for a place to buy. We still didn't have a car so being chauffeured about was a treat. We found what we wanted in the nearby suburb of Bondi Junction and my parents quickly paid the deposit. It was actually a brick house with two bedrooms with the toilet out the back in the yard. The backyard was not as large as I had hoped for, and much of it was taken up by an old jacaranda tree with branches that reached almost down to the ground. Dad said he could tidy the branches up and I could use the water-tank to practise my batting just as Donald Bradman had done. There was also a park nearby where we could go for a hit, or to kick a ball about. The house was just off the bus route to Bondi so there was no problem catching a bus to my new high school.

One personal confession came out that I had been

keeping a close secret for well over a year: my letters to Lynda. Mum and Dad were surprised at first but then accepted it quite happily. I think they were rather amused actually. I showed them my best photo of Lynda and they agreed she was very pretty. In the new year, Lynda started going into Goulburn High School on the bus every day and I began studying at Auntie Mollie's high school. Auntie Mollie was my French teacher.

Lynda and I are still writing to each other and sharing our innermost thoughts.

In February, we had some extraordinary news. Mum announced that she was expecting a baby! She had proved the medicos wrong! There was much celebrating. It was decided that the baby would sleep in Mum and Dad's bedroom when it arrived and we would now have to start looking for a bigger house, one with three bedrooms, a larger "cricket" backyard and an inside toilet!